Praise for David Park and *Ghost Wedding*

'A beautifully luminous and powerfully haunting piece of writing about the things that live in the shadows just beyond our reach, glimpsed occasionally, then lost again. I loved the way it crosses memory, the past, the secrets, the might-have-beens, the lost, and the paths that travel parallel with ours, without ever touching.'

Rachel Joyce, author of
The Unlikely Pilgrimage of Harold Fry

'David Park is one of Ireland's finest writers. He has written a symphony of extraordinary novels, not least *Ghost Wedding* which immerses us in a world where time interrogates history, passion, grief and war.'

Colum McCann, author of *Apeirogon*

'Time is fluid in David Park's masterfully constructed novel where the shifting plates of the past slip their boundaries, causing seismic waves in the here and now... A compelling and absolutely mesmerising read from the maestro of the quiet crescendo.'

Bernie McGill, author of *The Watch House*

'David Park is one of Ireland's great novelists.'
Roddy Doyle, author of *The Commitments*

'The Belfast Turgenev... One of the truest observers of life.'
Big Issue

GHOST WEDDING

DAVID PARK

ONEWORLD

A Oneworld Book

First published in the United Kingdom, Republic of Ireland, United States
of America, Canada and Australia by Oneworld Publications Ltd, 2025

ISBN 978-0-86154-974-0 (hardback)
ISBN 978-0-86154-998-6 (trade paperback)
eISBN 978-0-86154-975-7

This publication is supported by the Arts Council of Northern Ireland

Typeset by Geethik Technologies
Printed and bound in Great Britain by Clays Ltd, Elcograf S.p.A

The authorised representative in the EEA is eucomply OÜ,
Pärnu mnt 139b–14, 11317 Tallinn, Estonia
(email: hello@eucompliancepartner.com / phone: +33757690241)

Oneworld Publications Ltd
10 Bloomsbury Street
London WC1B 3SR
England

Stay up to date with the latest books,
special offers, and exclusive content from
Oneworld with our newsletter

Sign up on our website
oneworld-publications.com

For Alberta, in this world and all others

When thou art bidden of any man to a wedding, sit not down in the highest room; lest a more honourable man than thou be bidden of him...Then said he also to him that bade him, When thou makest a dinner or a supper, call not thy friends, nor thy brethren, neither thy kinsmen, nor thy rich neighbours; lest they also bid thee again, and a recompense be made thee. But when thou makest a feast, call the poor, the maimed, the lame, the blind.

The Gospel according to St Luke

The geological layers of our lives rest so tightly on top of each other that we always encounter earlier events in later ones, not as a matter that has been fully formed and pushed aside, but absolutely present and alive.

Bernhard Schlink, The Reader

1

They are always present when you walk through the city at night. Glance up at the oldest buildings, those that have survived the gutting, the ripping out; look up at the silent upper floors of the former linen mill, the warehouse, the bank or department store, accounting offices and hotels, and you sense them in the emptiness, on dusty stairwells, in boarded-up back rooms where even the brashness of the city's new light struggles to enter. They live on in their own realm, waiting and watching at the mouth of the river where the city started, built on reclaimed mud and the slime of sleech. The lives of all those who have dwelt here are layered, linked eternally through the ages from when time was nothing more than the rise and set of the sun and spectral stick figures foraged the shoreline for clams and cockles.

Now time is marked by the stream of the universe, the spin of the earth; the hands of a clock, tick after tock in the darkened hall when all are sleeping; the calendar on the kitchen wall that pretends to control the space of days wherein we live. They say time flows like water but in this place that they call the Manor House because they don't wish to use its older Irish name, something is happening to time, with its course diverted, its journey subverted, harnessed – who can say what the right word is and who can tell where it will carry us?

An old house with a newly dug lake that waits patiently for the water to fill it. Its owners stand expectantly at the best vantage point, behind them at a respectful distance their servants, separated in turn from those who have worked to excavate the void. The time has finally come. An excited order is shouted, then repeated. Slowly the water loses its accustomed direction as it seethes and rundles through the channel that men's callused hands have laboured to create. The river is confused, suddenly pulled out of its expected path, a path so familiar that the enclosing banks are shaped and smoothed by its passage, banks that have long held it tightly like the embrace of a lover.

Tumbling in a sudden surge of expectation, it rushes out of its preordained channel, thinking it is finally breaking free, but instead finds itself filling the great hollowed-out basin of earth that stands waiting. Its confused, skittering entry is greeted by cheers from those who stand watching it. An old house with a new lake and at its edge a boat house with red tiles and two stone dragons on either side of its doors. Men wave their caps in the air. And all around them, as if summoned from hidden cloisters, come the others, all those who are no longer bound by time's restraints. They stand at the lake's edge as if mesmerised by the water's flow, before vanishing again like some early morning mist sifting through the trees.

And here too amongst the unseen is a child, a newly born child, whom the water will wash clean and render timeless. Its cries are soft, momentarily lost in the rising cheer from the army of labourers who now toss their caps in the air and slap each other on the back. The lake slowly fills, but with it comes a sense of disappointment that the water is as brown as the earth it covers, its surface laced with a froth of milky suds because time has not yet had a chance to purify its essence. The child cries again. But still the water seethes and courses with excited rivulets running ahead, searching out the contours of its new home, layering and pooling in ever-changing patterns until the weakening cries slowly slip below its surface and time settles once more.

2

What did they expect? He didn't actually use those words, but they ran like an invisible thread through the condescension lacing his voice and along the lines of his expensive suit until full-stopped by the shiny glass squares of his cufflinks. A Saturday afternoon wedding in July? A year's advance booking was the absolute minimum and usually two were needed to secure the Manor House. He smiled at them as if they were naïve children who still believed that love's imperative had the power to transcend all obstacles, then pushing his leather-bound diary across the coffee table, told them that sometimes the pre-booking sadly lasted longer than the marriage itself. And of course they were still dealing with the backlog of those weddings that had to be postponed. Currently there were no cancellations, thankfully no dramatic changes of heart that always haloed tears like confetti over the heads of the unfortunates. He stopped speaking to sip the coffee he had arranged for them. His pearly-coloured fingernails were manicured.

Alex stared at him and wanted to tell him he didn't care if the Manor House wasn't available, that he'd be perfectly happy getting married in the local registry office, or on the beach, in

fact anywhere other than here. Wanted to tell him that everyone connected with the wedding industry was no better than
a low-life gangster making a killing out of people's romantic
fantasies, fantasies about which he cared very little. But looking
at Ellie and seeing the disappointment on her face, he knew he
needed to take back some control of the situation because it
was obvious that the Manor House's wedding planner was finding pleasure in delivering the bad news he obviously believed
enhanced the exclusive prestige of his domain.

'Well, thanks for your time,' Alex said, then rested his arm
on Ellie's shoulder in a gesture of consolation, but she felt
stiff under his touch as if the disappointment had calcified her
skin. She sat motionless until, feeling the slightest of tremors,
he worried that she was going to cry. She had set her heart
on this particular venue, saying she liked the sense of history,
the high quality of the facilities and the fact that it was easily
accessible from Belfast. He didn't fully understand her attrac-
tion but assumed it perfectly matched the wedding day she had
always imagined for herself. But they would find somewhere
else – and as far as he was concerned, so much the better if it
allowed them to get married without the pretension he saw
everywhere around him.

Perhaps it was the all-too-obvious attempts to make the
interior resemble some photograph in *Country Life*, with gilt-
framed landscape oil paintings, vases full of flowers that looked
as if they had just been cut from a meadow, wall lights with
velvet tasselled shades, thick carpets and dark wood upholstered
furniture that was supposed to signify gravitas. A carefully
curated selection of magazines fanned open across the coffee
tables like playing cards. Even the doormen were liveried from

some lost period of history. And while Alex was naturally drawn
to old buildings, this one seemed to him like a simulation
whose original character had long since been stripped away
and then dressed in a pastiche of someone else's fantasy of the
past. Whatever had been the original essence of the house had
been slowly suffocated by its supposed improvements. The
heavily advertised extensive spa facilities of course offered the
requisite balance between the new and the old and no doubt
justified the exorbitant prices.

He couldn't remember hating anywhere quite so much
since the time they had gone to Disneyland Paris and the Magic
Kingdom had left him feeling only that he was the victim of an
elaborate and shameless swindle. 'I think you probably need
to bring a child with you for it to work properly,' Ellie had
said, and he had nodded in agreement but secretly thought
that not even the biggest brood of children could alter the
way he felt about it.

Perhaps it was the unwelcome prospect of tears, perhaps
it was because he had extracted the maximum satisfaction
out of dashing their foolish expectations, that made this
middle-aged man in an expensive suit suddenly hold up a
hand – as if he was at the eleventh hour suspending the
court's judgement.

'There is one possibility that you might choose to consider.
Let me see,' he said as he flicked the pages of his diary forward
then placed his hand on his chin to simulate deep thought.
'There is the Boat House down by the lake. It's still being ren-
ovated and refurbished, but if everything goes according to
schedule it could be available if you were prepared to go for a
date in late September. We could reserve a small number of

rooms for guests who want to stay overnight. You would be the first party to use it.'

'What's it like?' Ellie asked.

'I think it will be very pretty,' he said. 'It's right on the water's edge and because you're not having a particularly large wedding it could accommodate your numbers.'

'Can we see it?'

'Of course. But if you don't mind I'll get my assistant Rosemary to take you down. I have another meeting scheduled.'

He made a call and then, standing up, shook their hands. As he walked away, the spicy scent of his aftershave lingered in his wake. Alex was glad he'd gone and was tempted to say something but stayed silent.

'What do you think, Alex?'

'I don't know. Let's have a look and then you can decide.'

'We both need to like it. It's not just my decision.'

'I know,' he said and then stopped himself saying, 'I'll be happy anywhere you want to marry me,' because it sounded trite but, as the assistant arrived, regretted not saying it anyway.

She was an older woman with a genuine smile and already he liked her better than her boss because she didn't patronise them as she introduced herself, then asked them if they had finished their coffee.

'It's just five minutes' walk to the lake,' she told them. 'But don't worry, the renovation includes a small bar so guests don't have to traipse up to the house every time they need a drink and all the catering is delivered in. There are bathrooms and a dance floor so you have everything you need, and if the weather's good on the day we can even arrange to have the ceremony outside right on the water's edge.'

They followed her through the gardens then down the gravel path that was bordered on both sides by glossy-leaved rhododendrons and azaleas still harbouring the lingering traces of blossom. Already they could hear the sound of work and when they reached the end of the path they saw the Boat House for the first time. It was larger than he had imagined and, despite its present state, grander in scale. There was a team of men busy on both the interior and exterior, the air riven by the high-pitched whine and screech of machines cutting wood and nails being fired home. A radio in some unseen spot struggled to make its music heard above the tumult. A web of cabling latticed the entrance and a generator close by throbbed angrily, shivering and shuddering with its own intensity. Two portable toilets, clearly intended to preclude any need to use the hotel's facilities, stood close to where a white minibus was parked.

The building was constructed mostly from wood, its brickwork base reaching about four feet in height, then topped with a roof of red layered tiles, some of which were missing. The two stone dragons guarding its double-doored entrance suggested it had been modelled on some Oriental pavilion. The original windows had been removed so the building seemed afflicted with a kind of blindness. Around it on the house side were some flower beds with dust-coated mottled shrubs and rowan trees still studded with red berries. Nearby, a narrow wooden jetty reached into the water, the dull surface of which was disturbed only by the light keening of a breeze which stirred the heavy-headed braid of rushes lacing the edges of the lake.

'We've tried to keep as much of the old structure as possible, then extended it on two sides. The final interior colour is going to be a particular shade of red which we think is close to how it was originally. It's not a listed building so the builder's been able to crack on. New windows will create plenty of light and afford lovely views of the lake. What do you think?'

'I like it,' Ellie said, 'but will it definitely be finished by September?'

'Definitely. There are penalty clauses in the contract if it's not, and knowing the builder I can tell you that he won't be paying any of them, even if it means working weekends.'

'What do you think, Alex?' Ellie asked.

He knew then that his default response of 'I like it if you like it' was the wrong one, so he stirred some enthusiasm and told her he thought it was great, and as far as he was concerned, it was great if it got them out of the suffocating atmosphere of the Manor House.

'How long has it been here?' he asked.

'The Manor House has been here from the middle of the nineteenth century. Then a family called the Remingtons bought it just after the First World War and pumped a lot of money into it – I believe it needed a lot of work. And we know the Boat House was built in the twenties: we still have the dated original plans. The lake itself was created at the same time – I think it was the fashion. Dear knows how many men it would have taken to move that amount of earth, but I suppose people were desperate for work then and labour was cheap.'

One of the workers ambled over to them. He had an aura of authority about him and they assumed he was a foreman. Squat and muscular, he was wearing a low-slung tool belt that made him look like a gunslinger, reinforced by the fact that one hand held a nail gun.

'Come to check on us, Rosemary?' he asked, smiling and letting the hand holding the gun drop down by his side.

'Someone needs to keep an eye on you, Alfie,' she said, sharing the same jocular tone. 'And you better get a shift on if these two young people are going to get married in it.'

He looked at them and nodded, his eyes bright with mischief.

'So you'll be wanting a roof on then,' he asked, 'and glass in the windows?'

'If it's not too much trouble,' Ellie said, joining in the game.

'I'll see what I can do,' he answered, 'but you could always do what my eldest boy did. Take yourself off to Vegas and get married for less than a hundred dollars. A bit more and Elvis will do the ceremony for you.'

'You trying to put us out of business?' Rosemary asked.

'The prices you people charge,' he said, 'would put a deposit down on a decent house.'

'We have a house,' Ellie said.

'Come on, Alfie, you wouldn't begrudge a girl her big day,' Rosemary said.

'Suppose not,' he said. 'Well, good luck to you – and I promise to have the place looking great, roof, windows and all.'

They thanked him and, as he wandered back to work, tried not to look at where the weight of the tool belt had started to pull his trousers low enough to expose the start of what they didn't want to see. Then suddenly he turned and, hitching up his trousers, said, 'You know the place is haunted, don't you?'

'Alfie, don't be spreading that old wives' tale.'

'Call it what you will but the local boys say they always knew it as the Ghost House.'

'We're not superstitious,' Alex said. 'And what're a few ghosts amongst friends? They're all welcome.'

'Why is it supposed to be haunted?' Ellie asked, staring at the building intently and narrowing her eyes against the bright light.

But whether he didn't know or didn't want to say they would never find out, because his reply was a slow shrug of his shoulders and then he turned again to take a phone call, during which his only contribution was to say 'No problem' at regular intervals while he pushed some gravel back and forwards with the toe of his work boot.

'Don't pay any attention to Alfie – he likes winding people up. But he's a good builder. He's done a lot of work for us. And always to a high standard. He's old school – takes pride in his work.'

They followed her to the entrance until she told them they shouldn't get any closer, and stared into the mote-filled interior whitened with a trembling snow cloud of dust and debris. From the ceiling, cables hung down like prehensile tails while the floor was coated with a yellow snowfall of planed wood curlicues.

As if anticipating the doubts that she imagined were taking root, Rosemary told them, 'You're seeing it at its worst but things change very quickly, and when the building work is done, the interior people will really transform it into something special. Somewhere you'd be happy to get married. I'll leave you for a while to talk it over. We can discuss the details when you've made a decision. I'll wait for you up in the house. I have some drawings from the architects that will give you a good impression of how it will look when finished.'

Alex watched her go, and suddenly the sound of her shoes scrunching the gravel made him think of his childhood seaside holidays. The shingle beach pressed against his skin and the vision of that sea's permanent unrest momentarily overpowered the calm of the lake. He remembered too the sun-glinted pebbles sharp against the soles of his feet, so he always walked across it with slow exaggerated steps.

When Rosemary had moved out of sight they walked towards the lake, its surface shifting in a sudden swathe of unfettered light as it lisped and seeped through the penumbral braiding of feathery-headed reeds. Two swans stalled calmly, indifferent to their presence. He thought he remembered that they mated for life and considered making a joke of it, but didn't know how to carry it off without sounding sentimental or crass. However, he hoped it was true because he told himself he loved Ellie. When he had announced their engagement his male friends had joked about a life sentence, and all the old clichés had got a boisterous airing, but he was tired of freedom, of all the energy that needed to be expended, of all the pretences and games that had to be played because of it. He was ready to give it all up, to be married in this boat house, however it looked, and set out on a new stage of the life they already shared.

Matty had been the worst. But Matty was always the worst. A friend since childhood, but as time went on Alex had grown weary of him, and had already decided that after he got married it would be his best opportunity to loosen the connection. He could justify it to himself with lots of reasons – Matty's recklessness, his lack of self-awareness, his insistence on the pursuit of a good time in ways that now seemed immature and even dangerous. But he knew too that there was a reason he could never fully free himself from the friendship they once shared: moments that could never be forgotten or vanquished. He shivered a little and told himself it was the wind skimming off the water.

Ellie turned to look at him and smiled. 'I think it's perfect – that it will be perfect.'

'That's good,' he answered. 'That's good.'

She walked out along the jetty, which was partially edged with reeds. The effect made it look for a second as if she was walking on the surface of the water. He followed her because he wanted to see her, see her the way he had at the start and not through the filter of wedding favours, endless lists of potential guests and seating plans. He wanted to have once more that simple freshness of vision and renewed sensation of what he had felt, not have it blurred and cheapened by every supposedly indispensable ingredient vital for the day's success, or all the other debris that had started to fall across the life they already shared. And as he put his arms around her and they both stared at the lake, he told himself that the coming day would indeed be another beginning, when everything they didn't need could be cast off and love itself would shine anew with the very lightness that now caressed the water's surface.

George Allenby had never constructed a lake before and if he had anything to do with it, would never repeat the experience. He had drawn the very short straw because of his university degree in engineering and because he was the least senior of his colleagues who worked for the Belfast architects of Wickets and Rodgers. And yet as Alastair Wickets, perhaps detecting his lack of enthusiasm, had stressed, it was by no means a job of low importance: because the Remington family was a longstanding patron of the practice who had frequently solicited their services, including to restore the Manor House itself, and also to draw the plans and oversee the construction of various commercial properties through-out the city.

Allenby had been compelled to do his research, both as a result of his ignorance of the mechanics of such a project and a desire to get things right. He had consulted a practice in Derbyshire who had completed a similar piece of work for a stately home being regenerated by the National Trust, had read books and written numerous letters to fellow architects and engineers. He had also gone to the Linen Hall Library and pored over musty tomes in search of historical examples.

But as he stood at the southern aspect of the lake's newly fashioned contours marked by red poles, the level of knowledge he had acquired did not ease his apprehension, or indeed the increasing sense of foreboding that had deepened and thickened with the advent of a week's rain. The resulting mud took full possession of the works as if the earth was exerting its primitive primacy and sullenly reclaiming what had been stolen from it. Wet splodges spattered the plans even though he tried to shelter them inside his jacket. If he stood too long in the same spot there was a danger that he might stick, so at intervals he squelched his feet out of the sucking mire. But it did little to repel the growing sense of paralysis he felt. The work was too slow, too beset by things outside his control. His increasingly damp tweed jacket smelt like cat's piss, but despite the rain he had not sheltered under an umbrella. He knew from the war that you couldn't lead men by rubbing privilege in their faces, that however much of a pretence, which couldn't resist any form of close scrutiny, it was a necessary gesture of solidarity. Solidarity in the face of the enemy. Many of the labourers had tried to improvise some protection from the rain by fashioning capes out of hessian so they looked like Owen's 'old beggars under sacks'.

The size of the proposed lake was far too big but Remington had refused to compromise. The lake's size, just as his acquisition of the Manor House itself, was clearly another element of his belief that there was no point having wealth unless it was fully displayed. It made the work involved enormous and the given timescale extremely challenging. He could have used twice the number of men that had been enlisted. But as grandiose as Remington's imagination might be, there was also an inherent meanness when it came to expenditure.

Allenby blinked rain away as in front of him a legion of men laboured at removing the soil with long-handled shovels, then spooned it inelegantly into wheelbarrows before struggling up the ramp to carry it where new landscaping would eventually transform it into a grass-covered, rhododendron-planted drumlin partially screened with native trees. But as the rain churned the mud so the men could barely move and as they compressed it with their feet, it made it even more difficult to extract. And the earthen ramp constructed to allow them to wheel their barrows out of the excavated basin had become a sodden quagmire, gouged ever deeper by the wheels. The planks they had then placed as tracks had slimed over and men were slipping, sometimes spilling the hard-earned barrow loads they carried. From a distance it might look almost comical, like some scene from a Chaplin film.

He looked at the sky, the colour of beaten tin, hoping for any glimpse of respite, but even though the earlier downpour had slowly turned into a light, almost invisible drizzle, there was nothing to offer hope or clemency. He had already dismissed the use of machinery, frustrated by one too many breakdowns and bog-downs where sacking and planks had to be put under wheels and long lines of men had strained on ropes to pull the marooned vehicle free, looking for all the world like a journey back through time where men such as these had laboured to move some building block or giant stone to a rising monument or a memorial to the dead.

A memorial to the dead. It was inevitable that the mud would take him back, even though he tried, as with all memories of those times, to resist that compulsion. And what was the point of it, he asked himself, except to relive once more the misery endured, the overwhelming sense of loss and, in its most bitter moments, its inexplicable futility. Sometimes, however, as in his dreams, or in some seemingly random and disconnected moment, he didn't get to exercise a choice – a shadowed glimpse of his profile reflected in a shop window as he hurried by, a particular smell that he wasn't sure belonged to the present or his past, the sound of a small bird heading for open sky smacking into his bedroom window, could shudder through him. But the time he had come closest to collapse, of falling into some void inside himself, was when it felt that nature itself conspired to overthrow him. The cries of foxes in the hour just before dawn, coming from somewhere in the woods behind his house on the edge of the city. The screams of a man caught on the wire slowly dying from his wounds, screams that after a while they all pretended not to hear, tried to drown out with the raised coarseness of their talk, even at one point with the breathy discordant hysteria of a mouth organ. A voice from somewhere down the trench shouting, 'Will someone put that poor bastard out of his misery!' while the others silently cursed their fallen comrade for inflicting his suffering on them. Suffering was not something that could be shared, so to lament it was to shoulder an additional burden that wouldn't help, might cause you to stumble, even when the shadows fell thickly, to lie down in the mud.

And everyone needed only things that helped them – the photograph of a wife or lover; some meagre little item that arrived in a parcel and whose significance was so much greater than itself; a dream of a dry bed or a glass of cider; a dream of a purer, unsullied future. The ever-present hope of a Blighty. He had no photographs of a wife or lover, only the reality of his own dream, a dream in which he bought a plot of land where he would build a house overlooking the sea, the sea in which he would wash himself clean in the early morning light. The nature of the house changed – sometimes it was big-windowed and flooded with light, other times its walls were thick and defensively sheltered against the world outside. Once, he imagined it with a glass roof and nothing except the motionless clouds above.

As dawn broke and with the cries of the foxes still in his head, he had got up and walked in the wood, until the burgeoning light and the stirring freshness of the air saturated his being. The foxes were long gone. Now there was only the soft press of his feet cushioned by the moss and a breeze stirring the branches into the slightest tremble of movement. He walked on letting his hands feel the reality of bole and leaf until a calmness found him again.

Class and education had seen him arrive in France as an officer. The men had laughed at him. Sometimes behind his back, sometimes with ill-disguised surliness or sarcasm in their answers. His sergeant had taken him aside after the first week and told him what he needed to do before it went beyond saving. His sergeant, who was twice the man he now found himself serving, who knew what had to be done in every situation and yet every day had to address him as 'sir' and pretend he needed his orders. So Allenby had waited for the right moment, the right trouble-maker, and then hit him with all the force he could muster, then stood over him with his drawn revolver and told him he would put a bullet in his head if he ever spoke to an officer like that again. The men were happy to fall into line – they always found a greater sense of security if they were able to believe that the person in charge knew what they didn't. There was no comfort in chaos. He came to feel their perverse respect, strong and enduring enough to follow where he led and in the knowledge that he would never ask them to do anything he wasn't prepared to do himself.

A fox crying in a wood. A sea of churned mud. In the trenches you were no longer fully human but a creature burrowing ever deeper into the bowels of the earth, slowly transformed in a backward journey of evolution into some kind of snuffling half-blind thing desperate to tunnel into shelter. And it was the earth that was your constant companion, a liniment lingering along the folds and crevices of flesh, caked in hair and ears, under fingernails, the smell and taste of it in your mouth and inveigling itself into your very consciousness. He would never forget the smell – ammonic, rotten, disfigured by the obscenities inflicted on it so it became a repository of noxious vapours that in vengeful response slowly released its putrid gases. And when it turned to mud it became a killer. He had never witnessed a man drowning in a green sea of chlorine gas but he had seen the corpses of men face down who had tried in vain to clamber out of shell craters that they had mistaken for refuge, their last breaths returning them to the clay from which life had once been formed. Some of them had slipped back into the water where their bodies bloated and fed vermin. At other times partial faces, hands, limbs broke free from the earth where some explosion had buried them, as if desperate to reclaim the light once more.

As he surveyed the shambles below him he felt a sense of foreboding. Once, he had thought of rain as bringing a cleansing to the world, a refreshing restorative to the dry withering of the sun, but after the war he knew it only as an enemy, indifferent to the suffering it delivered to those on whom it fell. Another man stumbled on the slope out of the excavation, going down like a collapsing horse in halters before he stumbled up again and reclaimed his balance.

'A good day for ducks,' the voice behind him said.

Edward Remington, the son of the Manor House, was coming towards him under an umbrella. He wore black leather riding boots, a long belted raincoat and a trilby hat – he could have been setting out for a day at Downpatrick races. He knew Eddie from the golf club they shared – once they had been drawn together in a four ball and he knew too that while winning at anything didn't seem particularly important to his partner, he was still prepared to cheat, and not averse to discreetly using his foot to nudge a ball into a better lie. Afterwards they had shared a drink and a smoke. Eddie had been too young for the war, and while Allenby wished that experience on no one, he couldn't help thinking that the consequence of discipline and the compulsion of collective responsibility might have shaped him into something better. Charm was the currency Eddie dealt in, the seemingly bottomless capital on which he drew daily and which, allied to his good looks and reputation as a source of fun, seemed to obscure the need for any meaningful or specific employment in his father's commercial empire. Allenby didn't harbour an intense dislike for him but he judged people now on one criterion only – whether they could hold up their end or not, and he had no great belief in Eddie's ability to do that.

'It's a bloody nightmare,' Allenby said. 'Going on in this weather is probably doing more harm than good. I'm going to call it a day if it doesn't stop soon.'

'The old man was complaining about it taking so long, but then he never was blessed with much patience.'

'Where is he now?'

'At some lodge dinner I think.'

'Orange?'

'No, Masonic. The Orange don't do much more than tea and sandwiches in some draughty hall. I've been to enough of them not to want to be at any more.'

'Creating a lake isn't just a case of digging a big hole and then waiting for it to rain, or suddenly turning on some giant tap in the sky.'

'Isn't it?' Eddie asked.

'I wish it were,' Allenby said, 'and if it was, I'd be sitting in a warm office back in Belfast by now drinking tea and making up the bill.' Though he knew Eddie wouldn't be particularly interested, he felt the need to unburden himself of the frustrations of the job. 'We have to divert the river by blocking and you can't get a stonemason right now for love nor money because they're all up in the Mournes working on the reservoirs; then construct a sluice gate to control the flow of water, work out stuff about water tables, dig pipes and drainage, find a way of stopping it silting up, build an outlet structure that allows the lake to be drained if needed, arrange for planting and on and on.'

'So it's not just a big hole in the ground,' Eddie said.

But before he could reply there was a loud cry of pain as one of the men pushing a barrow up the ramp fell suddenly. He didn't get up. Men gathered round but simply stood looking down at him. Allenby hurried along the edge of the excavation, careful to keep his balance and avoid slipping into it, and for a second he was running along the duckboards of a zigzagging trench. When he reached the fallen man he had to elbow the bystanders aside to see him. He lay on his back groaning and holding his hand across his face as if that might shield him from the pain – or perhaps it was his embarrassment at being the object of so many stares.

'Move away! Give him room!' Allenby shouted, then knelt down beside him and placed his hand on the man's shoulder, which felt like a sodden piece of rag.

'My leg's broken,' the man said, lifting his hand away from his face.

'Are you sure?'

'I heard the bloody snap.'

Allenby asked him his name and then looked round for Eddie Remington. He was standing about twenty feet away still sheltering under the umbrella. Allenby walked towards him.

'Can you get the car from the house. We need to get him to the doctor down in the village.'

'The car?' Eddie asked. 'He's in a bit of a state.'

And Allenby knew that the prospect of a mud-coated man laid out on the pristine leather of the Austin was more than Eddie was willing to contemplate. He turned away in disgust and told the foreman to bring the horse and cart round to the edge of the lake. Then dismissed the workers and told them to be on time in the morning.

'Are we getting full pay for today?' a voice shouted.

Allenby told them they were, and when the cart arrived they carefully lifted the injured man into the back, his cries of pain lacerating the air, then laid him on a bed of green tarpaulin before covering him with what was left of it. Everywhere was putrid with the smell of clay and the sodden phalanx of men moving away, their caked feet leaving a brown trail across the grass. The horse whinnied and flicked its head as if it too wanted to be gone. Allenby organised for someone to tell the man's wife about his injury, then shouted to the two men who had offered to accompany him to tell the doctor that the bill should be sent to the Manor House. He stood for a moment looking down into the excavation, its undisturbed puddles momentarily brightening with light, and wondered if he would ever see the job completed.

'You know what the name for the boat house is that we're going to build here? For all this?'

Eddie shrugged his shoulders.

'A folly, a bloody folly,' Allenby said, then tried to scrape some of the mud off the soles of his boots by sliding them back and forwards across a patch of clean grass.

In response Eddie reached into the pocket of his coat and brought out a hip flask. At first Allenby refused, but as the younger man continued to hold it outstretched towards him, he took it.

'Come up to the house and get dried out,' Eddie said. 'Warm yourself with a cup of tea. Or get the chill out of your bones with another wee Bush.'

'I'm in a bit of a state,' Allenby said, staring at him with barely concealed disdain, but he was concentrating only on screwing the cap back onto his hip flask.

'You can use the boot room,' he said, 'and anyway, we'll only be going into the kitchen.'

Allenby went to say something about the tradesman's entrance but stopped himself, then extricated his feet from the mud for the final time that day and followed Eddie as he set off across the meadow and onto the lawn that circled the house. He turned back only once to let his eyes follow the bruised trail through the grass left by the tramping feet of the men heading in the opposite direction. He knew that if the world wasn't in the state it was, where every job, however badly paid, was fought over, there would be fewer of them returning in the morning. Eddie's riding boots squeaked with each step he took, steps that seemed to slither over the grass as if lifting his feet was an unwelcome burden.

4

Alex's pleasure in old buildings was mitigated by the knowledge that his arrival was usually a forerunner to their disintegration. And if he had been told to think of himself as someone who brought new life to the dead, who helped exercise a miracle of regeneration, he didn't buy into that. His father harboured no concerns for history, and in their business, time was always money – big money. Alex had worked for him long enough to know that if he got his own unfettered way, he would have levelled half of the city centre – 'nothing better than a clean slate' was a favourite saying. In fact Alex had often thought his father's future headstone should have an image of a wrecking ball engraved on the marble.

Whenever Alex entered an old commercial building their business had acquired or intended to purchase, he often thought he should lightly kiss the front door like some Mafia don because he knew his entry was the beginning of a brutal betrayal. So it was important to savour moments like the one in which he now found himself, where nothing was destroyed, as much as he could, to show respect by being on his own. He always insisted on ditching the company of estate agents or architects and moved quietly from room to room – sometimes he even

put his phone on silent. When he touched doors and surfaces
he did so gently, as if trying to calm them before the trauma
that awaited was unleashed. Of course, there were planning
restrictions in place – restrictions and regulations that caused
his father apoplexies, then sent him scampering off to consort
and confer in search of ways to circumvent what he thought
of as the constant bureaucratic desire of 'pen-pushers' to put a
brake on a march to progress, to modernity. To making money.
And not just making money for himself and the company but
also for all those who would get a cut. For the new businesses
and interests that would flourish in their wake, even though
his father sometimes resented that they simply moved in like
carpetbaggers after the bloody business of war was over.

Working for his father paid well and provided him with a
comfortable lifestyle that included a town house in the right
part of the city for him and Ellie. But as with everything,
there was a price to be paid, not least a sense that somehow
he was, metaphorically at least, still living at home and while
under his father's employment forever subject to his rules, to
all his foibles and whims. That you were never fully grown-up
because you were never fully independent. And Alex knew he
hadn't even earned his position, because he hadn't acquired
any qualifications relevant to the job he did. He had started a
degree in architecture but had packed it in halfway through,
just before he had been forced to leave by repeated failure to
submit work. His father's frustration with his failure was clear
even though it was mostly wordless, but Alex didn't doubt
that he found some pleasure in it because it served to confirm
his opinion that his son gave up too easily, walked away too
quickly when things got difficult.

It was true, however, that he had imagination, the ability to look at a building and see what it could become, so perhaps it didn't matter that it was always someone else's job to translate those ideas into tangible reality. He didn't need to worry about the state of the Tea Merchant's roof that sprouted willow herb and buddleia as if in an attempt to simulate a ragged rooftop garden; he didn't need to inspect beams and structures; or carry out measurements – that had already been done by others – nor did he need to do a detailed survey of the building's fabric. None of this mattered because this brownstone Edwardian building was going to be gutted from top to bottom. To appease the planners, they would leave the frontage untouched, even refresh it to its original pristine state before years of the city's smoke and pollution had done their damage.

It was an old tea importer's office, with three floors and an attic. There was a wooden staircase winding up to the top of the building as well as a metal-grilled lift that had some half-hearted decorative features. Initially they had bought it for office space, but the city, like all cities, had a surplus of that now. At first they were considering the possibility of a boutique hotel and he was pondering if they might somehow theme it round tea. Afternoon teas, rooms named after particular blends, perhaps if an hotel it might be called the Tea Palace – there were lots of unfolding possibilities.

Although no tea had actually ever entered the premises apart from what the clerks and secretaries used at lunchtime, it felt as if the whole building had been washed in tannin. So the light edging surreptitiously through the empty rooms was as if tea-stained, only spearing sharply in a few places where the boarded windows had failed in their appointed task. Everywhere looked indelibly crepuscular, silently waiting for the coming of the night. He moved through the ground floor rooms that were empty of everything except the whispering resonances that lingered from the accumulated lives of those who had spent decades working in this place. Secretaries who answered phones and wrote letters on headed paper, clerks who wore shirts with detachable collars and jackets that had seen years of loyal service until the elbows grew threadbare and were patched with leather. Bookkeepers who wrote in giant ledgers with ink smudges on their fingers like blue nicotine and who used blotters to safely seal the columns of figures, and thought themselves a cut above those who laboured in the nearby shipyard. The incessant click clack and tinkle of typewriters, the trill of the phone, the scratch and squeak of pens, the constant scampering of feet on the wooden stairs before they were set free to hurry through the city's streets to wherever was home.

Soon, however, the clamour subsided. In one room on the first floor there was a single wooden chair. He suddenly felt weary and sat on it, letting the building slumber again in its dotage of must and memory. He didn't often have the opportunity to be solitary, so such empty buildings pleased him, seemed to offer a companionship and a refuge for which he was grateful.

There was the faint sound of distant music from somewhere – another place, another time? And for a frightened second he saw her face again. The girl whose name he couldn't remember or didn't want to remember but whose presence accompanied him ever closer as he moved towards his wedding day. Would it make it better or worse if he remembered her name? He was glad when the music faded into silence.

He tried to free himself from the shard of memory by making himself focus intently on his surroundings, saw how the wooden floor revealed where its carpet had been pulled up, exposing a lighter-coloured border. There was a little rucked remnant in one corner showing that its colour had been bottle green. Similar lighter patches on the walls marked where cupboards had been ripped away. The building had endured for a hundred years, had survived the car bombs of the seventies and eighties, but its time had finally come. And who could say that his father wasn't right in part at least and they were in fact preserving it by bringing a new form of life to it so that in time its locked doors would open and new voices would be heard in all its rooms? There would be pain for it of course with more ripping, more knocking down and putting up, more hollowing out before it was given a new identity. He wondered if it would even be able to recognise itself.

He sat on the chair and told himself he needed a drink, perhaps something stronger. He needed a lot of things and the most urgent of these was that he wanted to know if he was a good person. It was something to do with getting married to Ellie. It wasn't anything as antiquated and clichéd as wanting to be worthy of her, because worthiness was itself a meaningless abstract. It was rather he wanted to know if he really was the person she believed he was, that she wasn't deceiving herself or even worse that he was deceiving her. He thought of the ledgers that once covered every desk and tried to deconstruct his life into columns, into negative and positive, into deficit and gain, into what was true and what was false, but life couldn't be measured in this way and there were things that spilled out over the pages of his memory and refused to be confined in the rigidity of columns. As he watched the light squeezing through the edges of the boarded windows, he thought that life was mostly a chaos, a constant flux that flowed about and through you so it was almost impossible to find something fixed to hold on to, and he tried to convince himself that whether you were a good person or not was determined not so much by what you had done, but what you would do in the days that were to come.

It was the wedding that made him dwell on these things because on that day he would have to step into the public gaze, offer himself up to scrutiny and make vows in front of people, a few of whom were important to him and some of whom meant nothing at all. In a building called the Boat House beside a lake that had not been created by nature. He lit a cigarette and felt guilty – he had promised Ellie he would give them up. It would, however, be the only one he would smoke that day and as always it was requisitioned by a moment such as this where he was unobserved and solitary. Where he could draw out the pleasure.

Alex knew in part that it was merely a delay before he had to fulfil one of his less enjoyable duties. He looked up suddenly. There was a kind of stimulation in the air, a slight tremble of consciousness, but he had sensed it often in empty buildings such as these. He told himself that it was something brought with him, like burrs stuck to the clothing or the after-image you carried having looked in a mirror. But it is all of them coming to look at him, summoned by Joyce the office gossip and spreader of news, both good and bad. So they ascend and descend the stairs from their allotted places and file, one after the other, into the room and slowly circle him. Some of the more curious move silently through him, disappearing for a second before reforming again, unsure whether he's real or not. There's Agnes who collects money every month for the Cripples' Institute and who has never married; Eamon whose son somehow went to university and became a doctor; Eilish the reader of tea leaves, possessor of a sixth sense and frequenter of religious retreats; Lynn who knits in her lunchtime and whose husband keeps greyhounds; Kelvin who frequents the bookies and always wears a pencil behind his ear and Brylcreem in his hair; Arnold who breeds budgerigars and still lives with his mother in Sandy Row. These are those who exist in this place, a living part of the city's layered past and so part too of its present and even future.

It isn't the smoke that attracts them – they are used to men smoking – nor is it the sound of his feet moving from room to room, however quietly he manages to do it. It is to do with some almost imperceptible disturbance of the air, the shifting of what has settled for so long into different patterns, the slow ebb and flow of new currents. The dissolving and reforming of time itself, the constant layering of what has once been with what is still to come. So they slowly stir now from their past lives and form about him, just as they do in every one of the city's derelict or discarded buildings when Alex comes to mark them out for a different future. And Billy is still thinking of having to ask Mr Russell for next Wednesday afternoon off so he can travel to Derry to play in the cup replay and he knows Russell will enjoy giving him a hard time about the missing hours, but he knows the chairman of the club has already sweetened him with a season ticket and the promise of a future seat in the directors' box. And the conversation will inevitably end with Old Man Russell saying to him, 'The least you can do is stick one in the back of the bloody net!' And nothing would give him more pleasure but there is no predicting it because the Brandywell ground is a fierce little place that doesn't ever hold its arms open in welcome and having a team mate shouting 'Billy' is like a red rag to the hordes on the terraces. He holds his hand out to this visitor and asks Alex for a drag, a drag both to calm his nerves and to have someone listen to him.

'There was talk a few years back about going over the water for a trial, but it never came to anything and it's not going to happen now,' he says, taking his first drag. 'But part of you always thinks you could have made it,' the smoke fogging about his head. He looks around him and gestures with the cigarette so the smoke wavers through the air. 'So this is it, this is it now. Could be worse.' He hands the cigarette back.

'You shouldn't be smoking before a game,' Evelyn says.

'And what would you know?' he asks.

'I know you haven't scored the last three games.'

He wants to tell her that sometimes in his head he scores with her even though they're both married, and that it excites him to remember the Christmas she let him hold her in the store. There is an abundance about her he likes, just a generosity about her body that presses against whatever she's wearing that makes him wonder if there might ever be a moment when he could slip his hand inside her blouse and feel the little ripple of flesh just above the waistband of her skirt. Just cup it in his hand and somehow experience the soft fullness of her, even for a moment. But all he did was hold her a few seconds longer than he should have. In a different world there are those who think that they exist only as spirits, as hazy, half-formed memories whose bodies have vanished into nothingness. How little they know, how little they understand. He moves now in a corporeal dream of his hand kneading her little rundle of softness and then a light flares and he's running at pace with the smell of cigarette smoke and pungent liniment breezing about him, dubbin on his boots, the riven, rutted mud of the pitch, the bitter wind coming over the Brandywell wall bleaching his face and stinging his eyes. His back and neck arcing to meet the ball, his eyes fixed on its flight and never faltering despite the elbow being pushed into his chest. Rising to meet it on the tides of memory but where time no longer exists, so he's not even sure if it's something still to happen or something long gone. But he gives a little skip of celebration before vanishing, suddenly absorbed once more into the silent spaces, and he wonders whether if he waited in the store she might come to him, embrace him once again into new meaning.

But she won't come even though she sees the way he looks at her. Perhaps it's a natural consequence of working in close proximity – and she can't pretend she doesn't enjoy it – but she knows she holds the power. That whatever happens it will be what she has decided. And if she likes to flatter him sometimes by teasing him about the latest result, or getting his autograph for her nephews, it's only a game – something that eases the boredom of the long afternoons when dusk falls on the city and the steady flourish of sudden lights sent up like flares in the no man's land of time, signals that they are in the last hours of their day, the hours, however, that creep most slowly. He has asked her once if she'd like to go for a drink before home but she declined even though she knew that Bob was on night duty. Afterwards on the bus home as it passes the shipyard workers streaming over the bridge, each holding a tin lunch box, she imagines that perhaps she has gone for a drink. Gone just long enough to get home after Bob has left for the station, his police uniform hidden beneath his overcoat. Sometimes she thinks he spends so much time policing the city that he imagines he also polices her, so it pleases her to think that he has no jurisdiction over what is in her head. Those mornings when he comes home with all the frustrations of what happens at night and spoons himself into the warmth of her back with the smell of the drunks and petty criminals, the city's grimy industries and dangerous streets still clinging to him, and if she decides to let him spend everything that has brought him to her in need, then she faces out of the bed and it's Billy she smiles at.

Better Billy than Old Man Russell. But sometimes she isn't sure. She knows he'd like to, sometimes looks at her more than he should, and when he asks her to shop for his wife's Christmas or birthday present, she knows part of him would like to give it to her, to see gratitude and indebtedness in her face. Men have no guile in these matters, their faces an open book with their longings and needs pressed against the weakness of their flesh. But still, there's a lot of warmth in money and once after she'd been to the jeweller's in the Arcade to collect a bracelet and found herself desiring it, she'd thought how if he ever asked again whether she minded staying behind to do a letter for him, or sort some invoices, instead of using Bob's shifts as her excuse, perhaps she should be a little more accommodating, not exactly willing, but enough to let him think there was a vague prospect.

She goes back to the endless spiral of her book work as Russell appears, pausing to look at his pocket watch with the chain that girds the width of his stomach. She can't bring herself to imagine physical intimacy the way she can with Billy. Russell studies the watch before carefully pocketing it again. He believes it bestows a sense of his authority – he is the keeper of time as well as the ledgers, the list of accounts, the endless accumulation and distribution of tea. Tea – something the country takes for granted, but if each time someone raised a cup to their lips they had an understanding of everything involved with the journey from the distant shores of the Empire, the processes involved, then they'd give it a bit more respect. Give the custodians and suppliers of it more respect as well. He has only come into the room to show himself, to engage on a kind of tour of inspection, to show to everyone that he is there, in charge, that everything is in the safety of his hands. He looks at Evelyn and tells himself that she has recognised his entrance with the trace of a smile. Then he sees the young man sitting smoking and he doesn't quite like the cut of him, the way he lounges back on the chair and carelessly lets his cigarette ash fall to the floor. He doesn't like what he might portend. Never in his own life has he been careless, never cut any corners or fiddled the figures, never invested his money except in sureties. And yet recently he is increasingly aware of a dissatisfaction, a dissatisfaction that stirs both in his head and somewhere he considers more primitive, because it's true when they say you only get one life. So at the end of the day what exactly are the rewards of carefulness? The preservation of reputation? But what exactly does the reputation of a tea merchant ever amount to? And there is no warmth any more in his bed despite the presence of his wife, no sense of fulfilment in body or head.

He glances at Evelyn and wonders about the realities of risk and what the odds are of the dice rolling in his favour. He's getting on, put on weight – without the importance of his status he doesn't believe there'd be much chance – but sometimes he thinks he sees a kind of glimmer in her eyes, a little preening of herself when she brings him some document to sign. Perhaps what he wants could be bought in some way that isn't explicit or vulgar. His thoughts seem to break free and float round the room until they mingle with the wreath of the young man's smoke and he slowly waves his arms in the hope of dissipating them before they coagulate into a solidity that can be read and sniggered over. He fingers the watch chain across his waist, wonders if he should think of it as an enforcer of chastity, a reminder of the calamitous consequences of squandering a lifetime's adherence to caution. Yet as he glances again at Evelyn his eyes flicker to the top of her brassiere strap, briefly revealed as she stretches across her desk to reach some papers, and he hears a voice in his head saying: let the wheel of fortune spin.

Alex stubbed the cigarette out, looked round him one last time, and then walked through them, his movement melded with the final wisps of smoke. They became wraiths once more of their former selves, lost again in the city's memory and the memory of themselves, washed in the faded half-light of the shuttered building. Only Eilish lingered on, watching as the young man fumbled in his pocket for the keys, but although she saw a vision of what awaited them, she knew she wouldn't share it with the others because for them the future was only able to exist in the present. As he moved across the wooden floor he unknowingly wore a kind of transfer of all of them lightly pressed on his being, so light he might have dismissed it as a shiver or merely his own breathing, or the way in broken sleep a certain memory tries to break the surface of consciousness. Then the building embraced and enfolded them once more, brought them home and swaddled them in the stillness of the air, softened their stirring with a new soft wash of sepia.

As he turned the key in the lock he let his hand rest for a second on the panelled wood of the front door, traced the beading and carved floral insert. Touched it gently like a lover, but as he walked away he knew he had already been unfaithful.

5

Edward Remington didn't bother taking off his riding boots when they got to the kitchen door at the back of the house, so when Allenby took his off in the boot room he felt at a disadvantage as he slithered over the tiled floor in his damp socks, glad that there wasn't a hole that needed darning. But he was grateful for the sudden splurge of heat that greeted his entry into the kitchen. It came from a cavernous open fire boasting a pyramid of turf and also from the cream-coloured range where what looked like a large ham was on the boil, the water threatening to bubble over the lip of the pot. On one wall was a numbered board with a bell to show from which room a summons had been issued.

There were two young women standing at the kitchen table making what looked like apple tarts, surrounded by a mess of pastry offcuts and the cores of cooking apples. The air smelt sweet and sugary and Allenby was conscious of his plastered hair, the mud on his trousers and the steam starting to rise off his jacket. He thought it best to take it off before the women imagined he was about to spontaneously combust.

'Where's Mrs Sullivan?' Eddie asked.

'Gone into the village, sir, to complain to Rogan the butcher about his last delivery of meat.'

'God help him then if he's provoked Mrs Sullivan's ire,' he said, as he reached into one of the tarts and lifted a slice of apple, holding it tantalisingly in the air before letting it drop into his mouth.

The two young women smiled discreetly at each other but kept their eyes downcast. Allenby guessed they were in their early twenties and he thought they had been having some fun before their arrival because each had flour spots on their cheeks and the one with the pinned-up auburn hair actually had a spot on her nose so they both resembled badly made-up clowns. The taller one had jet black hair pushed tight under a lace cap, and a white apron over her black dress like a waitress in an hotel. The red-haired woman who was smaller, slim of build but also in a black dress and cap, glanced at him and blew a wisp of fallen hair away from her green eyes. Was it freckles or flour across the bridge of her nose? Both of them were pretty in an unostentatious way and spoke with Belfast accents.

'So in the absence of Mrs Sullivan I believe you must both be in charge of catering for guests. Chop chop, girls, and get Mr Allenby a cup of tea. And a bit of cake or something.'

Both young women gave a half-hearted curtsy and wiped their hands on a tea towel. But before they could get a kettle on the go he called out their names – Ida and Cora – then beckoned them towards him. Taking the cloth, he dabbed the flour from their faces, like a parent with errant children.

'Don't want Mr Allenby to think we run a circus here,' he said as both girls suppressed a giggle. 'When Mrs Sullivan's away the mice will play, isn't that right?'

Neither of them spoke, offering only smiles in reply, then busied themselves with the tea and cake. At Eddie's gesture, Allenby sat down on the rocking chair beside the fire and watched him leave the room. He was uncomfortably aware of the two women studying him but when he looked at them they quickly averted their eyes. A self-conscious silence settled, broken only by the bubbling of the ham and the slow strain of the kettle. He wanted to break it but didn't know what to say.

'That's a terrible day,' Cora said.

'A good day for ducks,' Ida added.

They both giggled again and, worried that their giddiness was inspired by his bedraggled appearance, he simply nodded in agreement. He was in a strange room with women he didn't know. Working-class women whose function was as always to serve. Blue light brothels for officers, red for other ranks – even in the fulfilment of sexual needs there had to be differentiation by class. And he didn't object because while he found it humiliating enough to parade his need in front of a woman who allowed him to use her for money, he found it an even greater humiliation to be a witness to the needs of others, not least those officers he knew were married. The exchange of money, a functional release with the illusory hope of tenderness and no need to make conversation, and when words were spoken they were thankfully in a different language and whatever eroticism that might have created was always ameliorated by a suspicion that what was being said might not always have been flattering. The male fantasy that she would think you different from all the rest, because in some inexplicable way your need was different to all those who had gone before, that some human connection might be made.

Perhaps it was his sense of leaving emptier than when he entered that limited the number of his visits, an experience much more reductive than anything that might or might not have been put in their tea. After the war a year's friendship with a woman named Sarah petered into nothing, so he was relieved when she called it a day. And there was something deathly about sex – not that he had ever even come close to experiencing any real form of physical intimacy with Sarah. The closer to the battle and the closer to death, the longer the queues outside those houses. What was it after all but a giving away of yourself, a kind of pleasurable pre-emptive dying in an attempt to momentarily escape what was pressing against your skull and he didn't know if it ever led you to another human soul, opened a pathway, so much as shut you down to yourself.

A ginger cat appeared from nowhere and looked around his feet, briefly pawing one of his socks as if it saw the possibility of play. He pushed it away and it scampered under a large open cupboard holding an array of pots, tureens, cooking paraphernalia and shiny metal moulds that, if anything, resembled an armoury.

The kettle began its high-pitched whine and both women turned to it. Ida used a cloth to lift it off the range and its black heaviness contrasted with the delicacy of the china cups and saucers that Cora arranged on the table. For a second they looked inexperienced, like children playing house. Allenby guessed they hadn't been long in post. Eddie reappeared carrying a bottle of Bushmills whiskey and poured a measure into the cups.

'That'll put some heat into you,' he said before he pulled a table chair to the fire. Then he winked at him and flourishing the bottle called to the two women, 'Any of you girls need a little heat in you?'

Allenby stared at the fire as if to separate himself from the man's coarseness but then he heard Ida say, 'If you're offering, Mr Remington,' and after the tinkle of more china both women approached with their empty cups held out like paupers waiting for a bestowal of charity.

'Not a word to Mrs Sullivan, and what happened to the cake?' Eddie said as he poured the whiskey.

Cora scurried back to the other side of the table and returned with two slices of Madeira cake on small plates. Ida, however, stood closer to Eddie than she should have and sipped her whiskey, holding the cup in both hands as if worried about dropping it.

'That'll warm the bones,' Eddie said, smiling at him.

In reply Allenby merely raised his cup. He was conscious once more of the fire steaming his clothes, that the tiled floor still bore the print of his feet and that his trousers were badly mud-spotted. He no longer felt comfortable in the kitchen and resolved to take his leave when he had finished his tea. He liked Eddie less the more time he spent in his company, and sought comfort in imagining situations that would have presented themselves in the war when certain realities might have been established, particular instruction given with ill-disguised relish. Younger men like Edward Remington rarely referenced what had happened to the generation before them. Perhaps some of the more stupid felt a silent resentment that they had missed the action and in so doing were thought less manly than those who hadn't. Others had simply consigned it to the pages of history, or felt it was a club from which they were forever denied membership. And Allenby, like so many others, never talked about the experience with those who weren't there. What was the point, because to talk about it was a form of reliving it and who would want to do that when every impulse was to forget?

As he started to feel warm for the first time since early morning and the whiskey slowly worked its effects, his resolve to drink up and leave began to fade. A squall of wind-driven rain lashed the kitchen windows. The light darkened and the gaze of all seemed to fasten on the fire. Unless Eddie offered to drive him he would have to make the trek to the village station for the last train to Belfast. The two women washed and dried their cups as if intent on hiding the evidence and Allenby watched as they slid the two apple tarts into the range. He suddenly felt weary. If it rained again so heavily tomorrow, the excavation work would be delayed once more. He resolved that in the morning, whatever the weather, he would give up his pathetic attempt to show comradeship with his workers and come appropriately dressed and equipped. Eddie was staring at his mud-covered clothes as if he was affronted by them.

'Cora, can you do anything about the mud on Mr Allenby's trousers?'

'It'd be better waiting until it hardens,' she said, making Ida snigger, 'then brush it off.'

'It's all right,' Allenby said, 'I'll have to be going soon.'

Eddie poured another measure into his cup and told him it was one for the road. Before he could raise the cup to his lips, however, the outer door slammed open and a black figure lurched in with the shoulder capes on her black coat flapping like wings, so she looked like some raven propelled on a savage current of wind. Under a black umbrella that sprayed droplets of water was a thin, indeterminate creature who turned out to be Mrs Sullivan returned from her foray to the village. Ida and Cora hurried to take her umbrella and shopping basket. Then she handed them her coat and hat and patted her face with the palms of reddened hands.

'It's shocking out there,' she said. 'Coming down like there's no tomorrow.'

Then as if noticing his and Edward Remington's presence for the first time, she tried to gather some composure, smoothing the straying grey tails of her hair back into place and twisting her dress straight as if wrenching free a locked lid on a jar.

'I hope you've been looked after,' she said, glancing at the two women, who in response stood a little straighter. 'I had some business in the village with Mr Rogan.'

'Hopefully sorted,' Eddie ventured.

'I believe so. I think I made my concerns perfectly clear.'

'This is Mr Allenby, our hole digger,' he said, gesturing to him. Ida and Cora looked downwards to try to hide their smiles.

Allenby stood up and nodded to her, conscious that she was looking at his socks and mud-spattered trousers with something close to disdain. He wanted to tell her that she didn't look so presentable herself but instead said that it was nice to meet her, thanked the two maids for the tea and cake and announced he needed to set out for the station.

'There's no train, Mr Allenby. Not tonight. The rain has caused a landslide outside the village – all the trains are cancelled.'

'Are you sure?' he asked.

'Perfectly sure, sir,' she said, bridling a little. It was obvious she wasn't used to being questioned. 'I heard it from the station master myself.'

'Well, that's that, Allenby,' Eddie said, shrugging his shoulders. 'Nothing else for it than to stay here tonight. You'll be able to have an early start in the morning.'

At that moment Allenby thought he'd rather spend the night in a foxhole, but knew there was nothing he could say except to ask Eddie if he too was sure.

'Nothing else for it, old chap, and it's not as if there's a Mrs Allenby waiting at home for you. Mrs Sullivan will see one of the guest rooms is ready, won't you, Mrs Sullivan? And I think some towels – I imagine Mr Allenby will want to have a bath.'

Mrs Sullivan nodded, then asked if she should set an extra place for dinner.

'Yes, of course,' he said. 'Especially now Rogan's had his card marked and no doubt we have better fare to look forward to.' Then turning to Allenby he added, 'And it'll give you a chance to provide an update to the old man in person. Explain the delay. Good luck with that. Mrs Sullivan will arrange a change of clothes – we look vaguely the same size – while yours are being cleaned. Isn't that right, Mrs Sullivan?'

'Yes, Mr Remington. I'll see to that right away.'

She offered a kind of wave to the two women and when their only response was to look at her, she shooed them away with another impatient gesture that hurried them out of the kitchen.

'I'll show Mr Allenby to his room,' she said, taking his side plate and cup from him, her eyes inspecting the contents with ill-disguised censure.

'You're in safe hands, Allenby. And after dinner we can have a couple of games of billiards. I imagine you play.'

'Yes, thank you.'

He followed Mrs Sullivan as she led him along the main hall that was darkened by wood panelling and swathes of floral carpet. On the walls were various landscape paintings that even a cursory glance revealed as amateurish and unworthy of the elaborate frames with which they had attempted to elevate themselves. There was a damp smudge on the collar of Mrs Sullivan's blouse, beads of water like seed pearls in her pinned hair. Then up two flights of stairs with more floral carpet and brass stair rods and at the end of each corridor a large bay window with stained-glass panels. She walked ahead in silence and he did not attempt to engage her in conversation. The guest room was at the front of the house, looking out over the formal lawn and across the space where the lake would be. It was cold and edged with mustiness and did not give the impression of having been aired or used in some time. Mrs Sullivan disappeared into the corridor and, raising her voice, summoned Cora and instructed her to light a fire. He looked out at the great morass of mud and felt a sense of shame that he had desecrated the earth in this brutal way, rendering it into a reflection of what they had done to it in the war. At the edge of the lake, the wide trail where the workers' feet had trampled the grass out of existence made it seem as if the mud had taken on a life of its own and was flowing out into the world beyond. Puddles and interconnected swirls of water had formed everywhere so the expanse was both pockmarked and fluid. Rain continued to sheet down, primping and stirring the gathered water so that everything looked as if it was about to burst into molten motion. They would have to pump the water out before they could excavate any further. More delays to explain to Remington senior.

Cora knocked the still open door and then entered with a coal scuttle and kindling. She raked at ancient ashes in the grate and then lit a fire, at one point blowing vigorous life into its reluctance to catch. He watched her kneeling at the hearth, the flame of her hair the only colour in the room.

'Thanks for that,' he said. 'I don't think it's been lit for a while.'

'It's a cold house,' she said, pausing before stirring more enthusiastic flames. 'Cold and damp.'

'You can blame my company for that. We did most of the repair work.'

'You own a business?' she asked, looking at him over her shoulder.

'No, it's a firm of architects I work for.'

'So you've been here before.'

'No, the work was done before I started. I just got the job of doing the lake – digging the hole.'

'Why do they want a lake?'

'A good question. It's a kind of fashion for houses like this.'

'A lot of trouble just to be in the fashion,' she said, getting to her feet.

'Have you been here long?'

'A couple of months. I came with Ida. We used to work in one of Mr Remington's mills.'

'And is this better?' he asked, staring at the greenness of her eyes.

She stared back at him but before she could reply Mrs Sullivan returned with a neat pile of clothes and a pair of black patent leather shoes. He thanked her but she barely acknowledged it.

'The bathroom is down the end of the hall,' Mrs Sullivan said. 'There should be hot water and I've left extra towels out. Afterwards you can leave your clothes in the kitchen for cleaning. I think these should fit.' She set the folded clothes on the end of the bed and then gave the fire an inspectorial glance. 'Don't smother the fire, Cora – you'll have it out before it's got going.'

After she had gone he smiled at Cora and she rolled her eyes in response.

'I know who I'd like to smother,' she said quietly, and then before he had time to thank her again for the fire, she too was gone. He looked at the clothes and should have been grateful but there was something discomforting about the thought of wearing what belonged to Eddie. He went to the window again. The rain had relented slightly but all the light was draining out of the day so everything he saw was rendered inert and devoid of any recognisable stir of life. It had been a terrible day. The men had laboured in miserable conditions for the pittance of their pay. He was tired of asking men to endure suffering, whether for the whims of someone with too much money, or by generals for ownership of some meaningless stretch of ground whose value existed only in their mind-warped idea of strategy. If Mr Remington wanted a lake let him take off his suit, take a shovel and join them. If a general wanted a piece of land then let him be first out of the trench and leading the way. He pressed his hand to the coldness of the glass and had a sudden vision of constructing a gigantic lake and then letting it burst its boundaries, flooding the Manor House and carrying everything before it.

He looked round the room, taking in the brass bed frame; the ugly dark mahogany furniture that stood stiffly on guard and which seemed to resent his presence as if he was an intruder; the floral wallpaper and dried flowers in a vase with a chipped rim. Only the fire seemed to offer any semblance of life so he went to it and stood at the edge of the slate hearth. On the mantelpiece were two stubs of candles in saucers, an invitation to a wedding long past, a clock that hadn't been wound and a tiny seed pearl whose milky lustre he rolled between his fingers before setting it back. The veneer of dust was white-spotted where the candles had dripped. He thought again of the house he wanted to build and wondered if he might indeed be able to find a plot close to the sea. It would be a house with large windows where light and air would flow in, dispelling forever any trace of must or decay and the sky would be welcomed. And it felt to him that it was the permanent restlessness of the sea that might be able to absorb his own, its restless motion able to subsume whatever it was in him that resisted his own attempts at stillness. A place that wouldn't have the imprisoned artificiality of this lake he was charged with delivering. He looked at the flaring fire that had finally quickened into life and for a second he remembered the blaze of Cora's hair, the paleness of her skin, then turned reluctantly away and lifted the pile of another man's clothes.

6

Ellie took a seat in the back room of the auction house and opened the file named Wedding. It contained a spreadsheet with detailed costs; numerous photographs of dresses – both brides and bridesmaids; floral arrangements and wedding favours; a list of guests complete with a seating plan and the wedding invite template; emails to the chosen florist, cake maker, the wedding band and DJ and the wedding car supplier. There was all her correspondence with the Manor House, a contract signed by her father, and numerous back and forths with Rosemary about various matters of minor importance. One folder even contained possible wedding vows and another all the details about the registrar and required certification. Each time she opened it the file had grown bigger so it had begun to take on the appearance of one of the wedding-themed magazines she had started to collect. Alex made jokes about it, but she knew he was glad that she was taking the lead. They still hadn't made a decision about rings. And she had started to feel uncomfortable with having everything on a spreadsheet because although she told herself she needed it to keep a track of it all, it was also true that she associated them with business, with income and expenditure, and she didn't want any echo of commerce to taint her wedding day.

She told herself she wasn't a trivial person, wasn't gullible or naïve in her understanding of the world. So then how did she explain the wedding file, or her preoccupation with the coming day? But she believed there shouldn't be any begrudging in relation to a wedding, whatever form it took, or even whether it took place or not, because at the end of the day what was love but the making of a promise? Even if promises were things that could be kept or broken.

Monday was the quietest day in the auction house, made quieter by the fact that her father Raymond had started to play golf in the afternoon if the weather was half decent. And she was glad of that because everything was well organised and everyone knew their jobs, whether it was the accounts office taking payment, or Brian and Declan locating purchased items from the previous Friday's auction and seeing them safely off the premises. She helped Sylvia to value incoming items and write them up, taking the photographs because online was crucial and more financially rewarding than the purchases from the same group of punters who arrived faithfully every week, some of whom enjoyed the social aspect as much as anything else. Her father still insisted on contributing to the descriptions, and clearly enjoyed the public demonstration of his knowledge, his access to a lifetime in the trade. Sometimes Ellie thought the real pleasure in his life came from using words like chiffonier, tantalus, cellarette, marquetry. His favourite sentences always started with 'A fine example of...'. Alex liked to tease her occasionally by using it, and most often to describe something mundane:

'a fine example of a bacon sandwich', or 'a fine example of a digestive biscuit'.

Money was the one part of the business her father was reluctant to let go, and he always insisted on seeing the books at the end of each week. Ellie had had to show him how to access them on the computer, and after some initial reluctance he managed to master the basics. She thought her father would retire in the near future, but any time she mentioned it to him he would make a joke of it by saying he couldn't afford to when he had a wedding to pay for.

Ellie closed the file again – it felt as if she was overfamiliar with its contents and that overfamiliarity prevented her from seeing it in the fresh way she wanted. And there was work to do. A man had brought in his deceased grandfather's war medals. When she had asked him if they were not something he might want to keep in his family, he had been dismissive and focused only on their financial value. She had almost enjoyed disappointing him because although it was a nice set there was nothing particularly rare about them, nor were there any accompanying photographs or documentation that would have created a human story. The preponderance of television programmes about antiques, and their inevitable focus on unexpectedly valuable pieces, ensured that she was always being presented with items that had little value by people who were convinced they'd found a way to get rich. She had checked the medals online and established a fair valuation – although if, as sometimes happened, two collectors locked horns it was possible they might climb much higher. She touched them respectfully with her hand. Then took a photograph.

Perhaps it is that click, that halting of forward time that summons him bleary-eyed and uncertain from the shadows, and it confuses him even more when he doesn't recognise his surroundings. He blinks as he falters into the light, falters into being. There has been confusion for a long time, the ebb and flow of a constantly moving sea that carries him adrift on whatever current forms around him. So who is this young woman and what does she want from him? He blinks again and thinks she may be his daughter, his granddaughter or one of the strangers who comes to his room every day and calls him by his name, speaks to him as if he is a child. Everything closes in and then he sees the medals and it is as if he has stumbled into a light that pierces his very being. So he moves about her, through her and everything comes down to wanting her to understand what her hand touches and the words tumble out.

How they come in the night like wolves. Hunting in packs, slipping silently under the radar of the destroyers whose job it is to guard the strung-out flanks of the convoys, then picking off their targets like shooting fish in a barrel. It is the waiting that is the worst of all, more cruel than even the white-teethed Atlantic winters that threaten to rip exposed flesh from the bone and ice the very soul. Whether on duty or down below, there isn't a moment when some part of him doesn't imagine the torpedo spuming towards them and it is raw fear that churns his stomach more than any storm or mountainous sea. And even though he does what he has to do and buries it deep, it is in the eyes and everywhere he looks he sees the reflection of his same own unspoken fear.

Now his gaze fixes on the three medals that sat on the mantelpiece between the clock and the photograph of his wife. His wife – where has she gone? Why can't he reach her? Why doesn't she come to him? What was her name? He looks at the dull glint of the medals that haven't been cleaned since the last time she held them in her hands and sees the way that the ribbon is threading at the edges.

Three medals – it doesn't seem much to compensate for what he has done, what he has seen. Afterwards it was the RAF boys who got all the credit, those public schoolboys with their silk scarves and swanky blue uniforms who were seen as the nation's heroes. But it was the sea that was the living hell, not the sky. Before they had worked out how to fight the U-boats. Never so much owed by so many to so few, Churchill had said about the fighter pilots; well, he bloody well wanted to make a winter crossing of the North Atlantic and see how many cigars he managed to smoke.

'Who was it put food on the tables?' he asks. 'Who was it put the fuel in the planes? Did they think it dropped down like manna from Heaven?'

He tried to spit and get the bitterness out of his mouth. He wants the young woman to see with his eyes. To see it all.

The sea suddenly bursting into fire. They'd hit a tanker – crewing one of those was like sailing your own coffin – and it lit up the sky like a vision of Hell. He hears once more the screams of burning men in his head and he doesn't understand how this young woman doesn't hear them too. He waves his arms frantically as if wanting to bat them away, claps his hands to his ears but it's no use. Despite their orders not to stop there'd have been a mutiny if they hadn't done so, just long enough to pull a pitiful handful of survivors out of the water. Men hauled from the boiling cauldron with their flesh pink and seared like meat. Some of them it would have been more merciful to throw back into the sea. And there were others too, completely covered from head to foot in oil. They hooked their clothes gently with boathooks and fished them out until they slithered aboard like tar babies, only the writhing whites of their eyes breaking their blackness.

Breaking the darkness. He asks the young woman if she understands, but she only looks through him as if he doesn't exist. He wants to take the medals but when he stretches out his hand there is nothing there except a void opening once more and then he lets himself fall slowly backwards and into the currents.

She closed the case containing the medals and wondered about the person to whom they were given and was sad that his family wanted to let them pass into a stranger's hands. But she knew that this is what they did in their business – took the objects that once formed part of a life, a life they never got to know, and placed them in the hands of someone so they formed part of a new reality, part of a new story. There was a call for her to come to reception. A woman had brought in jewellery to be valued, and because the more experienced Sylvia was on her lunch break, she knew she would only make an approximate valuation that would have to be confirmed. It was too easy to be wrong about jewellery, particularly where stones were concerned, too easy to mistake the inferior for purer quality or not to appreciate what might actually be the highest quality. The ability to discern only came with experience and she was still trying to master the four Cs – cut, clarity, colour, carat. And it reminded her again that they hadn't decided on rings, but she knew she wanted it to be something that already had its own story. She looked about her, conscious of something that had caught the corner of her eye – but decided it was only the momentary change of light from the skylight and that the movement was nothing more than the clouds drifting by.

The woman at reception was elderly and as she pulled her items from her handbag, Ellie saw that the skin on the back of her hands was shiny and stretched tightly, the raised veins coloured in the bluest ink. There was a nice cameo brooch, a charm bracelet of the type that was hopelessly out of fashion but which someone would buy for its gold value, a string of pearls that Ellie knew could be worth something or nothing at all – it was always hard to tell with pearls. There were three sets of good quality earrings, one with six heart-shaped clusters of brilliant-cut diamonds, one with yellow gold and pearls and one with emeralds. But it was the ring that caught her attention – it looked as if it was from the twenties or thirties with a row of five graduating pearls set within gold open-work and quite different to anything she had ever seen. She lifted it and held it to the light.

'It was my grandmother's,' the woman said.

'It's very pretty.'

'But I don't remember her wearing it very much. We found it when we cleared her house. It was hidden away in a drawer. Maybe she was keeping it hidden away for special occasions.'

'Are you sure you want to sell it?'

'Yes. I'm too old for jewellery now. And I've two sons so they're no use to them.'

'No daughters-in-law?'

'Two. But I wouldn't give either of them the skin of my teeth.'

'They can't be that bad,' Ellie said, smiling.

'You don't know them. They'd have me in a home and my house sold if I didn't look out.'

'I hope I'm kinder to my mother-in-law after I get married.'

'You're getting married then?'

'End of September.'

'That's a good time to get married. Autumn light is kind to the face.'

Ellie laughed and heard the woman say, 'No offence, luv.'

Ellie gave her an approximate valuation for all the items, apart from the string of pearls, and told her she'd phone her with a proper estimate for everything in a day or so, made sure she understood about the auction house's commission. The woman appeared happy enough and wished her well for the wedding.

'No use to me this stuff, at my stage of life,' she said as she closed her handbag. 'I'm going to put the money to a funeral plan. Spare myself the embarrassment of being bundled off in something cheap as chips.'

Ellie watched her go, held up the ring to the light again, then slipped it on her finger. Someone else's ring, someone else's story – it was how she spent her life, handling and charting other people's pasts. But there was something about this one that held her attention, as if it might become part of the future that awaited her.

7

Allenby was disappointed in his bath. The hot water ran out before there was enough to cover his body, and the plumbing rattled and complained as if it had been asked to do something wholly unreasonable. Once too he was conscious of giggling coming from the corridor outside. The modernisation his firm had carried out on the house – and he had looked at the file out of curiosity – seemed to have fallen far short of making it a place where any sane person would ever wish to live. It was in fact everything he had come to detest. Too big with too many disconnected and purposeless rooms, impossible to keep warm in winter or to air in summer so that there was always a kind of chill clinging to its empty spaces, all of which were redolent with the lives that had gone before and from whom you felt a lingering, sullen resentment at your intrusive presence. And there was the constant upkeep and maintenance, where owners were locked in a permanent battle against insidious and insistent decay.

It was a familiar story, the grandiose dreams and lifestyles of the Anglo-Irish, gradually eroded by time, the impact of the war where so many of their sons had been lost, and the increasing financial pressures of trying to maintain what was gradually moving beyond them. The roofs generally went first, and then the spread of damp in a house that could no longer be heated saw the family decamp from room to room, a bit like the Russian Matryoshka doll his mother had been given as a child, until in the equivalent of the smallest doll, they ended up living in whichever of the rooms could best be heated, the army of staff needed for the running of the house reduced to a cook, a maid and a gardener.

No doubt Remington believed that he required a house and land that reflected his rise in the world and, with all the surplus money he needed to throw at it, decided the Manor House was sufficiently grand. Allenby wondered if he was happy with his purchase, or whether it simply had to be maintained for reasons that had nothing to do with comfort. No doubt too Remington mentally compared it every day to the tiny terrace in a Belfast backstreet where he'd grown up, with its outdoor privy and gaggle of children sleeping head to toe in one of two beds. But it was also true that Remington's purchase of the property had prevented its continued slide into decay and eventual dereliction.

Allenby tried to imagine the house in its heyday and attempted to convince himself that the lake he was creating was part of restoring its previous grandeur, but was hindered by the fact that the water in the bath had turned the colour of days-old tea. Although he didn't despise natural comforts, one of the legacies of having lived in a trench was an instinctive aversion to unnecessary or ostentatious display. He knew too that a man could survive on very little but had no desire to speculate on what additional metaphysical component might sustain existence. He lived day to day and the only future dream he permitted himself was of the house he would build and live in. So he shrugged off his disappointment at the bath and dried himself on the single towel Mrs Sullivan had left, then reluctantly put on Eddie's clothes. There was one cufflink and betting slip in the pocket of the jacket for a horse called Summer Dancer and a flyer for a golf club New Year's Eve dance that stipulated fancy dress. He wondered what the young man had gone as and whether there was such a thing as a lounge lizard costume. Eddie's shoes pinched his toes and the trousers finished a little high on his ankles, but he was pleased not to be an identical match. Then gathering up his own clothes, he set out to find his way back to the kitchen. Three rooms down the corridor he paused at a door just long enough to know that two people were having sex. He tried to step soundlessly as he walked on, but the lighter he trod the more the floorboards started to creak. The room went silent for a few seconds, then he heard the sound of stifled laughter and the activity resumed.

In the kitchen Cora was draining the ham at the sink, steam clouding up around her. Without knowing why, he was glad that she hadn't been the woman in the room. But there was no dignity to be found in holding out his clothes like a child so he just stood silently and waited for her to finish. She hummed a little tune to herself and then slapped the pink slab of ham on a board. He coughed lightly and she spun round in surprise, though she didn't appear flustered at seeing him.

'I'll take those,' she said, reaching out for his clothes.

'I'm sorry you have to do this,' he said. 'I'm sure you have enough work of your own to be getting on with.'

'I don't mind. They'll be ready in the morning.' And then she added the word 'sir'.

He wanted to tell her his name was George but he knew it was not appropriate and she wouldn't thank him for the embarrassment, so he simply offered his gratitude and went to leave again. But stopping at the door he turned back and asked her what time he should come down for dinner, unsure whether he was supposed to call it dinner or tea.

'Seven in the dining room, just off to the left there.'

'Will Mrs Remington be there?'

'No, sir, she's gone to her sister's in Dublin. Won't be back until the weekend I think.'

And even though he knew he shouldn't, he asked. 'Where's Ida?'

'She's doing a message.'

He looked at her now in just the same way he had looked at his men when he knew they were lying, but she stood impassive and undeterred, her two hands holding the folded pile of his clothes as if she was waiting to make an offering of them. Then he went back to his room and when he passed the bedroom where he had heard what he imagined was Eddie and Ida, there was only silence.

At dinner he met Remington senior, who was already seated at the head of the table when he entered and acknowledged his arrival with a slow raise of his hand. He had given some of his features to his son but his face was florid and jowly and although he had a good head of hair, it was uniformly grey and somehow lifeless. Allenby guessed he had consumed a few drinks at his lodge meeting.

'So, George, you're stranded with us for the night. I think I'll send a bill to Wickets and Rodgers for your board and lodging.'

'I'm sure they'd be happy to pay, sir.'

'Only pulling your leg, George. You're very welcome. Where's that son of mine? He's always dragging his heels.' He held his hands out in mock exasperation. 'Edward tells me that you've encountered more problems.'

'The weather, sir. It's rained solidly for three days and that makes working conditions very difficult.'

'A bit of muck never harmed anyone, George.'

'No,' Allenby said as he saw a man's body floating face down in the bottom of a crater, the sheer side walls scoured and trailed by his desperate struggle to climb out, 'but it makes the excavation virtually impossible – everywhere's waterlogged. Sometimes the machinery gets bogged down and you need to spend valuable time trying to drag it back out. And it's dangerous. A man broke his leg today.'

'Sorry to hear that. So what's the answer, apart from praying for better weather?'

'We'll try and pump out the water that's lying tomorrow. See how we go.'

'We're making a lake, can we not just leave the water in?' Remington asked, pulling his linen napkin from its silver ring with a theatrical flourish and placing it on his lap.

'We haven't excavated enough yet. We need to go deeper if the lake is to hold the water we direct into it.'

'Who would have thought digging a hole would prove so complicated? And so slow? If Lydia hadn't got a bee in her bonnet about having one I wouldn't have given the idea the time of day. Apparently a lake raises us a couple of rungs up the ladder in some way I don't quite understand. But George, it all has to be ready for the open day in August, absolutely has to be ready by then – she has her heart set on it.' Allenby told him he believed that it would be. Then when Mrs Sullivan appeared silently in the doorway Remington asked her to find Eddie. 'Tell him that if he's not here pronto we're starting without him.'

Allenby admired the housekeeper's ability to appear and disappear almost seamlessly, sometimes not more than a passing shadow caught in the corner of an eye. It was probably a required qualification for her. He imagined there wouldn't be much she didn't hear and even less she didn't see and that she was a kind of walking repository for everything that happened within the walls over which she presided.

Allenby studied Eddie when he arrived with an apology but there was nothing visible in his face or his manner that revealed anything other than a desultory sense of unflustered ease. A few minutes later with Mrs Sullivan leading the way, Cora and Ida served dinner, their faces drained of their earlier frivolity, bodies held stiffly and everything concentrated on what they were doing. Allenby had an insight into fear – he could read it as clearly as he could read a book – and if the two young women didn't exhibit the nakedness of fear then there was an apprehension lining their faces and their movements that made him curious. He watched Ida serving Eddie but saw nothing pass between them, and when his own eyes met Cora's she looked away. Mrs Sullivan stood rigidly in a supervisory role until they had been served and then followed the two women out of the room. They had the ham he had seen cooking in the kitchen, with potatoes and garden peas washed down by a glass of red wine.

What fading natural light ventured in from the large windows behind Remington at the head of the table seemed to flow round him while the other lights made everyone's faces waxen and pinched.

'So how did you put in your time today?' he asked his son.

'This and that. Went out in the rain to see how things were progressing with the lake, helped out a bit there.'

Remington glanced at Allenby, who merely kept his eyes on Eddie and tried to register nothing on his face.

'Lydia took a real shine to the drawings for the boat house,' Remington said after a few moments of silence.

'I'm glad she liked it,' Allenby replied.

'Though I'm not sure why you'd want something to look Chinese in the middle of Ulster.'

'Unless it was a laundry,' Eddie said, smiling at his own joke.

'What's it called, George? Chinesy or something.'

'Chinoiserie is what it gets called. Right down to the dragons at the door.'

'Who'd have thought it, George, a lad from the Shankill with a boat house and dragons at the door.'

After the meal was finished and cleared, Remington poured them three glasses of port and offered cigars. Mrs Sullivan reappeared and switched on the reading lamps, and the smoke from the cigars seemed drawn to them and swirled round their luminescence like some sea mist curling itself round offshore lights. Remington asked his son to fetch his reading glasses from his bedroom and after he had loped off unenthusiastically, the cigar held down by his side leaving a thin flurry of smoke in his wake, there was a moment of silence before Remington spoke.

'He'll be a while. The glasses are in my study. I'm sure Eddie's engineering skills were a big help today. Surprised the lake's not ready with him at your side.' Allenby only smiled in reply. 'The problem with Eddie is that he's never had to work for what he has and so he doesn't know the value of anything. And getting things too easy rots the soul.' He paused to reach across the table for the ashtray and flicked some of his cigar ash into it. 'Maybe you could have a talk, spend some time with him when I take myself off to bed.'

Allenby nodded noncommittally and sipped more of the port before saying, 'Why can't he manage some part of your business?'

'Tried that. Unfortunately, Eddie likes a bet but he doesn't always pick winners. He almost ran what he was responsible for into the ground and in business you can't bet on anything you're not able to cover, or you risk being holed below the waterline. Eddie doesn't always understand that, tells himself over and over that there's always another race. There have been times when I'd have given him a hiding except he's an only child and the apple of his mother's eye.' He poured them both another glass. 'You were in the war, George, weren't you? I imagine you look down your nose at the likes of us, people who made money out of it.'

Before Allenby could reply Remington said, 'I fought my own war, George. And bloody hard it was. One of seven children. My father was killed in a shipyard accident when I was twelve. I had to become the man of the house, put food on the table or we would have starved. I ducked and dived, thieved off the back of lorries and from warehouses, did whatever needed to be done, and sometimes what didn't – a hundred years earlier and I'd have been transported to Australia.'

Eddie returned without his cigar and when he told his father he couldn't find the glasses Remington told him not to worry, that he must have left them somewhere else. Eddie draped his leg over the arm of the chair as if weary from his journey.

'How did the Masons go?' he asked his father.

'Same old people saying the same old things and the only point to being there is to be seen to be there. A waste of bloody time if you ask me. Everybody playing at being important. Next time I think I'll send you. You could play at being important as well as the next man, couldn't you?'

Eddie didn't answer but topped up his own glass from the port decanter then took a cigarette from a silver case and, lighting it with a show of concentration, angled his head as he exhaled. It was clear that this was to be his only reply to his father's question. Remington dropped his napkin on the table and asked Eddie if he would tell Mrs Sullivan to put a hot water jar in his bed because he had been cold the previous night. Eddie looked over his shoulder to see if he might be able to summon her without having to get up again then with a sigh raised himself slowly from the chair. Before he could set off Remington stood up and said he would do it himself. He offered them a goodnight but just before he left the dining room he paused and turned around and said, 'I must be getting old and soft, allowing the cold to get into my bones. You don't know the heat a woman puts in your bed until she's gone.'

Allenby followed Eddie to the room with the snooker table and when offered the choice between billiards and snooker chose the latter. He wasn't going to talk to him about the war; to do so would have felt like an insult to the men he served with and to himself. What was the point of talking about something that someone who wasn't there would never be able to understand? Why too would he expose his own experiences by dragging them into the light of day, when the only way to deal with them was to keep them buried as deeply as possible? Then just maybe eventually they would melt away like yesterday's snow or the morning's hard frost. Keep hoping that some sun, some unexpected warmth, might dispel what had hardened into the set of memory. So instead they talked about the people they had a shared knowledge of in the golf club and who had started a discreet campaign to secure enough votes to become the next club captain. At Eddie's insistence they played two games with a slight wager on both and Allenby turned a blind eye when his opponent twice fouled the cue ball without declaring it. Allenby won both but his winnings took the form of a verbal IOU, something he doubted he would ever see translated into cash. After the second game Eddie leaned on the table and taking the white ball rolled it down the table so it ricocheted between cushions.

'I suppose the old man gave you his self-made-man speech, how he single-handedly tunnelled his way out of Poverty Street and despite overwhelming odds managed to find his way into fields of clover.'

'Something like that.'

'When I was a kid he used to take me to see the house where he grew up. A backstreet off the Shankill. I'd have to get out of the car and stand and stare at it even though there was nothing to see. He'd even do the same old patter every time so I knew it off by heart.'

'You didn't enjoy it?'

'I'm sure I could have thought of better things a boy might have done on a Saturday afternoon with his father. And another thing, this open day, this grand showing off is a waste of time.

It's never going to impress the people they want it to. The old money, the horsey set, even including those who have no money but have the right names and right accents – they're like a bloody clam, tightly closed to the likes of us. So it doesn't matter how big the lake is, or how grand this house looks, we're never being invited inside that circle. And you can have fire-breathing dragons and build a bloody replica of the Great Wall of China – it's never opening that shut door.'

The cue ball had finally come to a halt until he set it in motion again. He offered Allenby a nightcap but he excused himself by saying he needed to be up bright and early in the morning. Eddie nodded and stared at the table, but just as Allenby made to leave and go up to his room, he heard the sound of his name.

'George, it's a cold night. Do you want your bed warmed?'

8

Alex knew that going to the Tea Merchant's had served no real purpose other than to put off his visit to the Arcade. If he could have avoided this second visit he would, but it was at his father's insistence. The building was only a short distance away and his spirits dropped as he got closer. Built in Art Deco style in the thirties by Wickets and Rodgers, it had fallen into decline although there were still original features remaining, including tiling, green marbling and black granite on shopfronts. It too had survived a couple of IRA bombs and decades of the same neglect that blighted the whole area so it was a long way from what Alex imagined had been its original splendour. His father owned the building but did so from behind a property company called Montgomery Holdings, the connection so well disguised that establishing any link would have required sophisticated detective skills.

Alex's father liked decay and commercial decline, saw it always as opportunity, and the Arcade – even in its run-down state – signified serious opportunity. Political contacts and insiders close to planning officials, all of them on occasional kick backs, had tipped him off that a large multinational property development company had received initial approval to submit plans for an extensive regenerative programme of the whole area. In response, his father had bought up several derelict buildings. The Arcade was a prime location and a potentially valuable asset. The problem that had somehow drifted onto Alex's shoulders was that the Arcade contained a number of occupied shops, small-time enterprises paying cheap rents but with long leases. There was a coffee shop, a second-hand bookshop, a tattooist, Tropical Tans, a jeweller, a vinyl record store, an artists' collective, a picture framer and a barber. Alex liked all of them, found them decent people working hard to make a living, so as he entered the Arcade for the second time that day he felt a traitor, a Judas, whose smile hid his true intentions. Everyone he would see in the Arcade believed he worked for Montgomery Holdings and that the purpose of his visit was to check everything was going all right with their tenancies or to respond to some small problem that had arisen – a dripping pipe, a warped door, a problem with someone's heating – when the truth was he was there to check things out, to make subtle soundings about the future and ultimately to convince all of them to vacate. He wasn't ready for that, wasn't sure he would ever be ready, and wondered how he might persuade his father to allocate the responsibility to someone else.

He went first to the barber's thinking that a haircut might help him shed some of what he was feeling. There was only one other customer, an old man.

'All right?' Anton asked without turning his head so their eyes met in the mirror.

'It's cold outside,' he said, as he took off his coat and hung it on one of the pegs just inside the door. He tried to push it away from the old man's coat, with its smell of cigarette smoke and cooked food.

'I wouldn't know,' Anton said, 'I'm too busy working, not swanning round town with my two arms the same length.'

Alex's supposedly easy job was Anton's favourite joke and even though he'd heard it many times he smiled in reply and took a seat. He liked the quiet intimacy of barbers' shops, the polite, silent waiting, the smell of leather and spice, the click of the scissors and buzz of the clippers. And if you wanted to make it a confessional you generally could do so, but without the prospect of judgement or penance. He looked at himself in the mirror and was taken aback by how old he looked, a bit frayed at the edges. Perhaps a haircut would actually help. Anton wore a short-sleeved T-shirt, and his tattooed arms looked as if a child had taken a ballpoint pen and scribbled randomly on his skin. A wall full of mirrors, no hiding place to avoid seeing himself. It wasn't his image he saw but in a blink of his eyes, the child he had once been, coming slowly towards him from some world beyond the glass. Walking slowly through the years, a child who thinks he's no longer a child because his mother sends him to have his hair cut for the first time on his own, handing over the money and telling him to repeat to the barber the instructions she has given him. Shadows on the glass, the sweetness of the scent, time coalescing then slowly splintering on some fault line and finally separating until it propels the present into the past.

The first time without his mother. Perhaps she isn't well enough to take him. There is only an old man in the barber's. His scant hair is grey and like a bird the barber pecks and teases at it with scissors, his metal comb that lifts the limp strands the same colour as the hair. His scalp is mottled and papery. The barber has a small television high on the wall. There is a broad leather strap for sharpening the razor. Bottles of lotion line the shelf in front of the mirror. It must be from these that the sweetness comes. The floor hasn't been brushed for a while and there is a circle of different colours of hair around the base of the chair. When a draught sneaks in under the door the little sheaves of hair shift slightly. On the walls young men peer down at him from black and white photographs. He thinks they look like Italians with their sallow skin and slicked Brylcreemed hairstyles. One of them is sitting on a scooter. Their heads are angled to the camera and there is always a smear of light in their hair. When the cut is finished the old man leans on his stick and searches deep in his pocket for the money. He has to reach so deep that his whole body slopes sideways and for a second it looks as if he might overbalance. Then he pays with the slow clink of coins.

'All right, Big Lad,' the barber says and he takes a flat piece of wood and sets it across the arms of the chair. He had hoped the barber would think him tall enough not to need the wood. In the glass he watches him flourish the striped apron like a matador's cape.

'So what are we doing with this?' he asks as he rests the palm of his hand on his head. 'A bit off all over?'

The barber's hand feels heavy and because he has got flustered he forgets his mother's instructions, so he simply nods. But when the cutting starts the barber's hands grow light again and, as always, he thinks how strange it is to see the curlicues coiling on the apron and then falling to the floor. Their ends look bleached by the light. The scissors skitter and sing round his head, the comb lifting and laying again. Then suddenly it all stops.

'I'll only be a minute, son,' the barber says and there is the sound of him scampering out the door.

So he sits and waits, the apron tucked like a bib under his chin and pushed into his shirt collar. When he glances at the television he sees horses being paraded round a ring. Some of them throw and roll their heads so it looks as if they might break free from their leads. The wait extends. He gets bored and blows some of his hair nestling in the folds of the apron to the floor. The locks drift down slowly like sycamore seeds. When the barber returns he's puffing a little – he feels the warm breath on the back of his neck and the barber asks, 'Where was I?' And then he cuts some more but stops again to turn up the volume of the television. He reaches for the shears and they buzz and then purr. The race has started. The barber is stopping and starting and he's saying, 'Go on, go on,' and in the mirror the small boy watches him stare at the television and both his hands are raised as if he's holding the reins.

He has to wait until the race is finished and he doesn't think the bet has been lucky. 'Do you want anything on?' the barber asks as he brushes hairs away from his neck. The brush is very soft. And then he pours some of the sweet-smelling lotion into his palm, rubs both hands together and anoints him. One last wet comb, the cape is lifted away, folded in on itself so that the hairs don't fall on him and then he hands over the money. The back of his neck feels cold and somewhere down his shirt a hair is itching against his skin. Later his mother will put her hands on his shoulders and turn him in a circle, then tell him that it's the worst haircut she's ever seen and he's not going on his own again. But for the moment as he makes the journey home he feels light as air and carries with him nothing but the sweetness of the scent.

The sweetness of scent blossoming and billowing down the vista of years until it was there seeping around him now. Then the light closed in on the past once more so there was only Anton standing behind him, looking at him in the glass, his comb hovering. Standing, awaiting instructions that weren't forthcoming.

'Just the usual then?' he asked and Alex nodded, then after he told him the story of his first haircut Anton said, 'I once cut a boy's hair after a night out when I was still a bit hungover but that's as bad as I've got. Made a complete balls-up of it. Apologised and everything, but he still slagged me off on Facebook. Can't blame him really.'

They talked about nothing and Alex wondered how he would ever broach the subject that was the reason for his visit. He knew that his father had previously owned the shop and Anton had a son with special needs. And as Alex sat in the chair he worried that somehow his hidden thoughts would be visible in the glass, and that the fall of his cut hair would reveal all the things that he was supposed to say. So he was glad when Anton finished and he'd paid him, heard him say as always, 'This is a good game. I take it off you and then you take it back off me.'

The shop was empty. This was the opportunity pressing itself on him. If he worked on his father then Anton and all the others might get a generous pay-off, enough to find other premises and set themselves up in a different part of the city. He put on his coat as Anton read something on his phone.

'It's Danny's school. He's had a bit of a turn and I need to take him home. I need to go now. Second time this month.'

'Sorry to hear that, Anton. I can't cut hair but is there anything else I can do?'

'I'll call my Da and he'll come down and fill in. Is there any chance you could hang on until he gets here? He doesn't have a key to get in. He won't be long. He'll get the bus.'

Alex told him he hoped everything with Danny would be all right, but Anton barely seemed to hear him as he flung on his coat, rattled the door and hurried out. The shop was suddenly intensely silent, drained of all the reverberations of its previous life, and after Alex closed the door and put up the shut sign, he went and sat in the barber's chair. Something was happening to him. He thought it must be something to do with the wedding because he found himself increasingly and involuntarily returning to what was in his past. What did it mean? Sometimes it felt as if he was making an inventory of himself, piecing together all the moments that made him who he was in the hope of finally reaching the verdict that he needed, if he was to marry Ellie with his face turned only to the future. He knew already that she was a better person than him, and it frightened him to think that in the months before the ceremony she might realise that, finally see him with all his failings exposed to the light. He had started to wonder if doing some good thing might obviate what he had done, if an act of kindness or generosity might set everything back in balance. But even as he speculated on this possibility, he remembered the purpose of his visit to the Arcade and it weighed against his previous idea, sending it scuttling into uncertainty.

There was a knock on the glass door. He looked up to see Rosie who owned the tattoo parlour next door waving at him and holding a takeaway coffee and a paper bag. He waved back but she stayed in the doorway and he had no choice but to go and open it.

'Has Anton taken you on then?' she asked. 'Where is he?'

'He had to go and collect Danny from school. I'm holding the fort until his father arrives. But I'll give you a trim if you like.'

'You're all right. No one touches my hair but me,' she said, then went and sat in the barber's chair. 'I'd love one of these old chairs at home. Retro cool.'

She sipped her coffee, then went in the back and made him one in a mug that said 'Best dad in the world'. She insisted they share her apple slice and while eating it Alex observed the paleness of her skin, a delicate parchment that seemed perfect for writing on.

'So how's the wedding planning going? It can't be long now.'

'A couple of months. All OK I think. Ellie's looking after most of it – she actually has a spreadsheet. Most things are sorted but we still haven't got wedding rings yet.'

'Never mind rings. What you need is a marriage tattoo. Both of you – it's a really big thing now. She gets your name and you get hers. Or get the same line of poetry.'

'Where?' Alex asked.

'Anywhere you like. Inner arm is always nice, though.'

'I think I'll stick to rings. I'm not a great one for pain. Why do you not have any tattoos? You're not a great advert for your business.'

'Who says I don't have a tattoo? Just because you don't get to see it,' she said, smiling at him in the mirror. 'But maybe it's not a good idea. I had a girl in last week who had one done with her partner – spent twenty grand on the wedding and it lasted six months. He cheated on her with one of her bridesmaids. I had to work some magic on his name.'

'What did you do?'

'Turned it into a two-headed snake. Seemed appropriate. You probably have to squint a bit, but under the circumstances…'

'How's business?'

'A bit slow sometimes but there's still a hardcore of customers – the type who always want just one more, who won't really be happy until they've gone the full monty.'

This was the moment he was supposed to say something, pose the question of whether she had ever considered a different location, but she told him she had an appointment due in and he said nothing as she binned her coffee cup, shook some crumbs off herself and headed for the door.

'If you change your mind about wedding tattoos give me a shout. I'll even give you a good deal,' she called back to him and he raised his hand first in acknowledgement and then in farewell. And as the shop returned to silence he thought once more of a young woman, a young woman in a tent with tattoos on her naked body. Shadows and light outside. Then slowly in the frieze of glass that held his gaze, the inkings bled into each other until their original form could no longer be distinguished, but as he closed his eyes and tried not to remember, they formed some new identity until they were a two-headed snake slithering across all his days.

9

Just as his bath had been, the bed was devoid of heat, enveloping Allenby in a miserable stiff-sheeted coldness. He told himself he had let himself grow soft, that once he would have considered a bed to be the height of luxury as he scrunched his body into a foetal shape and tried to tuck the eiderdown more tightly around him. The fire had smouldered and finally given up the ghost. Nor was there any semblance of silence, with the constant bronchial wheezing and throat gulping of pipes and a gurgling water tank that appeared to be directly above his head. Once, he heard a scurrying that suggested the presence of mice in the ceiling, and his first attempts to sleep were hindered by the intermittent shutting of doors, footsteps in the corridor and the sound of what might have been a trolley with rickety wheels being pushed past his door. It was as if the house disdained a nighttime silence, as if it refused to succumb to sleep, and Allenby tossed fitfully with jagged images of the day's disasters pressing against his consciousness.

He decided then that he would never stay overnight in the house again and would either find lodgings in the village or use the old labourer's cottage. He had been given the cottage as an on-site office where he could store plans and personal equipment, hold meetings with different people. It was one of the empty cottages situated in the grounds to the east of the house, and it was almost passable as a place to stay, after some of the debris had been cleared out. There were still a few pieces of original furniture and a cot bed. He resolved to sort it out in the coming days so that if similar events to that day occurred, he wouldn't have to avail himself of the Manor House's hospitality.

He hadn't slept well for a long time, couldn't remember the last morning he had woken up feeling refreshed. There were the nightmares, of course, but as the years progressed they had diminished in power so that often when he woke he couldn't remember whether he had even dreamed or not.

He tried to force himself into sleep by imagining the house he was going to build, but it was as if the Manor House exerted a greater power, all its defects seeking to impose themselves on his vision of the future. Once, he was able to sleep standing up or leaning against the side of a wooden post, but eventually he slipped into a shallow doze and did not hear the door to his room opening. He started awake when he felt someone slipping into his bed. A hand reached out to rest on his shoulder and he was being hushed and calmed like a child. Even before he turned to face her he knew it was Cora.

'What are you doing?' he asked, seeing her fully for the first time, her hair unpinned and wearing a striped cotton nightdress that made her look like a Victorian convict. 'You shouldn't be here. You'll be sent packing and I'll be not far behind you.'

'I'll be sent packing if I'm not here. Eddie sent me.'

Allenby's anger stirred him into life and he sat upright, pushing the blankets away from himself as if about to get out of the bed. He wondered if what Cora was doing was part of the required service, part of 'doing a message', part of the secrets he already sensed were engrained deep in the house.

'He can't make you do this. You need to go back to your room before anyone sees you.'

'I can't. Eddie's there with Ida. He told me to come here.'

'I'll deal with this,' he told her without knowing how he was going to, but as he started to get out of the bed she grabbed his arm and pulled him back.

'Please don't. I'll be out of work. He'll make sure I'm not taken on at the factory again. I'll have nowhere to go, nothing to live on and he'll make up stuff about me until no one else around here will employ me.'

'Can you not talk to his father? Let him know what's been going on.'

'You don't understand,' she said, speaking to him as if he was a child. 'If Eddie's embarrassed they won't take my side or Ida's, or anyone other than Eddie's. It's the way it is and we're not the first. It's what happens when you come to work in the house.'

'This isn't right.'

'Then nothing needs to happen if that's what you want. Just let me stay.'

He didn't know what was right. She still held on to his arm. Their faces were close and in the thick shadows of the room he knew already that he desired her, but only in the way he would have desired any woman who suddenly slipped into his bed. He resisted the temptation to reach out and touch her because in that moment there were only blue lights and red lights smouldering in dingy backstreets. Officers sitting at tables playing cards, light coming from oil lamps, the smell of smoke and drink. The constant coming and going on the stairs which everyone conspired to pretend had no significance or connection to them. Thought of how even in the most physical intimacy that could take place, vast and seemingly unbroach-able distances of different worlds endured. Knew he could take his pleasure with this young woman in his bed but then would carry the guilt and told himself he had enough things that were already blighted. So he hesitated, intensely aware of her scent – a fusion of cheap perfume, soap and the kitchen work she did, but it smelt honest to him inside the studied pretence of the house. He hesitated but then turned on his side and faced away from her, giving her a wordless answer.

'Thank you,' she said. And then after she had squirmed into a pocket of comfort somewhere behind him and the bed creaked a complaint, 'You keep a cold bed.'

'Cold as hell,' he said.

'Hell's supposed to be warm.'

She moved closer and stretched her arm lightly across him. He felt her breath on the back of his neck, her hand pulling the bedclothes over her shoulder, heard her chattering breathing. He hesitated again. And as in France he was invoking absolu-tion by telling himself that he wasn't like all the others, not just another nameless transient who had come to spend his need, trying to convince himself that perhaps a gesture of gentleness, a fumbling attempt at tenderness, however sincere, could somehow compensate in part at least for what was taken. And was it possible that even now something might be given so that it wouldn't just be a taking?

'Your name is George,' she said.

'And yours is Cora,' he answered, still facing away from her because turning to her would offer a temptation that he might not have been able to resist.

'The hole digger, Eddie calls you.'

'And what do you and Ida call me?'

'Mostly Mr Allenby, or just "the man". We don't really call you anything.'

'Would you not be better working in the mill? Better than this.'

'You don't know what it's like – the noise, the damp, the smells, the dust you breathe. Every day it feels as if you're having the life choked out of you. I hate everything about it.' There was a pause. 'This isn't the worst thing in the world.'

He thought of asking her how many times she had done this but stopped himself because he felt it stirring him and to prevent that made himself think about the battlefield of the lake, the sodden men trying to shield themselves with bits of ragged sacking, the way the churned mud stuck to everything and tried to drag it into its fathomless heart. But somehow she seemed to know his body's desire and snuggled a little closer.

'You can if you want,' she whispered, pushing her head lightly into the small of his back. Some of her hair touched his neck like the lightest brush of a feather on his skin. 'Nobody needs to know.'

He half-turned to face her but still resisted the urge to touch her. If he touched her there would be no going back. He could barely make out the detail of her face.

'I don't want someone in my bed because they've been ordered to be there. Eddie has no right to do this to you, or to me.'

'Ida thinks he loves her, that he'll marry her.'

'More fool her then.'

'I've told her that, but she's smitten.'

'In the morning if Eddie asks, you tell him I put you out, made you sleep in the kitchen. Do you understand, Cora?'

'Yes.'

'Now stop talking and try to get some sleep. The morning will come soon enough.'

'Thank you,' she said before turning on her side and moving to the edge of the bed.

She was gone before he fully wakened, a vague scent and the imprint of her head on the pillow the only tangible evidence she had ever been there. He smoothed the pillow's impression flat and wondered whether he had been a fool. If the war had done one thing it was to destroy any belief in the unalterable jurisdiction of a moral code. No one was saved because they adhered to any particular faith, no one suffered less because they acted according to some prevailing sense of decency. There was only a chaotic swirling vortex that randomly selected its victims, and which dispensed not the slightest concern for arbitrary definitions of right and wrong. No crucifixes or holy water brought immunity or mercy, no overarching sense of Divine purpose prevailed or offered protection. There was only what you yourself did to survive and what you yourself could manage to live with.

And there were so many things he had to live with and suddenly, as a momentary flicker of light edged tentatively through the curtains, it wasn't Cora he saw but Hawley. Hawley who was a living presence threaded through all his days and from whom there was no release. Just turned eighteen with a tumble of black hair and ruddy cheeks that always made him look as if he had been sitting too close to a fire. Hawley with his singing voice, his constant desire to please and be seen to do his bit. A boy still. A boy still and somehow unsullied by everything around him so that amidst all the cursing and darkness he carried a smile on his lips, as if part of him still lived in the world he knew back home. All his life before him, until caught in the blast of a shell with no way back, a blast that tore his limbs and left his innards spilling and sliming out in the mud. There was nothing that could be done. Allenby owed him this. Taking his revolver and with a hand that shook so much he had to steady it with the other, he had ended the boy's unendurable suffering.

So perhaps he should have taken what was offered to him by Cora if it helped him survive Hawley and everything else that he had witnessed. Helped him even for the briefest of moments. He wondered what it would be like, wanted too late to know the feel of her hair and if somehow that touch might absorb the richness of its colour and feel the intensity of its hue, the sudden shock of her naked body when she took off her shift. He could have taken nothing except what she was willing to give, then tried to be kind, as if kindness might prove some compensatory currency. A backstreet bar with its signal light. Step quickly inside. Only an outside queue at the red light, not at the blue. Tell yourself you've only come for a drink and the company. The thick smoke of pipes and cigarettes fogging the oil lamps, someone playing stupid music hall songs on an out-of-tune piano in the forlorn hope of inspiring a sing-song. But at least when money was exchanged it established what was happening and no matter how much he might have tried to convince himself that some human connection, however meagre and paltry, was being attempted, the coins were always a guarantee of its predictable failure.

He went to the window and peered out. There was a mist that swaddled the lake in its opaque embrace, but at least it wasn't raining. He was still standing looking out when there was a knock on the door and Mrs Sullivan's voice telling him his own clothes were ready. He wondered what the silent observer of everything that happened in the house made of Eddie's nocturnal activities and how she justified turning a blind eye. When eventually he opened his bedroom door there was a neat pile of his own clothes washed and pressed. Only his boots were missing. After he had made the bed, taking care to smooth the sheet on both sides, he left Eddie's clothes in a tidy stack at the end of it. Although it was still early he believed he would probably avoid Eddie if he started his day, because he wasn't sure how he would react to what he imagined would be his grinning face. But there wasn't any avoiding the kitchen, and when he entered still wearing Eddie's shoes both Cora and Ida were already there. The kitchen was filled with steam. Ida, her sleeves rolled up, was using wooden tongs to submerge sheets in a large vat of hot water, kneading and plunging them under the surface – perhaps they were the sheets off her own bed, perhaps not. Cora stood with her back to him at the range waiting for the kettle to boil. Her hair was pushed up under her cap so that only a few wisps trailed on the whiteness of her neck. Then Mrs Sullivan was suddenly in the room instructing them to serve him breakfast. Both women looked up as if surprised by his sudden presence. Ida simply stared and stopped plunging but Cora gave a quick bow of her head without looking directly at his face.

'No one should start a day's work without a breakfast,' Mrs Sullivan said. 'I hope you slept well.'

'Yes, thank you.'

'That guest room can be a little cold.'

He looked at her for even a hint that she knew about Cora but her face was as impassive as always.

'A cup of tea would do the job. Don't want to put you to any trouble.'

'I'm sure we can do better than that. I don't imagine a few rashers of bacon and some potato bread would go amiss. Cora will see to you.'

Perhaps it was his imagination, but he thought Mrs Sullivan looked at Cora a little longer than she needed to before she left. In her absence there was no sense of relief evident in the two women, no resort to play, and instead both turned their full silent attention to their separate tasks. He took a seat at the table and tried not to stare or be intrusive in the kitchen's busy space. Cora still hadn't looked at him and, wanting some response from her, he said, 'Thanks to whoever cleaned my clothes. Did a good job. Sorry they were in such a state.'

'Don't worry, sir, we're good at cleaning mucky things,' Ida said, without smiling, then plunged the tongs into the sheets making them disappear again, her face and forearms flushed red with the heat. Allenby wondered what Cora had said to her and whether she had invented something that hadn't happened, or said something disparaging about him. But he couldn't see Cora's face because her back was turned to him again. He wanted her to turn round then rebuked himself – he didn't need another complication in this world he found himself in. Whatever physical intimacy might have happened, and even if she had wanted it, he could never in the wildest reach of his imagination be with someone like Cora publicly, never turn up to Wickets and Rodgers' Christmas party with her on his arm because the moment she opened her mouth they would know who she was and who she wasn't. And there was no bridge could ever cross that chasm.

She was frying bacon in a pan. He heard the sizzle and spit. He wondered if her shoulders and back had the same light stippling of freckles as across the bridge of her nose.

'That's a better day, sir,' Ida said, taking a few seconds' rest and blowing some stray strands of hair from her forehead that her exertions had shaken loose.

'Yes, not so many ducks today.'

'Will you be able to sail a boat on the lake when it's finished?' she asked.

'A rowing boat. Not much more probably.'

'If it freezes over in winter could you skate on it?'

'In theory, yes, but probably not recommended,' he said, not sure if she was poking fun at him or not.

'Ida's always skating over thin ice,' Cora said, turning to look at her.

Ida stuck her tongue out in faux anger and in reply snapped, 'Don't burn Mr Allenby's bacon,' then went back to the pummelling of the sheets.

Cora still hadn't looked at him directly and it made him feel that she regretted whatever it was she thought he had done, or had not done. Either way, it was all just another muddy mess that he wanted to shake off. And yet when she brought him the breakfast plate and set it on the table before him, he let the tip of his finger touch her hand lightly, a touch that lasted the slightest of seconds. Her hand lingered before she lifted it away, still without speaking or looking at him. And he tried to tell himself that her voice didn't matter, that it didn't matter that she was a housemaid, or from a different class, but a louder voice told him he was a liar. Let that one touch be enough, be the end of whatever foolish desire swirled round his senses. He ate what she had served in misery while she busied herself about the kitchen and then Ida started to hum a tune he didn't recognise, the volume rising and falling in time with her prodding and pummelling. Some water sloshed over the side of the vat. He almost wished Mrs Sullivan would return and with her stiff-backed presence impose order on what felt like his hidden chaos.

'Everything all right, Mr Allenby?' Cora asked.

'Yes, thank you, Cora.'

'I've made you a few sandwiches with the left-over bacon. For your lunch.'

She set a small wax-papered parcel tied with string on the end of the table. He thought he heard Ida sniggering mid-hum.

'That's very kind of you. You're in danger of spoiling me.'

She didn't answer and when he got up and tried to take his plate and cup to the sink, she stood in front of him and reached out her hands to take them from him, but for a few seconds he didn't let go and so they stood facing each other until he relinquished his hold. The light band of freckles over her nose reminded him of the breast of a thrush in springtime. The green of her eyes. The light accenting the colour of her hair. He lifted the sandwiches, thanked her again, raised them in the air as a gesture of farewell then walked out into the mist.

10

Alex was going to be late. He had texted a story she didn't fully grasp about a barber's shop and someone's father, so she sat alone at the table and felt the self-consciousness of the single person in a restaurant. At least the waiter was kind and had brought her a drink and a menu with which she pretended to be preoccupied. At the closest table were two women, clearly a mother and daughter. She watched then surreptitiously. There was an ease to it, a frequency of smiles and even laughter, as if they were simply two friends in conversation. If she could, she would have strained to hear what they said to each other and in that moment she would have given everything to be sat with her own mother. As the wedding grew closer she missed her more and more. Missed her in the dress shop where every bride-to-be came equipped with a mother's advice, missed her for the help she would have given her with the wedding preparations, missed her for the friend she would have been. While Alex made a passable show of being interested, she knew wedding arrangements didn't matter to him in the same way they did to her.

The younger woman showed her mother something on her phone then, reaching across the table, handed it over. Ellie watched her scrolling through what she guessed to be photo-graphs. The mother smiled in response and then pointed to particular ones before handing back the phone. Because her own mother had died when she was a child, Ellie's limited understanding of who her mother was allowed her to construct her in whatever image she found most comforting at any par-ticular moment – but the more comforting the construction, the greater the sense of loss. Many people lost their mothers, but to do so as a child, and with the suddenness of her mother's death from a brain tumour, was a constant source of sadness that accompanied all her days. Sometimes she resented the fact that her father had never remarried, never offered his daughter a second chance of having a mother. Sandra, her older sister, had done her best until she grew bored with the role and sought her own solace in a succession of usually worthless men.

Her mother had died when she was seven, so she was never sure whether the images she carefully preserved arose from a fidelity of memory or whether they had been col-our-washed by wishful thinking and sentimentality. She still had her mother's CDs and so she had tangible evidence of her love of Joni Mitchell. Although she had no personal memory of the music, she tried sometimes to evoke her by playing *Blue* or *The Hissing of Summer Lawns*, but it never helped her mother form in any clearer definition. Her main memory of her mother's physical appearance was a piled-up tumble of black hair – the colour she had inherited – which always looked as if it might slide into chaos at any moment. Hair that she remembered being allowed to comb, sometimes with the tip of her finger surreptitiously touching the little white seam of a scar that was the legacy of a childhood accident. And then she couldn't comb her mother's hair any more because she wore a turquoise turban that made her look like a character in a story book. A story that didn't have the right ending.

There was also a very limited library of shared activities. A couple of trips to the seaside and a visit to Belfast Zoo. Did she imagine it or had her mother said she didn't like it and that animals should be back where they belonged and not halfway up a mountain in Belfast? Outside these meagre recollections there was only an album of photographs, all taken by her father. The pictures were mostly formal, with the family arranged into poses that drained everything of spontaneity, obstructed the disclosure of anything that revealed intimacy or insight.

There was always pain in the loss but as when she played Van Morrison's 'Sometimes I Feel Like a Motherless Child' on repeat, she had to begrudgingly concede to herself that there were occasions when she sought a self-pitying, sentimental comfort. So she would construct a multitude of scenarios that were never marred by fall-outs, or indifference, but always predicated on an emotional closeness, a happy sharing of everything that life might bring. And then there was too a lingering sense of guilt, as if she wasn't fully appreciative of what her father had done to fulfil the role of both father and mother.

Alex texted to say he was five minutes away and so she called the waiter and ordered for them both. As far as food and drink were concerned, he was a creature of habit. The first thing she noticed when he arrived was that his haircut was a bit too short, made him look boyish, as if he had just got his 'back to school' trim at the end of the summer holidays. He didn't kiss her and so she knew he had been smoking even though he had promised to give it up, but as she glanced again at the mother and daughter she wished he had shown her public affection.

'He scalped you,' she told him as he hung his coat on the back of the chair.

'I probably distracted him by talking too much. It'll be all right in a couple of days.'

'Did you get it done in the Arcade?'

He told her about Anton and having to mind the shop, about Anton's father arriving later than expected. The mother and daughter were toasting each other with what looked like glasses of champagne. She heard the light clink of glass on glass and felt it sting like a paper cut. She wondered what they were celebrating and what had been on the phone that so engaged their attention.

'Did you make any progress in the Arcade?'

'No, and I'm thinking of asking my father to get somebody else to do it. It's doing my head in. I made the mistake of getting to know them all, and now it feels as if I'm about to stab them in the back.'

'Why can't they stay and make it the problem of the developers?'

'Because it complicates the sale and impacts on the potential price.'

'What will they do with the Arcade if they buy it?'

'I don't know. Turn it into upmarket boutiques or bespoke office space for trendy businesses probably. Maybe even turn it into a location for arts and corporate events. If they invested money in it, the place could look pretty special – it has a lot of history in it and Art Deco never goes out of style.'

The waiter arrived with their starter. Alex nodded his approval of her choice. She wanted to talk about the wedding but knew it best to wait a while. She had a list of items in her head, a photographic image of her spreadsheet of unresolved issues, but wanted to address them with him without throwing a shadow over the evening.

'I had a suggestion for our wedding from Rosie – the girl who owns the tattoo place. She says we should get matching wedding tattoos.'

'Like hearts with arrows through them?' Ellie asked, smiling. 'Something out of *Game of Thrones* like dragons, or what about Chinese script? Maybe beautifully coloured butterflies.'

'Probably something more subtle. But I told her we'd likely just stick to rings.'

'Alex, we haven't got our wedding rings yet and time is running out. It's a late-night opening so I thought we could maybe look at a few shops. I want something a bit different – not like everyone else's – and I'd like both our rings to be engraved.'

'Engraved?'

'Yes, engraved with something we want to say to each other,' she said, while watching to see if he squirmed at the suggestion.

'That's a nice idea,' he said. 'So I guess you've already got yours worked out.'

'Might have.'

'And what is it?'

'You don't get to know that until the day, until I give it to you.'

'Pressure's on me then. To think of the right thing.'

'Yes, it is,' she said and then after glancing again at the mother and daughter asked him if they could have two glasses of champagne. The truth was she hadn't yet decided what she would have engraved on Alex's ring.

'What are we celebrating?' he asked while trying to catch the waiter's eye.

'Being here together; being able to afford being here; getting married in a couple of months; a new haircut. Take your pick.'

After the waiter had brought their drinks, she made Alex propose a toast and when he asked her what it should be she insisted it was his choice.

'To us,' he said as they touched glasses.

'That the best you could think of?'

'Right now it's the best I can think of. But I'll think of something good for your ring. Promise.'

'You promised you were going to stop smoking.'

'I had one. I swear, just the one. I needed it before I went to the Arcade.'

'You're forgiven. But stick at it, Alex. No sliding back.'

He nodded and then took his phone out of his pocket and, just when she was about to complain, told her that there was something he wanted her to see. It was photographs of the Boat House with only a few final touches to be completed.

'When did you go?' she asked, excited to see the photographs.

'A couple of days ago. And it looks great, really classy. Perfect choice.'

She was pleased as she scrolled through, often pausing to magnify one of the images with the pinch of her finger and thumb. She was pleased that Alex had taken the trouble.

'And Ellie, what about you and your dad arriving in a boat? Coming across the lake. Like something in those Netflix series about Vikings.'

She didn't deign to reply, concentrating instead on one of the final pictures of the interior of the building, holding it closer in the hope of seeing every detail.

'And you and the best man could arrive in a speed boat, James Bond style,' she said, handing him back the phone and asking him to send her the photographs. 'It does look great. And finished in good time. That's one less thing to worry about.'

'Why must everything be a worry, Ellie? This is something you're supposed to enjoy.'

She could think of many reasons to worry, not least that somehow she wanted to please her mother, for her mother to be proud of her. But he wouldn't understand because how could you please someone who was dead, make someone who no longer existed outside of the confines of your own head proud of you?

'And if you want something to worry about then I'd be more concerned about our families getting together for this pre-wedding do.'

'It was your parents' idea!'

'My mother's, really. I don't imagine my father's over-fussed at having yours looking down at the furniture because some of it comes from IKEA.'

'Your dad can just say, "A rather fine example of flat-pack circa 2022",' she said, wryly.

'Fair enough,' Alex said, smiling at her.

She liked it when he smiled at her because it was a smile that said, this is just for you. It always made him look lighter, less preoccupied with all the stuff that had no intrinsic value compared to whatever it was they shared. Sometimes in bed before he touched her he would look at her with that same smile and tell her his greatest pleasure was in the looking, and she almost believed him.

After their meal they headed down the steps of the hotel. An older man in a black overcoat and his wife who was wearing a leopard-print coat with a beehive hairstyle that looked as if it was modelled on Dusty Springfield were crossing in front of them, their walk unsteady. Both looked as if they had spent the afternoon drinking. The man stopped at the foot of the steps and looked up at them with what appeared to be scorn. Ellie felt as if they were being accused of having money, physically looked up at while being looked down on at the same time. She took Alex's arm. The man squinted at them and then at the building.

'All right?' Alex said in a voice that he had instinctively stripped of any trace of privilege.

'The Merchant Hotel,' the man sneered, 'I liked it better when it was a bloody bank.'

'You're not far wrong there,' Alex said as the woman pulled her husband's arm and dragged him back to their unsteady journey.

It was an omen for the evening. They went to the Victoria Centre and visited a jeweller's that had a security guard on the door. But the young woman who came to serve them seemed tired, the vividness of her lipstick belying the weariness of her movements and expression – perhaps it had been a long working day – and her manner, while polite, was flat and mechanical. She produced trays of rings but Ellie saw nothing that she liked. Even under the well-positioned lights, the rings in the black velvet trays looked characterless – as lifeless as the young woman behind the counter – and she didn't want the rings they would wear for the rest of their lives to be tainted by the lacklustre memory of their purchase. A second shop produced no better results. A wedding had to be personal so she didn't want something that was the same as everyone else's, but nor did she know exactly what it was that she did want. She tried to tell herself that she had invested too much importance in the choice. That everything was becoming inflated and out of proportion in her head.

When they admitted defeat and had grown weary of shops and crowds, they headed for the car park in the basement. Alex was standing at the pay machine looking for his parking ticket, rummaging in the inside pocket of his coat, when there was a flurry of movement and the sound of running feet. A teenager with a skateboard under his arm fired down the escalator multiple steps at a time, the board clacking against the sides and almost clattering into them, and then there were two other young men of similar age running too. She thought they were being chased, evicted from the Centre by authority, but then understood they were in pursuit of the first boy. And after almost careering into them, his feet skidding on the polished tiles, he slipped in the doorway to the car park and the other two were on him in an instant and they were punching and kicking at him. He pushed back against them windmilling his free arm and managed to stumble to his feet and started to swing the skateboard at them but they grabbed it and tore it from him. The three locked again in a flurry of punches and screaming swear words before they slammed into the glass window at the side of the doors making it vibrate and shudder like a sudden strike on a drumskin.

Alex shouted, 'For fuck's sake, lads!' but his voice was lost in the screaming as the boy being pursued was knocked to the ground and sprawling open to the damage his attackers' feet wanted to inflict. Before she even knew she was going to do it Ellie screamed at them, screamed at them to stop and that the police were coming and when they didn't stop she grabbed one of the attackers by his collar and tried to pull him away, her arm jerking again and again as if she was reeling in some fish. But then the arm on her shoulder dragging her back was Alex's and it was his voice urging her to get away, telling her to let go before she got hurt but it was a voice she ignored. And then the boy whose collar she had hold of turned round and smashed her grip away and fixing his eyes on her as if seeing her for the first time called her 'a fuckin' bitch'. For a second she thought he was going to hit her but in that same moment there were other people arriving and two men in high-viz jackets shouting. In an instant both attackers were gone, pausing only long enough to administer a final kick each, and as they ran to the escalators she heard the sound of their voices shouting something indecipherable, the crackling static of the security men's radios and the angry voice of Alex, asking her if she was crazy, if she had a death wish and telling her that one of them could have had a knife. But she didn't speak to him and as the Centre staff turned their attention to the boy, who despite what had happened seemed most intent on retrieving his skateboard, she walked away. She walked on even though she wasn't sure where Alex had parked, through a world that consisted only of the dull metal flanks of cars and concrete pillars. She walked because the forward movement helped stop her from shaking and she thought if she stood still she might be sick. She heard him calling her name, his footsteps on the concrete, then telling her the car was in a different part of the level but she kept on walking. And then he was beside her and asking her if she was all right but she said nothing and kept on walking.

11

When Allenby stepped outside, it felt as if there was a cobweb on his face, but the mist wasn't a settled entity and instead consisted of drifting swathes of different intensity. Men huddled in tight groups round the edge of the lake and only the nods of their cloth-capped heads or the occasional raising of a hand to emphasise a point prevented them looking like stone statues or calcified figures from some folk tale. Even though the rain of the previous days had gone there was no discernible improvement in the mood of those waiting and it felt as if the miseries of the rain-sodden days had permeated deep into their spirits. In the war they would have distributed an early morning rum ration because the impact on morale of even small comforts could be considerable. But there was nothing he could give them and one man spat on the ground as he walked by.

James Gregson, the foreman, approached out of the mist and touched the peak of his cap. Allenby told him to light some fires in a couple of braziers he had found rusting in the stables and said it might soften the early morning cold, lift morale a bit, and then asked him if they had a full complement. Stothers, the man with the broken leg, was missing but all the rest, bar one other, had returned no doubt driven by the desperate need to put food on their families' tables. As he looked about him Allenby thought the huddles grew tighter, as if intent on repelling his imminent direction to start the day's labour. He imagined that some of their clothes had barely had the chance to dry out and doubted that their boots had shed all of their dampness. If there was another day of similar rain he didn't doubt that at best a gradual desertion and at worst some kind of rebellion would take place. But as he looked at the sky, he hoped that the strengthening morning light would dissolve the miasma of misery. He blew a whistle, tried to subjugate the memories that the sound inevitably brought, and saw the tight huddles slowly stir, displacing the mist and fanning out in front of him, their faces shadowed by their caps, until it felt as if he could have reached out and touched their collective sullenness. So he started by thanking them for the work they had already done, told them this was the worst part of the job and expressed the hope that they would never experience such extreme conditions again.

Gregson managed to get the fires going and the whole scene took on the feel of something primitive, as almost instinctively men sidled towards the flames. Allenby thought all they needed to complete the tableau was some slaughtered sacrificial animal. He explained that first they had to start by using the pumps to remove whatever water still nestled on the bed they had dug and when that was done, they needed to excavate just a little more. Another couple of feet, that was all. One of the men launched into a rasping cough. It sounded as if it originated so deep in his lungs that Allenby suspected it probably signified a case of pneumonia. As the man throatily spat phlegm Allenby made a silent note of his face and resolved to put him in charge of keeping the fires lit.

As the mist slowly began to clear Allenby saw that there was less lying water than he had dared to hope. He oversaw the placing of wooden planks for the thin-rimmed rickety wheels of the two pumps to run along, and when the hoses proved too short to clear the edge of the excavation, organised lines of men with buckets to carry the water away. In the areas where the pumps couldn't easily access they removed water by simply scooping it up like children playing at the seashore. It was a slow process, but they were making progress and at least establishing a welcome sense of momentum even though there were many months of work still ahead of them. When he was satisfied that things were moving as best as they could, he went to the cottage that had been allocated to him for an office. There he had a meeting with Walter Clarke, the Manor House gardener, and discussed the landscaping and planting that would be needed. Clarke was English and had worked in similar properties in Wiltshire and Sussex. He'd done his homework and had already created lists of plants and trees, had even completed some drawings of how he envisaged the final appearance of the lake and its environs. He spread the drawings on the wooden table that occupied the middle of the front room. Allenby looked at the rough working hands of Clarke and wondered how they had produced the delicate illustrations that included two accomplished watercolours.

'If we end up with it looking like this we'll have done well, Walter. You're a bit of an artist.'

'An amateur. But not much to do around here at night so I suppose it's my hobby. I started when I was in the trenches. Passed some of the time.'

'You were in the war?'

'East Lancashire Regiment – the Accrington Pals. Weren't many pals left by the time it was over. The Somme saw to us. And you?'

'Yes. The Somme too.'

There was silence for a few seconds, as if out of respect for those they had known, and then Clarke gathered up his lists and drawings.

'This weather hasn't helped,' Allenby said.

'If you were at the Somme you know that nothing ever helps.'

'I imagine not. It always feels personal.'

'Personal?'

'Yes, as if the weather wants to punish you.'

'Everything wanted to punish you and never let up. After the attack on Serre, the Accrington Pals didn't really exist any more. Sometimes when there's no one about I hear myself talking to the plants, telling the soil about it.'

They stood in silence for a second but each of them knew that they would say nothing more about what had happened to them. There was always an unspoken constraint, an understood limit to what might be shared.

'And is Remington hard to work for?'

'He doesn't know a flower from a weed. But that's no bad thing as it means I can draw up my own plans, get on with the business without interference. Remington just stumps up the money.'

'And Mrs Remington?'

'She's happy so long as there are plenty of roses and flowers to cut for the house.'

Allenby felt a sense of ease with Clarke drawn from the shared bond between those who had served. He tried to imagine him sketching in the trenches but baulked at the images that might have been his subject matter, nor could he imagine any form of paper unsullied by the mud or unstained by the hand that held it. But before Clarke left he asked him if he could hold on to one of the watercolours and have it displayed in the cottage so that he could use it to help others see what the end goal was. Clarke handed it over and watched as Allenby propped it on the wooden-beamed mantel that was stained black from the fires that the hearth had once known.

After Clarke had left, Allenby went back to the lake to inspect progress. The mist had all but gone with only a few skinny tendrils lingering through the branches of the trees and some garlanding the house itself that looked like smoke trails from its many chimneys. There was a rising wind that he hoped would help see off the water. He suddenly shivered. The coldness of his bed, the warmth he had spurned. He looked at the fire in the braziers and tried to scatter the unexpected and unwanted chill that seeped into his body and mind by remembering the offering of her body, then imagining himself subsuming his need in the soft fold of her embrace, his mouth against her skin, his hand lost in the fall of her hair. He dropped his hand into his jacket pocket and reassured himself that the small parcel she had given him was still there.

He drew closer to the braziers, held his palms to them. Looked at the scrubbed whiteness of his skin. He always tried on those times when he went to the blue light to go with clean hands, but he could never be as thorough as he would have liked. There had been earth permanently grimed in the crevices of his skin, grimed so deep so that no haphazard ablutions ever rendered it fully clean.

The man he had allocated to the fire had amassed a pile of wood, harvested from the grounds. The wetness of much of it made the fire hiss and spit. Allenby threw on a couple of sticks as an offering. The wood-gatherer sat on an upturned bucket, hunched over, his collar turned up and his face staring at the ground. He didn't acknowledge Allenby's presence in any way and sat almost motionless in his own misery, only an occasional shiver disturbing his stillness. Allenby knew he should have sent him home but knew too he represented a family that couldn't afford the loss of his pay. If his pockets had contained a bottle of Remington's whiskey or even some of his cigarettes he would have shared them with the man, but he had nothing to give him except the briefest commendation for the fires.

Strange to worry about clean hands when going to touch a woman's body in the blue light, because in war the human body lost all semblance of integrity, every single vestige of dignity. He thought of the desecration of Hawley's body with everything unseamed, everything spilling and slathering on the ground, his helmet blown aside and only the untouched black mass of his hair leaving him recognisable as the man he once was. Why worry about hands that weren't perfectly clean to visit a whore? Perhaps he had indeed been foolish to refuse the previous night's offer, an offer that would surely have left him enough residual heat to survive the days that lay ahead. A fantail of sparks showering out of the brazier suddenly startled him and made him take a step back.

Once during training Hawley had come to him and requested compassionate leave, sheepish, blushing as he asked for permission to visit his family farm.

'It's not far from here, sir. And I'd be back first thing in the morning. Parents are getting on a bit and it's meadow cutting time. With the war and all, not many helping hands about.'

And he hadn't let him, told him he might miss something that was important, something that might save his life one day. Said it all with a pomposity of voice that still shamed him when what he should have told him was to go, go and never come back, hide in the mountains, live the life that was owed to him.

Gregson approached and told the sitting man to get off his arse and go and find more wood.

'I've had a deputation,' he said when they were alone. 'Five of the men, with Crawford doing the talking. They say they're not getting paid enough. That conditions weren't safe yesterday.'

'Are they speaking for themselves or all the others?'

'Say they're all of the one mind. And there's talk of laying down tools.'

'They're bluffing. Where else are they going to find work?'

'It's back-breaking work,' Gregson said, 'and yesterday just about scundered them. Thomas Stothers breaking his leg hasn't gone down well either.'

'That was regrettable and I'll see he gets paid for the next couple of weeks but I'm not holding the purse strings. Tell them that and tell them if they'd rather be building stone walls in the Mournes they're welcome to give that a go, see what shifting boulders up mountains does for their backs.'

'Is that your last word?'

Allenby stopped himself from saying it was. He couldn't afford to lose more time but nor could he be seen to instantly submit to blackmail, so he told Gregson to find out what exactly their wage demand amounted to. That would at least buy him time to see what scope he had, but not even for a second did he believe Remington would contemplate any additional costs as a result of paying the men more. And he was sick of being in charge of men, constantly having to consider the collective need rather than his own. There were times when he barely knew what was best for himself and when he felt as if his natural instinctive state had been reduced to a kind of sleep-walking. It was an existence, however, that he had no desire to lose because mostly it kept him safe from everything that sought to spring him awake and into a fuller consciousness. For a foolish moment he wondered if he could contract some appearance of pneumonia and thus be absolved from the task he had been allocated, given a Blighty that would see him return to the comfortable offices of Wickets and Rodgers, but as always, and for better or worse, he knew that the judgement of whether a man could hold up his end irredeemably applied to himself. There was no escape from that.

As the day wore on the men began to remove more earth. The soil had not fully dried out so it was still difficult, but the wheelbarrows gradually carried away new loads. When it was the middle of the day and a halt was called Allenby went to the cottage and took some time to make it more worthy of an office. He found an oil lamp in the back room that seemed in working order and placed it on the wooden beam over the fire that served for a mantel. The windows of the cottage were small and he knew that the lamp would be needed when light began to fade. The tiny back room where he found the lamp had a narrow cot bed with a straw-filled sliver of a mattress and a dresser with a cracked mirror. A jug with a floral pattern and a chipped handle that looked as if it hadn't seen water in a long time sat in an enamel basin. The narrow window was blackened over with grime so that little natural light made it into the room, and there was a prevailing coldness that made it an uninviting place to sleep. The front room had a wobbly table with a ledger containing the names of the men and accounts of payments made, two chairs, an open hearth and little else. Some marker poles and shovels were stored in one corner.

He looked again at Clarke's drawing, almost as if by looking at it intently enough he might be able to translate it into a working reality. Then he took a brush and swept the floors of the two rooms, the dust skirting up round his boots. Still using the brush, he ran it along the top of walls and flailed it into corners to dispel the cobwebs. It was as good as it was going to get. Sitting at the table he studied the costings, looking for a way to cut some corner that might allow him to pay the men a little extra, but there was nothing that instantly revealed itself. To buy some time he would tell Gregson to assure the men that their demands were being considered, and that they would be informed of the outcome in due course.

He took the sandwiches from his pocket and carefully untied the string and opened the waxed paper. On top of the two sandwiches was a little square of paper and written on it in black ink were the neatly formed words 'Thank you'. He tried to stop himself inflating its significance into anything other than the kindness it was meant to be. A kindness in return for a kindness, he supposed. At least it felt like an equal trade, if not a trade between equals. He thought too of the family who had once lived in the tiny cottage, and how an entire network depended on their ability to provide comfort to those in the house, a whole chain of gardeners and labourers, housemaids and cooks whose existence was entirely predicated on loyal service.

Work continued throughout the afternoon and Allenby was conscious that in another month or so the days would lengthen, a thought that brought him closer to the deadline and rising apprehension about meeting it. Inevitably as the day headed to its darkening end, the pace of work slowed and Allenby knew that some of the men were reduced to merely giving the impression of industry. Perhaps they were physically weary, perhaps they needed to demonstrate that their complaints about their pay were deeply held. Whatever it was, Allenby called it a day half an hour earlier than he normally did and stood watching as the men quickly dispersed, hoping that they hadn't interpreted the gesture as a sign of weakness. He observed Crawford who had been spokesman for them, standing talking to a small group of men. He looked animated as if making some forceful point. Every army had a barrack room lawyer – it was a simple fact of life. Sometimes if they were worked right and their self-importance flattered, they could even prove useful in the long run.

Back in the cottage he lit the oil lamp, turning the wick down a bit so that the sudden heat wouldn't crack the glass. He had a little while before catching the last train back to Belfast and he sat at the table and looked again at the thank you note. He imagined it was the only one he was likely to receive on this particular job. There was a knock and Gregson appeared in the half-open doorway.

'Something you need to see,' he said. 'Bring the oil lamp.'

'What is it?' Allenby asked and already his mind was turning towards some consequence of the men's request for more pay. Perhaps some act of sabotage or expression of defiance, perhaps something connected to Crawford's animated discussion he had observed.

'Better you see for yourself,' Gregson said.

Allenby followed him along the gravel path through the garden and down into the pitted surface of the lake that in the rapidly fading light could have been the surface of the moon. But the moon itself was misted behind thin clouds. The smell of the lamp was strong and Allenby held it stiff-armed in front of him, its flame quivering and smoking the air. Gregson walked steadily towards the far corner of the lake where soil had not yet been excavated and his feet made little squelching and slurping noises. Allenby no longer had any idea of what he might be shown but the silent impervious walk of Gregson made him feel nervous.

Finally they arrived at a spot close to the far perimeter. Gregson stopped and looked back at him as if to check that he was still there before carefully beginning to scrape back the soil. Although little physical energy was being expelled, Allenby could hear the strain of his breathing like the tick of a run-down clock. A matter of seconds later Gregson stopped and straightened.

'Bring the light closer,' he said, his voice wavering like the smoke from the lamp.

'What is it?' Allenby asked as he bent over it with the lamp.

But Gregson didn't answer. Instead, he carefully drew back the piece of rotting cloth to reveal the tiny skeleton of a baby.

12

The bed was too big, yet at the same time not big enough. The space between them seemed to expand in the darkness where each of them lay in total stillness, as if a single movement – the press of a spring or creak of the carved wooden headboard – might take on the form of words. Neither one of them knew what those words might be, or trusted what they would signify.

They had already done the best they could. Ellie had listened passively as Alex told her about what could have happened, about single-punch deaths, about stabbings and the unpredictable effect of drugs where users were off their heads. About the need to witness and report rather than participate, about a city that – like every other city – had its share of dangerous people and that it only took a single moment of intersection, the briefest random crossing of lives, and everything could spin into tragedy. And he had stories to draw on – a father who had gone out to hush lads in the street who were being a nuisance: stabbed to death. A young woman stabbed for her mobile phone because she resisted. A long list of fatalities struck down without cause or meaning – all of them the briefest flare of tabloid headlines but permanently serving as portents.

And he patronised her by telling her that she had led a life protected by money so that in the normal course of things her path didn't cross those who were disturbed, desperate and given to violence, so when, God forbid, it did happen they should do nothing but extricate themselves as quickly as possible. He spoke to her as if somehow she didn't know the reality of the world and the people who inhabited it. And he tried to scare her by saying that although their lives mostly kept them safe, nothing could be taken for granted and there were sick people out there, probably more than they might imagine. And he had been frightened that she would be hurt, hurt in a moment of reckless, impulsive violence that couldn't ever be taken back or undone. Then in the car on the journey home he had imagined using the coming wedding as justification for his reaction to the fight was a good idea and she had hated him a little for that because she knew the wedding had never crossed his mind.

It didn't matter that she knew everything he said was true, didn't matter because in the unaccustomed silence of their bed she knew she had felt some stronger instinct that he didn't have, and it frightened her a little. It made her question what she knew and what she didn't know about the man she was going to marry. But perhaps she was inflating a few sudden and deeply confused seconds in a shopping centre car park into something it wasn't, and perhaps his judgement was clearer and truer than hers after all. There was the sound of a passing car, the far-away hysteria of a car alarm. All through the world outside their comfortable town house was a continuous course of human existence and interaction, of strangers following the ley lines of their lives in streets unknown to her, living in ways that were unfamiliar to her. She thought of the child she wanted to have with him and how she would be the best mother a child could have, filling all the missing moments of her own motherless life with an abundance of love. And she wondered how she might keep her daughter safe – because it was always a girl she envisaged. Safe from the predatory, safe from random acts of violence in underground car parks, on badly lit streets late at night, safe from men who wished her any form of harm.

'Are you all right, Ellie?' he asked as he let his arm fall lightly across her.

She didn't know what to say so it was easier to pretend she was, and when she told him, he pressed his arm a little tighter around her.

Alex, meanwhile, felt that this was the start of everything being OK. He didn't know what she had been thinking, felt she had acted in a crazy and reckless way that could have ended in tragedy, but he knew too that he had let her down even as he had tried to do the right thing, the sensible thing. He had been in bars and once in a Dublin club where fights had broken out and seen the damage that anger could inflict after the male ego felt itself subjected to any form of disrespect. Sometimes all it took was a spilt pint, a passing remark or a brush of a shoulder and that was enough to result in the shedding of blood, the breaking of bones. He couldn't bear to think of Ellie's body disfigured and defiled by the infliction of such damage. But he knew too that this was in part at least because he thought of her as his, and that his own male ego nurtured a fear of public humiliation if he ever proved unable to prevent that hurt.

When he stretched his arm across her she didn't flinch but didn't yield to it either so he let it rest there for a few minutes before he took it away again. Faint sounds of the night briefly filtered into the room. For a second he thought about getting up but knew it would only serve to make the sense of distance greater when what he wanted was to make it go away. He didn't like conflict. He didn't like arguments and never really had the energy to sustain one even when he knew he was in the right. He told himself that everything would be better in the morning, that they would move on together as they always did. But he couldn't sleep and, after making sure that Ellie had drifted off, gently eased himself out of the bed and went downstairs to the kitchen. The brightness of the main lights and their angry reflection on the marble worktops hurt his eyes so he turned them off again and used his phone. He found the packet of cigarettes and lighter hidden inside the piece of kitchen gadgetry that they never used and opened the back door. Stepping out onto the patio in his bare feet he sat down at the wrought iron table and lit a cigarette.

There was the smell of smoke from some other garden. Perhaps the smouldering embers of a barbecue or a kindred spirit whose habit banished them to the outside. A hazy little drift of music from a car or open window. The stars lingering lightly overhead and the moon lolling lazily like it was too weary to hold its head up. Everything in his mind and in the world around him felt vague and lacking definition. It was the only way he could think of the girl with the tattoos. The girl in the tent. Everything then had been muddled and so nothing could be extracted and confronted with certainty. And it was that absence of clarity that served to smother the realities of those moments, the separating protection from everything that was now and in the present. He tried to concentrate on the cigarette, on only the physical reality of the moment, to draw himself into a shell that nothing else could permeate. But it didn't work like that and the harder he tried, the more his defences felt as insubstantial as the wisps of smoke he exhaled.

The tattoos were always changing in his memory. There had been flowers perhaps, a pattern on the side of her neck, something spidery on her hands – was that a temporary henna decoration, the type you could get done at one of the festival stalls? They used henna in weddings in India, didn't they? A wreath of flowers under the swell of her breast. A peacock's tail, a hummingbird on her shoulder? He wanted to hold the calm of the suburban night that surrounded him, where everything was in order, but instead there was the intense noise of music amplifying in his head, the constant passing of voices and shadows on the side of the tent so that everything was always in motion and there was only the slightest separation from the outside world. He tasted the guilt, no matter how many cigarettes he smoked, but what he felt more than anything was the thinness that separated him from some unspecified form of retribution, of a calling to account.

He thought it was dope he smelt from one of the neighbouring back gardens. There was no sound of a party so it was probably a solitary smoker, sat like him on some garden furniture in search of respite from whatever swirled inside their head. For a second he tried to distract himself from his own thoughts by imagining himself burrowing through garden hedges and over fences to connect with this stranger, share the sweetness of the night and block out everything that he didn't want.

Ellie hadn't been sleeping, couldn't, even though she tried, because her mind kept homing in on a late-night car park as if it was permanently trapped in an underground world constructed from concrete and infused with metal, where everything was hard-edged and cold to the touch. The brightness of the overhead lights from which there was no escape, an open exposure to everything that was brutally unyielding. Her hand on a stranger's collar, his fist knocking it away, swearing at her and calling her a bitch. His face distorted with hatred. Everything feeling unmasked and whatever it was that permitted some cocooning belief in the best that people are, splintering in a second. Of course she would rediscover that belief, but for the present she was frightened by its absence, shocked by the seeming fragility of the veneer.

She had felt him leaving the bed but went on pretending to sleep. They had said all they needed to say although he had been the one doing most of the talking. She didn't have a full understanding of what she felt so it was mostly easier to listen. Perhaps silence now wasn't such a bad option for a short time. After a while, however, his empty side of the bed grew oppressive and the silence she had invoked as protection was invested with apprehension. Where was he? Where had he gone? So she got up and went to look for him. The earlier sound of the patio doors opening suggested he had gone outside, but instead of following him, she went into the back room he used as a den. She didn't put on the light but there was enough from their bedroom filtering across the landing to let her see his CDs and DVDs that he no longer played, his computer and PlayStation dark and mute at his desk, his acoustic guitar on the wall that he had never actually learned to play. She touched one of the dumbbells with the palm of her foot and it rolled a little across the floor. She thought they were perfectly named. Then going to the window she looked down to the patio where the red tip of his cigarette moved languidly through the shadows. He looked lonely, locked inside a world from which she was excluded.

Something swooped through the air, a black pulse of wheeling, careering speed. He thought it was a bat. A fellow creature of the night that was gone as swiftly as it had appeared. The stars seemed as if they were fading further into the sky. He suddenly felt cold. There was a knocking. At first he didn't know where it came from and then, still startled, he looked up and saw her pale face watching him from behind the glass.

13

Neither man spoke, but stood staring at the tiny remains before them. Allenby cursed under his breath. He had seen his share of bodies emerge from the earth, revenants trying desperately to reassert their claim to a shattered memory of life, but he had never seen anything so small. It could have been the skeletal remains of some little creature but for the unmistakable human skull. The lamplight bleached the bones that looked so perfectly intact, and yet so fragile. Just for a moment he wondered if it was one of Eddie's bastards but he could tell the bones had been in the earth for a very long time. He moved the lamp so that Gregson retreated into shadow, because suddenly the intimacy of it made him feel like a voyeur, like the first time he had seen the dead body of a man and been mesmerised by its similarity to his own living flesh before recoiling at the relentless and inescapable insistence of its eternally changed reality. The cloth the baby was wrapped in might have been a piece of linen. After Gregson had uncovered it, the remains seemed to look up at them. Both men turned their faces away instinctively so that they looked only at each other, then Allenby knelt down and covered it again.

'What do we do?' Gregson asked. 'Will I get the house to send for the constable?'

'If we get the police involved there'll be an investigation, an inquest. They'll clear us out of the site. We'll never make up the time, never get the work finished.'

'We can't just ignore it.'

'Look, James, I've seen lots of bodies, lots of remains, and I'm telling you this has been here for a very long time. Maybe even hundreds of years. There are probably more remains dotted all over these grounds. But it hasn't got anything to do with the present.' Then uncovering the bones for the second time, he said, 'Look, it's perfect. There's no injury, no marks anywhere. Can you see that? This is probably a baby that died almost as soon as it was born.'

'What are we going to do?' Gregson asked again. Then reverting to the church-going Presbyterian that he sometimes remembered he was, said, 'We have to do the right thing.'

'The right thing, James, is that we take this child and we bury it again with all due respect. That we stop it being carried away from where its mother buried it and don't pass it into the hands of strangers who will handle it for no purpose other than to satisfy their own curiosity. And to what end other than to bury it again? And while we wait for that all to happen there'll be men with no money to put food on their family's table.'

'I don't know,' Gregson said. 'I don't want to get into trouble.'

'You won't. I'm going to look after this, and believe me these are bones from distant history. It has no name, no family. I'll bury it somewhere with proper respect and the work can go on and men can earn the money they desperately need. And

I was going to tell you that I've thought of a way to pay the men a bit more.'

Allenby could tell Gregson was wavering and after bending down to cover the remains again with the cloth asked him, 'Does anyone else know about this?'

'No, I found it. I was walking over at the edge just after the men had left, looking at where we need to dig next, placing some poles, when I caught a glint of something through the cloth. The truth was I thought I might have stumbled on treasure, buried coins – that sort of thing. Give me a terrible shock when I discovered what it really was.'

Allenby's instincts would have been to offer him a stiff drink from the half-bottle of whiskey he had stored in the cottage for emergencies but he knew already that his foreman was teetotal, so instead he told him to go home, that he would look after everything, and it would all be done properly. That the decision was his alone and he would take full responsibility for it. And then as he held the light between them, painting Gregson's face in chiaroscuro, he could tell that he wanted to be gone, gone far from the bundle of bones and whatever was going to happen to them. So it took only a final encouragement and he was walking away, his feet once again lisping and squelching the clay until he finally disappeared into the dusk.

Allenby looked up at the house whose lighted windows could be seen through the screen of trees. He suddenly felt alone, alone and standing in a basin of clay with a ragged bundle of a baby's bones resting at his feet. Looking around him he tried to take his bearings because he would have to return to the cottage for a shovel. A strengthening wind, a left-over residual energy from the day stirred the trees, then scudded clouds across the half-moon. It was too late to catch the train – he would have to sleep in the cottage. But first he had to do what was needed. Taking one last look at the small offering of bones, he set off back through the darkness that was closing in all around him.

Back at the cottage he hesitated, asked himself if he was doing the right thing. The front room musted with damp and cold. He would try to light a fire on his return, hoping it might usher some warmth into the back room with its iron-framed cot. No one was going to be happy with further delay in constructing the lake, not Remington, not Wickets and Rodgers, and the thought of such a delay only served to intensify his growing desire to leave the Manor House behind. He told himself that it wasn't good for him, that there had been too many reminders of what he wanted to forget, so part of him felt as if there was a danger of regressing, when all along he had wanted to believe that he was moving forward from what lay over his shoulder. He knew too he had done much worse things and in the scale of those this was surely small and inconsequential. But the secrecy with which he now had to act made it feel insidious and a little dangerous.

He extinguished the oil lamp – this was a task that would have to be done in darkness – and taking a shovel from the group that leaned together in a corner and a hessian sack, went back out. The unlit world seemed strange, hesitant and not fully formed as the wind sifted through the shrubbery and creaked the branches of trees. He walked quietly, not letting the blade trail when he crossed the gravel path, but when he made the mistake of glancing back at the house it seemed as if the upstairs windows were watching him. Hawley had looked up at him at the final moment, but his eyes had been wild and unseeing. Afterwards he had told himself that they were imploring him to do it but he knew in that moment there was nothing left with the capacity to think, only the involuntary spasm of a body ripped apart and unrecognisable to itself. Told himself once more that it was the right thing to do.

'A bit late for digging.'

Allenby kept a resolute hold of himself and looked into the shadows under a tree where gradually Walter Clarke became visible. He lifted a pipe to his mouth and lit it.

'I didn't see you there,' Allenby said. 'I'm just going out to check a few things. I think we might have reached the right depth in some places.'

Apart from a few seconds when Clarke was lit by the flare of the match, they were far enough apart to prevent each of them seeing the other's face clearly, so he couldn't tell whether the gardener believed him.

'Do you need any help?' Clarke asked.

'I'm fine, thanks. It won't take me long.'

'Well, goodnight then.'

He stood still for a moment as he watched Clarke walk away, then disappear into the darkness as if a curtain had been slowly pulled behind him. He knew he had sounded ridiculous, but he believed that Clarke wouldn't seek to intrude, that in some unspoken way each had the other's back. Stepping down into the excavation, he leaned on the shovel to prevent himself falling. The deepening night made it more difficult to return to the exact spot, but he remembered to align himself with a particular tree. There was something unsettling about walking through the darkness, as if he was venturing into no man's land where, if suddenly subjected to an exposing incandescent flare, disaster might shatter the night.

At first he couldn't find it and wondered if it had all been part of some hallucination, some dream spun by the disturbance of the past. But eventually he reached it. He looked about but there was neither sight nor sound of another human being. He didn't want to use the shovel for fear of damaging it, so he had to kneel down, feeling the dampness seep into his trousers where his knee touched the ground. He wanted to lift it, still wrapped in the rotting cloth, and put it whole into the hessian sack. But he realised that wasn't physically possible, so there was no alternative but to lift it bone by tiny bone. But he didn't allow himself to think of it as a human life, and if he had to think about it all, it felt to him like an ancient religious relic that only superstitious people would venerate. Whatever well of sentimentality about the dead he might once have drawn upon had long since dried up. Folding the hessian sack's surplus neatly, he tied the folds in place with string then carried it back out of the lake bed and towards the part of the grounds that they were using to deposit the excavated soil. He started to dig deep, shovelling the soil he had removed to one side. Sometimes his feet slipped and the smell of the damp soil made him retch. It was a smell he recognised and associated with death. Hawley's remains had to be shovelled up by two of his friends. One of them spilled the meagre contents of his stomach, heaving and heaving until there was nothing left. Hawley, who was a farmer's son and who worked land under the shadow of the Mournes, had his dismembered body shovelled into a bag. Lime sprinkled like the first snow of winter.

The hole was deep enough now. Taking the hessian parcel he lowered it into the ground gently. He remembered he had spoken to Gregson of burying the remains with respect, but this was the closest he could come to any form of ritual or religious service. Then he filled the hole, tried to cover the prints his feet had made in the damp earth and walked away, using the distant light of the house as a guide.

Afterwards he had written a letter to Hawley's parents telling them nothing but lies, and as the wind rustled the shrubbery and skirted around him, then filtered through the copse of trees, it seemed to whisper every one of them back to him.

14

Alex came back to the bed. They said nothing to each other at first but when she felt how cold he was she pulled him close. His clothes and his breath smelt of smoke but she didn't care. He tried to make a joke and told her that someone was having a barbecue. Their bodies shared a closeness in the bed but when sleep eventually came they were separated again by their dreams, while in the world outside, a city existed that didn't sleep, even in the darkest hours of night, because all its neural circuits and systems still coursed and pulsed. So even in the silence there was the hum of what kept it alive until morning light. And even when the computers pretended to sleep they sometimes blinked themselves awake, or recorded some piece of information, a silent transmission through motherboard, processing units and random access memory before being lodged securely and invisibly forever. Cameras watching at roadsides and on buildings. Cameras watching and recording the speeding car, the act of violence, the intersections across which the old hatreds might ignite and spark the night. The river still flowing steadily through, the mountains still stiffening and girding the city. The living and the dead moving silently through the streets.

Alex and Ellie were troubled, but after they had moved apart neither reached out to the other as their dreams played out in a welter of images that ebbed and flowed, moving backwards and forwards in time, then out of time, but always shaped by a flare of intensity. For Alex it was a small tent that felt like a dome over all his life with loud music playing nearby. The whole world outside a single cry away. For Ellie, a cavernous underground car park where the softness of human flesh was exposed to the unyielding force of concrete and metal. And while they both slept, in the world they had tried to shut outside, taxi drivers ferried their passengers home – drinkers from late-night clubs and backstreet drinking dens; women and small children fleeing the dangers of their home with possessions stuffed into bin bags shining like black plums in the street light; the shift workers; a wife summoned to the hospital for a death, a husband summoned for a birth; the flitters from rent arrears or the racist slogans screaming on their door; the sex workers; the disturbed who had no money in their pockets to pay their driver. And all of them moving through the city thought it strange in its emptiness, that the buildings were dressed differently and stood in unfamiliar relationship with each other, and they felt uneasy whenever the taxi had to stop momentarily at lights, where the solitary walker they saw first made them feel curious and then nervous because they didn't know which world he belonged to. Some of the night travellers summoned by the dreams came and stood at the end of Alex and Ellie's bed, watched them sleeping, then moved back into the shadows of the city.

A world where everything was washed under yellow sodium lights. Everything bathed in the light that shifted remembrance to a different time and world. The ambulance with its human cargo wailing by. Delivery drivers hoping to be able to park up soon and sleep in their cabs. The homeless layered in doorways, their bodies slowly squirming in search of some vestige of warmth and hoping the drunk or the evil didn't vent their self-loathing on them, while in side streets and apartments off main roads a kettle boiled or a bottle sat open at a kitchen table where the newly lonely or the permanently unloved tried to speed the slowest hours of night away.

Alex turned to face out of the bed. In his dream, the girl's face always changed, one image morphing into the next because he no longer remembered her face or even her name. He had searched deep in his memory but could recall neither with any certainty. Matty and Will might have lodged this information somewhere, but he doubted it and he couldn't ask them. They all knew this was a subject that could never be spoken of. And the tattoos that he could not fully remember, either, began to blur and bleed into each other again then slowly move and this one that looked like a serpent, a serpent with two heads, slithered across her body and he was frightened that it would infect him with its venom. Infect him the way he had poured his poison into her.

In a different world a taxi passed the Arcade. Its closed grey metal shutters and the ugliness of the painted metal clashed with the sculptured delicacy of the interior. Before it was bombed. Before the fire. Before forward time. Nothing could get in, but inside was everything that lived now and had once lived. And in Alex's dream time, the once gleaming shopfronts formed again under skylights and the circular dome, each decorated with green marble and bronze trim,

globe lights, tiled floors. Anton and his son. The boy he saw
in the mirror.

*

And outside his dreams but along those same tiles clack the
heels of Evelyn. Dispatched by Mr Russell to collect his wife's
new ring, she is in no hurry, glad to be released from the
office and a little giddy with the unaccustomed freedom. It
is a position of trust he sometimes bestows on her, making
her a momentary confidante, an advisor about what a woman
would like. She knows it was a kind of flirting, but she likes
it well enough and thinks there is no harm in it. The harm
will come if at some point in the future he offers her what
he usually bought for his wife, because she isn't sure how
she will react. If she could have the one thing without the
other it might have been all right but she knows her boss to
be a recorder of times, a watcher of pennies, an observer
of every office coming and going, so she can't imagine he
won't think himself short-changed without the appropriate
recompense. But perhaps he himself doesn't know what
recompense he dares hope for, and if that is the case then
she might be the one in the fullest control, able to mould
him to her will.

She pauses at different shops to inspect the windows. Her
tardiness can't be criticised because she is on an expedition
requested by him. When she comes to the jeweller's she stands
and inspects the window display intently, letting her eyes
move along the rows of rings, the bracelets and necklaces,
the watches. She has a love of jewellery but only has a meagre

little collection to sustain that love. A sign says HP is available and there is already a Christmas Club. But Russell doesn't need either of these things and when she enters the shop and a small bell announces her entrance she feels the vicarious confidence of those who can buy what they want.

'A collection for Mr Russell,' she tells the man behind the counter, the same man who has served her before and who clearly recognises her.

'Certainly,' he says. 'I'll just get it for you.'

He disappears into the back through a beaded curtain that shivers and clinks after he has gone through. When he returns with a small black box he asks her if Mr Russell would like it wrapped but she asks to see the ring first and when he looks quizzically at her she doesn't care. She has picked it herself and so believes she is entitled to try it on. Let him think what he wants. And as she draws closer to the counter he opens the lid of the box. She tries it on – she already knows it is her size – and holds her hand out to look at it as if she is offering it to the jeweller to kiss. She tells him it's very nice, that the five little pearls are beautiful and then hands it back to him so he can replace it in the box and wrap it. Then she is on her way again, past the shop where in the future Anton will cut hair and Rosie turn unwanted names into two-headed serpents. Past all the shops that come before and after. Past Alex sitting looking at himself as a child in the mirror as he waits for Anton's father to arrive. Her heels clack the tiles again until they fade into the night and the Arcade falls silent once more.

★

Ellie has dreamed this before. A stress dream, the type she has had as the wedding gets closer. They are in front of the registrar in the Boat House and he's asking for the rings and suddenly they realise they don't have them. Are they momentarily lost? Are they in the best man's pocket? They stand looking at each other and then realise they haven't got rings. People offer to lend them theirs but she wants her own ring, doesn't want someone else's. She's crying and then she's standing in front of the lake and Alex is telling her that it doesn't matter, that they can still get married. And people's faces are pressed against the windows of the Boat House trying to see what's happening. There are two swans out on the lake but they're far away and the water looks cold. The rushes bend and rustle their heads in the wind and her dress flutters about her. Someone else is crying but she can't see who it is.

Then it's all gone and she's in the car park of a shopping centre. The high-pitched squeal of tyres as a car navigates one of the tight corners. The angry metal clang of a boot being shut. Being lost. The terrible feeling of being totally lost. And everything looks the same, every level indistinguishable from the other. She's frightened she'll be trapped there forever, unable to find her way back home. And then she hears someone calling her by name, the voice loud and clear and it's her mother's voice. Her mother's voice but she can't see her. She looks about frantically to find her but then the voice fades and then the voice belongs to Alex and he's telling her they have to run, run and run to get away from the people chasing them.

She awoke with a stifled whimper. She wanted him to hold her and tell her that everything would be all right but he was still asleep, wanted to ask him who was chasing them and whether he had heard her mother calling her name. But slowly the reality of the day broke over her and she forced herself wider awake because it seemed better than the world she had just left. What was there to do other than to keep going and hope everything would turn out the way she wanted? So she got up and went down to the kitchen and made herself breakfast. She wanted to look at her wedding dress, but it was in her father's house safely stored away from Alex's prying eyes. She flicked through photographs of it on her phone but it wasn't the same without being able to touch it. As with everything, she hoped her mother would like it. She heard Alex stirring and looked out at the garden where he had sat and smoked his cigarette. Light was breaking more brightly, causing the dampness on the grass to glisten.

On impulse she phoned her father, but when he answered she found she didn't know what to say, so she was grateful when he took the lead by asking her if everything was OK. It was the question he always asked when she phoned, as if he assumed every call was a prelude to her telling him that something was wrong.

'I might come over later and look at my dress. Check it's all right.'

'No problem,' he said. 'Are you worried the mice might have been at it or something?'

'Don't, Dad! That's not even funny. I just want to look at it.'

'A bit late to change your mind now.'

'I'm not changing my mind. It's the right dress and you're not to look at it. It's only to be seen on the day or it's bad luck.'

'I promise I won't. We don't want to invite bad luck.'

There was a pause. She could hear Alex's footsteps on the

stairs. In the garden a small yellow-breasted bird was perched on the hanging feeder.

'Are you OK, Ellie?' her father asked again.

'I suppose I'm just a bit nervous. I want everything to go smoothly.'

'It'll be perfect,' he told her.

'Keep telling me that.'

'You're not having doubts, Ellie?'

'No, Dad. Do you want me to have doubts?'

'All I want is for you to be happy. That's all I've ever wanted.'

'I know that and I am happy. Will be happy. Promise.'

She wanted to tell him that there was a sadness that her mother wouldn't see her married but didn't want to upset him because she knew, however much he hid it, he too must harbour the same feeling. And to speak of it now might breach some restraint they had both always exercised and risk it spilling into the happiness that was supposed to be ahead.

15

When he got back to the cottage she was waiting for him in the darkness. She was wearing a caped black coat that was much too big for her, and which he recognised and knew she had borrowed, probably surreptitiously, from Mrs Sullivan. She was holding something covered that he couldn't distinguish against the blackness of the cloth coat. It was wrapped in a towel, and when she removed it he saw that it was a stone hot water bottle.

'I thought you might need this if you're staying here tonight,' she said, handing it to him with the towel placed back over it so he didn't burn his hands.

He set it carefully on the table, acutely conscious of the pleasurable warmth on his skin.

'Thank you. That's very kind. How did you know I was staying?'

'Walter told me. Walter knows everything.'

He lit the oil lamp and placed it on the mantel. She looked about her, taking everything in, then placed both her hands on the stone water bottle.

'Does Walter know you're here now?'

'Probably. But it doesn't matter. He's one of us, not one of them.'

'I'm going to light the fire. I can't offer you very much but if you have a minute I can find a drop of something.'

He gestured to one of the chairs at the table and she sat down, Mrs Sullivan's coat hunched and rucked over her shoulders but she made no attempt to take it off. For some reason he thought of Little Red Riding Hood but it made him think too of wolves and he knew already part of him felt coldly predatory. Then putting a match to the kindling he added some of the peat from the wicker basket at the side of the hearth. At first some of the smoke blew straight back into the room and when he tried to disperse it with waves of his hands he only provoked more. Behind him he could hear her laughing, then announce that he'd never get a job in service, but gradually the fire took hold and some of the room's mustiness slowly dissipated as the silhouettes of the flames began to play hide and seek on the whitewashed walls. He found the half-bottle of whiskey, but rejected the two glasses he found in a cupboard as not fit for use. So after apologising he offered her the bottle and she took a hesitant sip before tightening her face in apparent disgust. The smell of peat grew stronger and as it caught, the fire glowed a deeper red. He didn't want her to go.

'Will you stay a while?' he asked.

'If you'd like me to. If you're happy no one's forcing my company on you.'

'Is anyone?'

'Well, Eddie's in Ida's bed. But no, I wasn't told to come to you if that's what you're thinking.'

'So you're homeless again,' then hesitated before adding, with a forced casualness, 'You can stay here if you like.'

She glanced towards the darkness of the small bedroom. He handed her the bottle again and she sipped as lightly as she had done the first time.

'Are you offering as a gentleman who feels sorry for me?'

'No. I'm asking because I hope you might stay. But it's your choice. I don't think that bed offers much comfort,' he said, pointing to the back room.

She looked at him as if she was studying him. He lowered his eyes but held her after-image in absolute clarity – the piled smoulder of her pinned hair, looking as if the fire had somehow reached inside it, the pale openness of her face, the way her eyes absorbed everything in silent evaluation but without any harshness of judgement. And in that moment he needed someone who wouldn't judge him because he knew he would come up short. He thought of the tiny bundle of bones he had buried a short while earlier, but then forced himself not to slip into cataloguing all the failures his life had accumulated lest they frighten her away. So many secrets that could never be shared or understood, because to do so would seemingly reveal him as someone other than who he really was, or the person he had always wanted to be.

She took her coat off. She was wearing a black dress with a white collar, the uniform given to her by the Manor House. Only her cap was missing. Then she disappeared into the back room, returning a few moments later pulling the thin mattress after her.

'We'll put it in front of the fire. It'll be warmer there,' she said in a matter-of-fact way that left him having to hide his shock, 'and we need something to cover it. I don't know if you've looked at it.'

He could see enough to understand but there was nothing in the way of sheets to hide the blemishes that covered the surface of the mattress. It was all he could think to do, so going to one of the corners where spades lolled lazily against each other, he lifted some of the hessian sacks and spread them on the mattress.

'There's nothing else,' he said. 'I'm sorry. You deserve better.'

'Please don't tell me I'm a princess or I'll know you're not to be trusted,' she said, straightening the sacks with her foot. 'I've had worse. Much worse.'

He looked at her face to see if she was having second thoughts but it was turned away from him and shadowed. It felt a terrible thing to need something so much, to need someone who was a stranger and about whom he knew almost nothing. But he had already started to invest new belief in the idea that being with her, being with anyone, might serve to block so many other things out. And it wouldn't be like the last time, when all they shared was sleep, because his impulse wasn't kindness but rather desire and it didn't matter that the colour of the lamp was wrong, that he had come where he wasn't supposed to be. Nothing mattered in that moment except the need to sate his desire and he counted it only a matter of small good fortune that she was attractive to him. But it wouldn't have mattered if she wasn't. He knew that. And there was an openness about her that he didn't think of as brazen but something he found compelling and devoid of all the inane rituals and game-playing he associated with women of his own class. The way she spoke to him so fearlessly, so different from the manner in which she was meant to address him. He wondered if her presence was somehow just another part of such women's lives, lives he knew little about but which he imagined were in large part predetermined and constantly shaped by the need to survive, by commerce rather than the luxury of romance. And yet what would she gain by coming to him like this? Did she think it would lead to something better for her? He attempted to tell himself that perhaps it was just a kindness for a kindness, but knew his decline of her offer had been nothing but common decency, whatever meaning those words held. Her motivations, however, meant little to him as he watched her go into the back room and heard a drawer opening in the dresser with the cracked mirror that sat beside the cot, then return with two grey woollen blankets that also smelt of must.

'The best I can find,' she said, wrinkling her nose at them.

He took them off her and was immediately conscious of their coarseness.

'I don't care,' he told her as he spread them on the top of the hessian sack-covered mattress, then turned away and fed the fire again.

'As good as the Ritz,' she said, slipping the hot water bottle under the blankets he had spread.

'As good as the Ritz.'

When the makeshift bed was ready they stood looking at each other and he felt a sudden shiver of embarrassment before she smiled at him in a way that seemed to recognise what he was feeling.

'So what now, Mr Digger?' she teased him.

'I don't know,' he said, momentarily bereft of his self-confidence, and suddenly he was in a smoke-filled room with someone playing music hall songs on an out-of-tune piano and men were ascending and descending the stairs, indistinguishable from each other except for the speed of their movements, those going up faster than those coming down. The exchange of money made everything more straightforward. For a second he thought of offering what was in his wallet but he knew what that would make her and he didn't want to risk losing her. So instead he simply lay down on the mattress with his back to the fire, his head propped on his hand and covered himself with one of the blankets.

She stepped carefully over him and, lifting the oil lamp, went into the back room for the second time. He listened to her movements as intently as he had listened to the night sounds in the world beyond the trench, constantly searching to ascertain the significance of what was heard, reality and the ceaseless conjuring of the imagination often at odds with each other. Then the light that funnelled in from the back room was suddenly extinguished and when she came back in, only the glow from the fire revealed her nakedness, the almost unbearable whiteness of her skin, the loosened cascade of her hair. She slipped under the blankets and shivered. He felt her feet seeking out the stone bed jar, pushing his own away from it.

'It's cold,' she said, pulling the blankets high on her shoulder. 'And the blankets itch.'

'Here,' he said, 'come to this side,' and he raised his body high so she could slip under it and feel the direct heat from the fire. As she moved under him he smelt the same scent of soap and perfume that he had before. It made him feel unclean – he still had the stale sweat of the day on his body. There'd been no time to wash it off.

'That's better. You're a gentleman,' she told him but it wasn't what he wanted to be.

She lay on her side facing the fire with her hair tumbling down her back. He hesitated then touched it lightly for the first time with the tips of his fingers. He wanted to bury his face in it but stopped himself. It wasn't as soft and yielding as he had allowed himself to imagine, instead it felt intensely alive as it moved under his touch. He drew his hand back as if shocked and then the white glimmer of her shoulder was a siren call he could no longer resist and he kissed it once and felt the intense pleasure of it.

'Are you sure?' he asked.

'If it's what you want,' she said, still with her face turned to the fire.

'Why?' he asked.

'For the company. For something… For – I don't know. You talk too much, think too much. Not everything has to have a reason.'

She turned and looked at him with the fire colouring the side of her face and he needed no further surety. But then as he took off his clothes he realised he didn't have anything. She told him it was all right, that she couldn't have children, mumbled something unfinished about an accident. She didn't explain and at first he imagined an accident in the factory, then started to wonder about previous lovers. About a pregnancy suddenly terminated. But he asked no questions and then lied to her, telling her that he was sorry, when really he was grateful for the convenience. She made no reply and when he was ready he arched over her on his elbows and kissed her but he was too rough and she moved her mouth away after a few seconds, levering him away a little with the palm of her hand on his shoulder. He didn't care about his roughness because all he wanted to do was to obliterate himself and if that meant pressing his need into her, so be it.

It was the price she would pay for lying naked with him on a makeshift bed and he was even glad about the bed, with its hessian sacks and coarse must-ridden blankets, because what he wanted to do was primitive and came from some far-off country where love or giving had no meaning or purpose. So he kissed her again, forcing her mouth open as if demanding her submission, but she pushed him back again and moved her head away.

'Who taught you to kiss?' she whispered.

'It's been a long time,' he told her.

Suddenly she cupped his face tightly with both her hands and kissed him. He knew she was showing him how to kiss her and he had to fight against the impulse to knock her hands away and subjugate her with the physical expression of his will. But instead he only shivered a little and then all he felt was the strengthening press of her hands, all he wanted to do was submit himself to the enduring pleasure of her mouth.

'That's better,' she said and her voice was soft and so close that he felt her breath mingle with his. The light of the fire was in her hair once more, burnishing and sparking it and then she told him to kiss her and he did it the way she had shown him. Already he knew that his power over her was ebbing away but he no longer cared and in a matter of minutes he had resigned it so completely to her, so that when she moved the blanket away and cupped her breast, he accepted the offer with gratitude and let his lips gently kiss her nipple hard. She put her hand to the back of his head while he did it and kneaded his hair. He kissed her mouth again and again, and then she held him only with her smile so for a few seconds they simply lay facing each other, the stipple of freckles across the bridge of her nose tiny embers, before he let his hand wander across her body and knew its tautness, a body with nothing surplus or self-indulgent. It felt to him like a map across which his fingers moved slowly, a map that might lead him home if he could follow its contours, come to know its hidden places. And then when he knew she was ready he arched above her again and she helped him and he looked at nothing except her green eyes.

A homeward journey was what it seemed like at the start because it had been so long but as he moved doubts entered his mind about where he was travelling to, and before he could stop himself, his thoughts slipped into freefall, tumbling into a world of mud, lime from a bucket sprinkled like flakes of snow, Hawley's face. He thrust harder to try to stop the lessening he felt, but she calmed and slowed him and she was whispering in his ear, repeating something that at first was lost in the broken splay of his own breath and desperation. Then he understood what she was saying and she was telling him to say her name, telling him she wanted him to say her name and he did so in a rhythmic whisper, over and over, until everything else slipped away and there was only the moment and even when his breath broke in a final frantic rush it still burst from his lips. Her hands fanned lightly across his back as she gently hushed and stilled him, then he slowly dropped his head to her breasts and resting it there tried not to humiliate himself by crying.

Afterwards they draped themselves in the blankets and sat shoulder to shoulder on the edge of the mattress, facing the warmth. When he thanked her she told him it wasn't charity so she didn't need to be thanked and there was an edge to her voice. He worried that he had disappointed her. They drank a little more and stared intently at the fire.

'What do you see, Cora?' he asked.

'Tomorrow's drudgery.'

He was disappointed again, somehow hoping that what had just happened might have changed something for her, though he didn't know what that change could be. Then, as his own sense of reckless release streamed through him, he was tempted to think that he could offer her some escape, something better than she knew in the drudgery of the Manor House. But he knew it was a fantasy.

'What do you see?' she asked, leaning into him.

'Tomorrow's drudgery,' he said. 'Men with shovels and wheelbarrows, mud everywhere. A bloody hole in the ground that's never deep enough.'

'Your drudgery is different from mine. You've an army of men at your beck and call. I've Mrs Sullivan in my ear all day long, so sometimes when I'm in bed at night I can still hear her voice as if it's trapped inside my head.'

She turned her face to him and then he saw her looking at the thick white ridge of scar etched on the inside of his forearm. She stretched out her hand and took it so she could look at it more closely, then lightly traced her finger along its length.

'How did you do it?'

'In the war. Caught it on the wire one dark night when you couldn't see your hand in front of you. It's nothing,' he told her, knowing it was caused by a piece of shrapnel, a tiny piece from the shell that blasted Hawley further down the trench.

'There were men in the mill – lots of them – who didn't come back. First day of the Somme mostly. Some of them young, some of them decent.'

He wondered if one of the decent young men had been her lover. The father of a child neither of them would ever hold.

'Sometimes there were accidents in the mill as well. People got tired or were distracted by something, got damaged by machinery. Ugly it was.'

It suddenly struck him that he knew nothing about her. They had just done the most intimate of things and yet he didn't even know her second name, nor where she had lived before the Manor House, nothing about her family. But part of him wanted to believe that it was a good thing they shared such an ignorance of each other because the more they knew, the greater chance of complications. And when he told himself he couldn't risk that, he heard a voice in his head accusing him of being no better than Eddie Remington. It seemed to him that all the men he had ever known could justify their actions, if not to others then certainly to themselves, and no pardons were so easily given and so eagerly received as those that a man granted to himself.

Her arm rested against his shoulder as she leaned into him so that some of her hair touched his skin and something from that touch flowed into him and after a while he wanted to lie with her again but she told him she needed to sleep, needed to be gone early in the morning. Then she simply lay down again facing the fire and draping the blanket round her as best as it would reach, pulled her body into an embryonic pose, but she let him snuggle into her back and when he stretched his arm across her stomach she didn't remove it, so he lay there absorbing her scent, absorbing the heat from her body, and despite what she had said he thanked her again. She didn't reply and he didn't know whether she had heard, for in a few minutes she was sleeping with her breathing a steady, threaded rise and fall through the gradual dying of the fire's light.

He hadn't made her. She had come to him. Nor was she some innocent child unfamiliar with the ways of the world or a man's body. He would treat her with whatever kindness was possible. She didn't strike him as someone like Ida, naïve enough to let herself be deceived into a foolish fantasy about love or shared futures. And he tried to tell himself that some-how it balanced out some of the misery that had befallen him since he came to the Manor House to construct this lake. That he could use it as an omen of good fortune, a protective shield against all the misfortunes that had strewn his days and would continue to do so until his task was finished.

In the morning she shoved him awake before light had broken and made him get dressed and draw water from the pump in the yard. During the night, she had added most of his blanket to her own but he hadn't claimed it back, content to draw his warmth from the closeness of her body. When he returned with the water, she covered her nakedness with a blanket, told him not to look and went into the back room to wash. He heard the water splash and when he called her to ask if he could heat some for her she told him that she hadn't time, that she had to be gone before Mrs Sullivan started her rounds. He wondered what would pass between them when the moment came for them to part, whether they would kiss or at least embrace, but when finally she emerged from the back room dressed in the uniform the house had given her, she seemed intent only on smoothing out creases in her dress and checking her hair was safely back in place.

'Will I see you again?' he asked.

'I'm not going anywhere,' she said, taking a pin out of her mouth and sliding it into her hair.

He didn't know if she had deliberately misunderstood his question or in fact was answering it.

'I can't sleep on hessian sacks,' she said, looking at him properly for the first time that morning. He wondered if she was speaking in code, but then she added, 'They itch too much. It's like sleeping on nettles.'

He nodded and held the door open for her. It was still dark outside except for a thin ridge of light pressing high above the trees.

'If you come up to the back door of the kitchen later I'll slip you some breakfast.'

'Thanks, but I don't want to get you in trouble.'

'That'll make you the first man I've ever known who didn't.'

He wanted to say something more, but before he could find the words she was gone, moving silently away, hidden by the blackness of her coat and replaced by the uncertainty of what the day ahead might bring.

16

Her father liked Eric, Alex's father, well enough but didn't wish to show it too openly. There was always a bout of jousting between the two men, mostly playful in nature, when they got together. Eric called him Ray in an artificially matey way – the only person she had ever heard do this. And although it was clear her father also liked Alex, she didn't doubt that he secretly harboured a belief that he wasn't quite worthy of marrying his daughter. He never criticised Alex to her, or made a negative comment directed towards him, but occasionally he would ask Alex a question out of the blue. She knew that there was a subtext when he asked if Alex liked working for his father, if he'd really never thought of striking out on his own, what his ambitions were. And she knew that Alex was never fully relaxed around him, even after he had given his blessing to the wedding and – just as his own parents had – been generous when they needed help to buy their first house. Perhaps there had been a little competitive edge to the generosity, both families keen to match the other's contribution.

He appeared to like Alex's mother, Angela, best of all and although he didn't exactly flirt, he was always complimentary about her – enthusing over her appearance, her cooking, keen to discuss their common enjoyment of golf, in a way that she suspected was occasionally intended to make Eric feel as if he was being blindsided a little. So the evening, which had been arranged as a kind of joint planning meeting about the wedding, threw up potential pitfalls, if not the prospect of looming disasters.

Her father arrived punctually. He'd taken some trouble over his clothes, wearing a smart jacket and shirt. She didn't think the tie was absolutely necessary but knew it was part of his vision of what he thought appropriate. He shook hands with Eric and kissed Angela on the cheek, then handed over a bottle of wine.

'Asda having a sale?' Eric said as he took the bottle from his wife and, studying the label, ignored her exasperated telling off for his rudeness.

'Sadly Asda doesn't sell a wine like this,' Raymond said. 'Or it'd get my business.'

'I'm afraid we don't go much further than the latest Virgin deals, so I'll look forward to this.'

Ellie looked at Alex, but he just stared back at her blankly, as if anything that was liable to happen had nothing to do with him. She felt a flash of irritation recognising that he was going to leave her to do all the navigating, in the way he so often abdicated responsibility when things became difficult.

Everyone sat down and the conversation was dominated by harmless small talk. When it petered out, she heard her father ask Eric how business was.

'Always challenging – you never know whether it's boom or bust round the next corner. But can't complain I suppose,' Eric said.

'This still seems to be a town where wads of money in brown envelopes is common currency.'

'The way of the world, Ray, the way of the world. Still, don't suppose we're much different from anywhere else. But at the end of the day the columns all have to add up or you're in trouble with the tax man, so it's not something I'd ever recommend.'

'I've heard it said, Eric, that the most creative people in this city are the accountants.'

'In case you're wearing a wire, Ray, I've no idea what you're talking about.'

Everyone except Alex laughed – she imagined he didn't want to be tainted with guilt by association. Glasses were filled with the wine her father had brought, and Eric led the admiration. She updated them with wedding progress and showed them photographs of the Boat House on her iPad, everyone going out of their way to say the right things. Then before the meal was ready to be served and after Angela had gone into the kitchen, her father performed his favourite joke. He went and stood in front of the worst painting he could find, put on his reading glasses and stared intently at it.

'Who's this by?' he asked.

'Rembrandt,' Eric said.

'Obviously one of his early works.'

'Would you like to give a valuation of it?'

'I don't want to cause offence.'

'That'll be a first,' Eric said. 'And you know, Ray, I think you boys have it made.'

'How's that, Eric?'

'Well, first of all you sell stuff people don't want any more, stuff that should probably have ended up in a skip, and then you charge the seller and the buyer at the same time. It's a double whammy. Quids in all round.'

'Never thought of it like that. But I'll do you a deal. To save this painting from the skip I'll put it in the next sale and not charge you for it.'

'How do I know it's not really an Old Master and you're trying to pull the wool over my eyes?'

'Because you know I wouldn't deceive someone with whom my family is going to be joined at the altar and because Argos, or wherever you bought it, generally don't sell Old Masters.'

And so it went on while they waited for the meal to be ready. Alex looked bored and restless. She thought he wanted a smoke the way he fidgeted with his hands and from time to time touched his mouth with his fingers. Outwardly things had been better between them, but the very fact they hadn't talked about what had happened in the car park silently implied that to do so would be dangerous. She went into the kitchen and offered her help to Angela but everything was well under control and there was a yellow Post-it note stuck above the hob with precise timings written on it. The table was already set and then Angela asked her to go into the dining room and light the candles. On the sideboard were some family photographs. She stood looking at them, lifting them one by one.

Family groupings mostly. Alex with his father and mother sitting squeezed up in the entrance to a caravan. Alex must have been five or six and he had told her that first seaside holiday was the best one he had ever had. She could remember some day trips with her mother, but had no memory of shared holidays or ever staying overnight somewhere other than her home. She envied him the photograph. At one point she had hoped

Angela might be a kind of surrogate mother, but as friendly and relaxed as she was, she hadn't shown any great inclination to play that role, nor – apart from a couple of lunches – had they spent much personal time together.

But the other photographs came from moments about which she had no knowledge: Alex with his parents seated at an outside restaurant table on holiday abroad; Alex, his wet hair plastered to his head, with his father, both in wetsuits holding bodyboards on a beach; and one of a young, unsmiling Alex in tennis whites with matchstick legs, standing in front of a net with a small trophy held tightly in both hands.

The boy in the photo comes forwards to meet her gaze. The trophy he's holding is no good because it's for second place and his father is only interested in coming first. And because he's paid money for lessons he expects his son to be a winner. But sometimes it's hard to be that because you meet someone with more natural skill, or someone who wants it more than you do and he can hear his father's shouts in the final, flailing about his ears. He'll never lift a racquet again, even though he has to listen to his father's admonitions about not giving up in life, because the game is tarnished with the memory of failure, of coming up short of expectations. He wants to tell her that the happy photographs are not all truthful because the camera often lies, only tells the stories the world wants to hear. So she's wrong when she assumes that everything in his family was always the way she wants to imagine and then envy. Let her know, as she lightly handles the frames and lifts them for a closer look, that they don't show the years when his mother was depressed and became more like a shadow than a real person, when his father would caution him not to expect something or other by saying, 'Your mother's not feeling well, Alex.' Nothing ever explained, not even the stay in hospital where he wasn't allowed to visit. Her sister coming to stay with them for a while and taking over the functioning of the house and her not liking his father, as if she blamed him for what was happening. Going to see his mother in her bedroom with the blinds always pulled so it was always a half-light and his mother assuming a kind of jolliness with him and always telling him that 'she was on the mend', that it 'wouldn't be long before she was up and about'. That soon she'd be 'right as rain'. Afterwards, it was as if none of it had ever happened, except once a week when she went to talk to someone as part of her treatment, and on that afternoon she always left a little snack for him on the kitchen table to have when he returned from school. A little offering he ate in abject loneliness. Loneliness, Ellie, that's not in the photographs you hold in your hands.

He wants to tell Ellie as she turns away to light the candles that as a young boy he always wondered what his mother discussed and whether she talked about him. Was he part of her problem, part of whatever it was made her unwell? There was only his father and him so the talk had to include them. What else would she talk about? And sometimes when he was with his mother he tried to study her when she wasn't looking or was preoccupied with something, to discover by stealth what she really felt about him, but she never revealed that secret. There was the time when he was older when she went to stay with her sister for two weeks, and it didn't feel like she had gone on a holiday because his father would be on the phone with her late at night in calls that lasted ages. When he'd tried to ask his father about it he'd been told that 'it was just one of those things', that his mother 'needed to clear her head a bit'. And later when things seemed to have settled into a more predictable pattern there were problems with his father's businesses and the recession or perhaps something else that was never explained. And for about three months he became an absence, his arrival late at night signalled by the sound of his car keys dropping in the bowl on the hall table. Their absence marking his departure.

There's something else he wants to tell Ellie, but he's embarrassed and he waits until she turns her gaze back to the dining table to check the candles. He's a teenager and his mother asks him to caddy for her because the wheel's come off her golf trolley and she hasn't got time to get it fixed. She tells him she'll pay him the going rate if he shapes up, so he agrees. And afterwards they have their tea in the club house and a man comes over to their table and he's joking with his mother as if they know each other well and his mother responds to him in a way that seems different from her normal self, as if she's acting out a part and she's quickened into a kind of alertness or receptivity that he doesn't fully recognise as something she has ever displayed to him. After the man moves away and he asks her who he is, she tells him that he's 'just one of the members' but the nature of her dismissal is unconvincing and she too quickly changes the subject. So, Ellie, he silently tells her, light all the candles that they might chase the shadows away, reveal the hidden stories and just for a while amidst them all see if you can find a small boy with a botched haircut but anointed with a sweet-smelling scent who believes he has stepped into independent life, stepped into his future. When for a moment the way ahead seems suddenly clear and look how he walks towards it unburdened and with yet no premonition of what loneliness will feel like.

Ellie heard Angela calling everyone and went into the kitchen to help her serve. When Alex entered the dining room there was only the slight trace of her perfume, the scent of the lit candles and the boy he once was and it seemed such a world away that he struggled to know if the person in the frames had any real connection to himself. He was conscious too of Ellie being somewhere else, her scent the only tangible evidence of her former presence. What happened in the underground car park had only made that distance worse.

He knew Ellie had an absence in her life after the death of her mother because she had talked to him about it but he had never told her about the space that existed in his, the space between two parents who he believed didn't always love each other the way they were supposed to. And even as he stood in the house he had grown up in, part of him felt homeless, unsure where he belonged, so he went on hoping that marriage to Ellie would change that forever. They would build a life together where each felt safe if only he could be the person she believed him to be. But to do that he knew he would have to keep things away so he could come to her untainted by the past. Untainted by the girl in the tent whose tattoos were always moving across his memory, a transfer print of garish unnatural colours.

He wanted to smoke but knew it wasn't possible to parade his failure in front of everyone and anyway they were coming in to take their places at the table. His father and Raymond were continuing their conversation about whether they should wear matching suits.

'What do you think, Alex?' his father asked.

'I'm going to leave it to Ellie to make that call,' Alex said. 'I'm hiring suits for me, the best man and the groomsmen. They do the full package – suits, with waistcoats, shirts, ties. I think you guys can probably wear whatever you're comfortable with.'

He didn't want to talk about this, found it too difficult to pretend to be enthusiastic about it when in reality it was near the bottom of the list of things that he worried about. But as Ellie and Angela served the starter then joined them, his father asked was he supposed to make a speech or was it just Raymond.

'Do you want to make a speech?' Alex asked, hoping the answer was no.

'Well, I think if my son's getting married I should do, don't you, Ray?'

'Up to you, Eric.'

'But we're not throwing the floor open,' Alex said. 'That just encourages people to stand up and spout nonsense that goes on forever.'

'We've all had to sit through weddings like that,' his father said. 'Meanwhile the food's getting cold.'

'Never stand between your audience and their food,' Raymond said. 'And if you have to, keep it short and sweet.'

'You could bring your gavel, Ray, to call for order.'

'I could, Eric, and if you prattle on too long you might hear me shouting, "Going, going, gone!"'

'I aim to be well gone by the end of the evening.' Then looking at his wife, 'Angela, do you want to tell Alex and Ellie what we decided earlier?'

For a second she looked a little confused, as if unaccustomed to being the one to make announcements, but then lifted her wine glass and told them that they would like to pay for the honeymoon. Ellie and Alex offered their thanks and everyone raised their glasses to the gift. Ellie pushed her foot against his under the table in a gesture that was meant to encourage greater gratitude on his part, but all he really wanted to do was to go home. Go home, go anywhere else and have a smoke. More and more, he was aware of Ellie telling him what was the right thing to do and he wondered who would be the first to tire of that. He glanced over her shoulder at the photographs on the sideboard and knew that if she had to tell him what the right thing to do was as often as she did now then sooner or later the shared knowledge that he had come up short would fester in them both. For a crazy second he wanted to stand up at the table and tell them he was done with it all, tell Ellie's father that he was right after all and he wasn't worthy, tell his own father that he too had been right: he was a quitter, the child in the photograph with his tiny trophy who didn't have enough of whatever you needed to win. Voices were complimenting Angela on the food, but they didn't register with him. He heard instead car keys dropped in a glass bowl – the same one that was still there in the hall. Keys gone again. A lingering absence. The same stairs he climbed to visit his mother in her bedroom when she wasn't well. The bottles of tablets on the bedside table. The drawn blinds and the half-light. Soon she'll be on the mend, soon she'll be as right as rain – that's what she would tell him. Right as rain. He felt as if he was drifting on some current, floating weightless in space, further and further away from where he was supposed to be.

When Ellie lifted his plate away she rested her hand on his shoulder for a second and he didn't know whether she was telling him to pull himself together or whether it was an expression of intimacy. Afterwards she took the car keys because he'd had a couple of drinks, and he let her, even though he hated being driven. When she asked him if he was all right he told her he was but knew that she didn't believe him. So mostly they drove home in silence and then when she started to ask him where they should go on honeymoon he couldn't think of an answer and threw the question back on her. But as she suggested places they might travel, he could only nod and warn her that there was a speed camera up ahead.

But she wasn't driving him home and at first he didn't understand until they were in the Craigantlet Hills at a vantage point overlooking the city, which unfolded before them in a simmering cauldron of light. Where they had come the first time, the sex fumbling and awkward but blessed with laughter and the right words spoken by both. They sat staring in silence at the gridded yellow pathways below.

'If you didn't know better you would think the city was beautiful,' Alex said. 'If you squint at it and concentrate only on the lights.'

'I don't remember you spending too much time looking at it. That first time.'

'No, maybe not. There were better things to focus on.'

There was a pause before she turned to him and asked, 'What's wrong, Alex?'

The unexpected directness of the question startled him.

'I'm just nervous about the wedding,' he said, instead of telling her that he was frightened. Sometimes so frightened it almost made him feel sick. He didn't have the words to explain, so instead he fixed his eyes on the lights again.

'I am too, but it will be all right,' she said and took his hand. 'And you'll want to see me in my dress.'

'I know you'll be beautiful. As beautiful as that first time.'

Then they fell back into silence and watched the lights of a night plane traverse the city that lay sleeping below them.

17

In the weeks and months that followed, Cora brought sheets from the house, clean pillows, proper blankets, a couple of towels and various bits and pieces intended to civilise the cottage. He worried that she would get in trouble for what she had taken, but she dismissed his concerns saying that Mrs Sullivan's husband wasn't well and that her attention was mostly focused on caring for him, so it was easier to smuggle out what was required. She attempted to justify it by saying that they had been told by Mr Remington that he was to get whatever he needed while working on the lake.

He stayed over in the cottage one or two nights a week. As if in some story in a book or a penny dreadful, he left the lit oil lamp in the window so she would know he was there, and he also made his own effort to make the cottage more presentable, bringing some items from home. It was never going to be the Ritz, but it had become passable. They still didn't use the back room but always put the mattress in front of the fire. Often they didn't have sex but merely talked and then slept. She liked to talk, sometimes even sing songs from the mill, and when she sang her stipple of freckles made him think of a thrush again, singing only for him. There was one song in particular she liked to tease him with:

> You might know a weaver
> When she comes into town
> With her old greasy hair
> And her scissors hanging down
> With a shawl around her shoulders
> And a shuttle in her hand
> You will easy know a weaver
> For she'll never get a man
> No she'll never get a man
> No she'll never get a man
> You will easy know a weaver
> For she'll never get a man.

Sometimes she would close her eyes and angle her head to one side so that it was as if she was singing only to herself. But once when she did this Hawley came to him, his voice ringing out in the trench as first light broke, the laughter in his voice as if he had just woken up to a summer's day back on his farm and there was nothing but pleasure stretching in front of him with country lanes to be walked and fields to be sown. Round an improvised fire at night the men would pay him in cigarettes to sing some sentimental song of home or love and then despite everything the world seemed to fall silent and still, as if a single voice held it transfixed.

As time went on, however, he began to worry that Cora might have started to create some private fantasy about what was happening between them, that her previously cold grasp of reality might be slowly loosening. He imagined he saw it in the little sprig of flowers she put in a jar on the window sill, the dainty china cups she had inveigled and out of which they drank tea. But then she would offer some disparaging insight into the world that dispelled those same fears, or swear vigorously about something that had annoyed her. Less readily dismissed, though, was his awareness that he felt increasingly bound to her. He couldn't bring himself to use any other form of words. Drawn to her completely blunt attitude about physical matters, her uncowed cynicism about the world and the way she showed him no deference. It was that lack of deference that allowed him to persist in the self-justifying belief that perhaps what they did was, after all, something equally shared, and entered into on an equal footing. But no matter how much he found things to like in her, he knew that it was her body joined with his that he liked most, the way she gave herself but also took what she wanted from him without embarrassment or shame. And her hair unpinned always seemed akin to a miracle, especially when the room was dark and it was quickened by the fire. His hand moving slowly over the pale tautness of her body, the thinness of her waist and flatness of her stomach, the gentle cup of her breasts, the way his hand found a little hollow above her hip in which it liked to nestle. The way when they lay together she held him in her unbroken gaze as if observing him anew and as if it was always the first time, the first time again and again.

Sometimes too in the midst of passion she used words he had never heard from a woman and it stirred him because it was best when it felt that what they did was primitive and instinctive, far removed from what the world expected of them. He understood too that in some way it was a rebuttal of what had been done to him, done to them all, because society's moral code was a lie and deserved only to be shattered in a million pieces. But he felt too his own cowardice, because he knew he could never reveal whatever it was that existed between them or have it flourish anywhere other than the darkness of the cottage.

At first they had deliberately displayed minimal curiosity about each other's past, as if there was an unspoken rule that to ask too many questions was to pry, and it was best if they just knew each other as they were in the present, inside that small room. Perhaps each understood that behind them stood disparate worlds and to venture into them would only accentuate that. Despite the first time when she had made him repeat her name again and again, she rarely used his and he wondered if she felt that to do so was too big an intimacy, regardless of what their bodies did to each other. Gradually, however, he started to ask her questions about her family, but it was a subject about which she was so blatantly evasive that he was left thinking of her as someone who had just suddenly appeared on the earth without parents. Questions too about how she had ended up in the Manor House.

One night as they sat at the table he poured some beer in the glasses she had brought from the house and she revealed things she hadn't before. She told him about her father but in a voice that sounded tentative, stripped of its customary force.

'He worked in the shipyard. He was a drinker and when he was drunk he liked to fight – sometimes he'd stand in the middle of the street and challenge all comers. Mostly he kept his drinking and fighting outside the house. Then to everyone's amazement he found religion, got himself saved on the Shankill Road in a gospel campaign led by some man called Nicholson. He wasn't the only one. In the shipyard they had to set up a special shed for all the stolen goods that were returned by the newly saved. The drink went out the window and instead it was holy, holy, you can't do this, you can't do that. Soon I liked it better when he was a drinker. I couldn't stick it any longer and moved out to live with Ida. Her mother didn't give a toss what you did or didn't do so long as there was rent money at the end of the week and enough left over for a packet of fags and a bottle of gin.'

She sipped the beer unenthusiastically and then dried her mouth with the back of her hand as if trying to brush away the taste.

'Ida and me worked in the same mill. Mr Remington hardly ever came near it,' she said. 'He had places all over and managers running them so it was only every so often that he'd appear in his car with his chauffeur. We all used to try and catch sight of him, probably more a sight of the car and despite the overseers shouting at us to get back to work. Fancy thing it was. All cream colour and shiny metal. Chauffeur with a cap and everything. Some of the women called him jumped-up to each other because they knew his family came from nothing better. But he only ever went into the offices and he never stayed long. Sometimes he had Eddie with him.'

She held her glass up to the light examining its contents.

'I don't know why men drink beer so much. Sometimes I think it tastes all right but mostly it tastes horrible,' she said. 'Eddie always had an eye for the women. Always sniffing round them, casting his eye over them, the way you would if you were going to buy something in a shop. Some of the women used to joke that they'd let him for a ride in the car.'

She laughed at the joke then sipped more of the beer before giving an exaggerated grimace. He wanted her to talk about Eddie but instead she continued talking about the women.

'We all stood together – it was the only decent thing about that hell-hole. They'd look out for each other, cover when needed. So if a woman had to come back to work soon after giving birth, they'd cover for her when she had to nip home to feed her baby. And they were always singing – anything to make the time go quicker. But except for that I bloody hated the place. Freezing cold in winter and the air filled with fibres from the flax, and there was so much noise from all the looms belting away that you had to learn to lip read.'

'And you can lip read?'

'Pretty much.'

'So what am I saying now?' he asked, using words he would never have said to her aloud.

'You've no chance, mister,' she said but she was smiling.

He went to pour her more beer but she put her hand over the top of the glass.

'And getting me drunk won't improve your chances either,' she told him before asking if he had ever had champagne.

'A couple of times. Why?'

'That's what I'd like to drink. Not this muddy bilge but champagne in crystal glasses.'

'Perhaps you will,' he said and then saw by the expression on her face that he'd made a mistake, knew she resented it when he let himself slip into some statement that denied the realities of her existence. She might think whatever she wanted in private but she wouldn't let him patronise her. He got up from the table and stirred some new life into the fire as a form of apology. When he turned back she was pouring what was left of her beer into his glass.

'Now you're trying to get me drunk,' he said.

'How long will it take you to make the lake?'

'Many months more, at least six, even if things go smoothly. Much longer than I ever thought when I started out.'

'You're only dragging it out because you met me,' she teased.

'That's right. Every night I go back out in the darkness and shovel the earth back into it.'

'So it'll never get finished.'

'Has to be finished for the open day the Remingtons have planned. If I don't meet that deadline there'll be hell to pay.'

'There's always hell to pay.'

They sat in silence for a few moments and he suddenly felt far away from her as if talk about finishing the lake, however distant it was, brought an understanding that its completion would see what existed between them also come to an end. That knowledge renewed the residual sense of guilt he felt about her, made him feel the force of his inevitable betrayal. He knew he could never give her champagne, never even give her loyalty, and yet he understood too on the times when she didn't come to the cottage he experienced a deep well of loneliness. The blind physical need he had felt at the start had lessened, so he understood what stirred in him was now something far deeper. If he didn't choose to dwell on whatever it was, it was because he was wary of the answers. He wanted to break the silence.

'You said Eddie often came with him.'

'Yes, but apart from eyeing up the women, no one knew what his job was supposed to be. Always fancied himself – that was clear enough. Last Christmas they held a party for the workers. Tea and biscuits. Dull as ditchwater it was, and the buggers put it at the end of the shift so no work was lost. Eddie spoke to Ida, said he was looking for a couple of housemaids for the Manor House. It was board and lodgings, a bit more money than in the mill but not much. Ida said yes if I could come as well. We thought we were on to a good thing. Living in a big house, moving up in the world. It was only later we learned there'd been others before us and even though I wear this outfit instead of an apron in the mill, the drudgery's the same. Morning to night, at someone's beck and call.'

'And Eddie... Did he ever?'

'No, I think I'm too scrawny for him. He only ever had eyes for Ida. But there's been a falling out. Eddie's started drinking too much. He goes to McCartan's in the village and sometimes the landlady lets him stay over. And if he's tired of Ida then he'll find some reason to move us both on. Bring in new girls from some other mill where they don't know what's what any more than we did.'

They sat in silence again until it was interrupted by a sudden knock on the door that made them both start. Cora went to the window and looked out without revealing herself.

'It's Ida.'

'What does she want?'

Cora didn't answer but when she went to the door she opened it just wide enough for her to slip outside, and was gone only a matter of seconds.

'I have to go. Mrs Sullivan's come back up to the house and is looking for me. Ida told her I wasn't feeling very well and went outside to get some air.'

She straightened her dress and put a hand to her hair.

'Do I look all right?'

He told her she did, but suppressed his impulse to tell her she was beautiful in case she thought he was patronising her again. Perhaps he would have been. He wasn't sure. But the night was cold without her and he felt an emptiness seeping through him.

He thought again of the parcel of bones he had buried. He was certain he'd been right about the possible consequences if the discovery had been made public, and knew he couldn't brook any more delays. There were months of work ahead and it would result in ignominious failure if he had to admit to Remington that there wasn't going to be any water in his lake on the open day. Sometimes he fantasised about setting explosive charges and blowing the earth to pieces, at other times with a greater grasp of reality he debated whether he could persuade him to employ more men. But Allenby didn't doubt that if he paraded too many obstacles in front of Remington about the lake's construction, his employer would be on the phone to Wickets and Rodgers to tell them that their man wasn't up to the job. Remington struck him as a man not gifted with much patience and it was clear that disappointing his wife's wishes was not something he would tolerate.

He imagined an ancient and ragged group of people huddling against the wind as they buried the child. He never believed he would ever be a father, had no desire to be one, because the idea of having responsibility for a child in the world as he knew it, was not something he could readily contemplate – he could not be someone bringing life into the world as well as someone who had ended the life of another person. But sometimes he couldn't fully shake off the belief that, in some way he didn't understand, he was now connected to the buried child. Perhaps it was the way he was eternally linked to Hawley. Hawley who himself wasn't much more than a child, with his boyish smile and love of mischief. The black cap of his curls, his voice in the morning singing and making up his own words to familiar tunes. His talk of the family farm and his occasional work aboard his uncle's fishing boat out of Kilkeel. Bones wrapped in cloth. Perhaps an offering to some nameless god. The war's killing of the firstborn. Their bodies buried undiscovered in the bowels of the earth or under rows of white crosses. Sometimes in his dreams he was digging in the lake, digging alone under a feeble moon that sheltered its face behind clouds when he discovered more bodies, his spade jarring and juddering in his hands as he struck bones again and again. And in the worst of his dreams, grotesque faces with distorted, grinning mouths would suddenly spring out of the clay. On those nights he would instinctively reach his arm out for her comfort and when he drew it back empty, feel an inexorable sense of loss.

When he resumed work in the morning the images still lingered in his mind so he had to force himself to focus on the work ahead as he discussed it with Gregson. He was startled by her sudden presence. She did a kind of half-curtsy before saying, 'Excuse me, Mr Allenby, but Mr Remington senior would like to see you up at the house when convenient.'

'Do you know what it's about?' he asked, as he stepped a little distance from Gregson.

'I'm sorry, sir, he didn't say.'

The word 'sir' clanged in the space between them but when he stared intently at her, the face he saw was emotionless and after he thanked her, she turned away.

'Wonder what he wants,' Gregson said, and Allenby knew the fear of the discovered bones was already flaring across his thoughts.

'Probably nothing. Nothing to worry about.'

'How can you be sure?'

'Because I haven't said anything and I assume you haven't either.'

Allenby looked at his foreman and wasn't sure if his assumption was correct.

'He probably just wants a progress report. Keep the men working.'

Allenby walked away hoping to catch up with Cora but there was no trace of her and so instead he went to the cottage to change out of his boots and make himself presentable. But she was waiting there, standing in the entrance to the back room, and as soon as he had closed the cottage door she pushed herself against him, one hand round his neck while the other slipped the bolt closed. He went to say something but she smothered the words with the forceful press of her mouth and then there was nothing for him beyond physical intensity, the impulse of the moment and a shared unquenchable urgency that consumed everything else and for the first time they stumbled into the back room with its tiny blackened window and cracked mirror, and he no longer knew where his body ended and hers began as they removed their clothes and pulled at each other's with a rising desperation. It was over quickly, almost as quickly as it had started, and they both lay entwined in a fused breathlessness, hers a descant over his deeper stream.

'That's how you deliver a message,' she said, starting to laugh.

'A message I don't think I'm ever liable to forget.'

There was a knock on the door of the cottage. She started to giggle and he lightly cupped his hand over her mouth and whispered for her to be quiet then took his hand away. His head was tight against her and he could feel the racing of her heart. There were a couple more rasping knocks and then whoever it was appeared to leave.

'Did anyone see you coming here?' he asked.

'No, you've made me an expert at sneaking around unseen.'

'We shouldn't take risks like this,' he said then regretted it because he knew it made him an hypocrite.

'I didn't force you. Don't remember you ever sending me away.'

'I wanted what happened – you know that. But we need to be careful. And I need to go and see Remington. You better be back up in the house.'

'Back in service then,' she said as she started to disentangle the knotted chaos of her discarded clothes.

It was on his tongue, the words already forming forcefully in his head with which to tell her that he would take her away from the toil of service, but as she slipped into her uniform and slowly reformed into who she was in the other world, those same words froze unspoken and he wasn't sure whether he experienced the sharpest of regrets or a deep relief. He knew, however, that he was allowed to feel gratitude and when they were dressed he put his arms round her and held her tightly, trying in vain to smooth the anarchy of her hair. She nestled against him as if she had found a place of shelter, and he was grateful for that too. But despite the morning light outside, the back room was still shadowy, and when they slipped apart the blackness of her dress drew her further away again.

He asked her to wait a few minutes until he had left the cottage before she departed. She nodded to show she understood, then started looking for the hair clips that had fallen everywhere and as she recovered them and stored them in her mouth, began to carefully repress the wildness of her hair. He tried to make himself respectable, although that too felt like an hypocrisy, someone constantly moving between two worlds at eternal odds with each other.

Being summoned to the house always presented a problem, namely whether he should go to the front door or the back kitchen door. As he was responding to an invitation he thought he should use the main entrance, and a good few minutes after he rang the bell the door was opened by Ida.

'To see Mr Remington,' he said as she wordlessly held it open but even though she angled her face away from him slightly, he saw that her right eye was blackened and her cheek bruised. She gestured for him to enter and he followed her to a study where Remington was ensconced behind a desk, Mrs Remington standing at his shoulder. He had never actually spoken to her before and had only glimpsed her when she was leaving or arriving in the car. She was sharp-faced and dressed in sombre colours, slightly younger than he had imagined but looked frail beside the physical strength of her husband. Although younger than her husband, she was grey-haired. Some of that greyness seemed to have leeched into her face so that the only brightness in her appearance came from the string of pearls she wore. She had her hand on Remington's shoulder and Allenby thought it was for his benefit, either to assert her status or to draw strength from their closeness. She greeted him with a smile and a nod. Remington told him to take a seat.

He felt as if he was in the headmaster's study and suddenly wondered if his – and he struggled internally to find the word before he settled unsatisfactorily on 'liaison' – had been exposed. So perhaps he was to be sent packing, dispatched immediately to Wickets and Rodgers in utter disgrace. But as he waited for the sentence to be passed, Mrs Remington rang a little bell on her husband's desk. Ida reappeared and tea was requested. He saw Mrs Remington looking at Ida and almost imperceptibly shake her head in disapproval, as if she was letting the family down by displaying a black eye in front of a guest, a feeling confirmed when she told Ida that Cora should come back to serve the tea. At Cora's name, he immediately thought that perhaps his first impulse was right after all, and there was to be some kind of staged denunciation, a form of melodramatic performance in which he and Cora would be told never to darken the door of the Manor House again.

'Now, George, I don't think you've actually met Lydia,' Remington said.

She extended her hand, and Allenby was conscious of its slightness as he shook it. They exchanged appropriate niceties and then she resumed her position by her husband's side but didn't replace her hand on his shoulder.

'And how is Lydia's lake coming along?' he asked, leaning back in his leather chair so that it squeaked with the strain.

'Moving ahead. More than half of the earth has been excavated, so there's a bit still to go. But we're getting there.'

'It's been a big task,' Mrs Remington said.

'It's going to be a very big lake.'

'No point doing things by half,' Remington responded. 'It's not a piddling pond this house needs.'

'It'll be a proper lake. I can assure you. And I've worked with Walter Clarke so the planting and landscaping will be ready to go once the water starts to flow.'

'We have a problem, George. A problem about water.'

Cora arrived with a tea tray. She set it carefully on a side table and poured, but when she reached the third cup Mrs Remington told her she wasn't having any by the slightest movement of her hand, as if she didn't need to use words to a servant to make her wishes known.

'I'm going to leave the problem with you gentlemen to solve. Mr Allenby, nice to meet you,' Mrs Remington said.

And then she was gone, her pearls a brief wash of milky light. Cora walked behind Remington with a cup and saucer but as she set it down it was Allenby's eyes she held. Remington was stirring sugar into his tea. Allenby had a sudden reckless urge to silently speak to her. To let the words form on his lips if not his tongue. To tell her he wanted her. To tell her he loved her. Even just to say her name. But the moment passed. She handed him a cup and saucer, offered him a biscuit off a Willow pattern plate, and then she too was gone. He wanted to turn his head to watch her leave but knew he couldn't and all that was left for him to hold was the receding echo of her shoes on the parquet flooring.

Remington slurped his tea then concentrated on dipping his biscuit almost as if he had forgotten what he had just said about the water.

'A problem, you say?'

'This was delivered by hand this morning,' Remington said, as he threw a letter dismissively across the desk. It was hand-written on expensive paper with the sender's address printed at the top. As Allenby read it quickly he saw that its author, Frederick Stewart, was giving notice that he intended to take legal action against Remington if he proceeded to carry out his proposed work on the river, 'through damming or diverting its flow for any purpose', as this would have 'serious consequences for my fishing stock and long established fishing rights'.

'Who is he?' Allenby asked.

'Has the estate on the other side of the river and a house falling down around his ears. These people are a bloody joke. Never worked to earn a penny in their whole lives, living on what was handed down to them and the rents they squeeze out of their tenants. And looking down their noses at the likes of me because I wasn't born with a silver spoon in my mouth. Fishing rights! It's not his bloody river.'

'It will delay things if we can't create the structures for filling the lake. It's on too big a scale to rely on a natural watershed. But it's not as if we're simply diverting the river away from him – if we were to feed it straight into the lake we'd get a build-up of silt that would need to be cleared in a few years.

So he's still going to have his river and his fish. Do you want me to go and see him, explain things?'

'No, I pay my solicitor an arm and a leg to deal with people like Stewart.'

'But what if we get caught up in a long, drawn-out legal dispute? We'll not be ready for your open day.'

'There's no open day date publicly announced yet. If needs be, we can push it back to the very end of the summer. In the meantime you can go on with what you're doing, can't you?'

'Yes, we're still digging out, and there's pipework to be laid to an overflow drainage area if we need to empty the lake. We also still need to build up the retaining banks and of course there's the boat house to construct. But you won't have a lake if there's no water to fill it.'

'There'll be water, George. Don't doubt it. Bloody Frederick Stewart doesn't have a pot to piss in so he's threatening the wrong man. I'll not be doffing my cap to the likes of him.'

For a second Remington looked as if he had exhausted his anger, but when Allenby stood up to leave he gestured him to sit down again, saying there were other things he wished to discuss. So for a second time he thought of Cora and wondered if his relationship with her might be about to arrive at a public judgement in a man to man exchange. Remington trailed the back of his hand across his mouth as if to clear it of the remnants of his anger.

'I've been thinking of going into politics, George, taking a seat in this new government. For far too long people like Stewart and his ilk have been running the show. The landed gentry – inbred, lazy-arsed and a bunch of snobs. Maybe it's time that people who live in the real world, build factories, give people jobs, should be the ones making decisions.'

'Have you been offered a seat?'

'Not yet, but if I keep on doing the rounds of the Masonic and the Orange Order, keep putting my hand in my pocket, it shouldn't be too long.'

'And you'd get the local vote?'

'They'll vote for anyone standing in front of a flag. Anyone who's not a Home Ruler. Don't you worry about that. So what do you think, George?'

'I don't know. Politics can be a messy business.'

'I like mess. Like getting my hands dirty. There's some might even say I enjoy getting in a fight from time to time. Keeps the blood flowing.'

Remington sat back again in his chair and the room fell silent. For a second time Allenby thought the conversation was over, but didn't want to stand up in case there was more to come. Remington stretched his hand across the desk and reclaimed the letter, scanning it rapidly again before setting it down and tapping it with his finger.

'If Stewart wants a fight then bring it on, but let him know I don't do Marquess of Queensberry rules. To the victor the spoils – that's my motto. And talking of boxing, George, there's one thing I want you to do. Eddie took a bit of a bruising last night. A set-to in McCartan's, some shenanigans I don't doubt he was probably to blame for, but that's not's the point. One of the men involved was called Crawford – I've been told he's one of your diggers. Get rid of him. Whether Eddie provoked it or not, I can't have my son struck in public, for that's the start of a slippery slope.'

Allenby nodded to show he understood. Crawford was a trouble-maker and he'd be better shot of him. This was the excuse he needed. Remington tapped his desk twice to signal that the conversation was over and, after setting his cup and saucer back on the tray, Allenby headed back to work. But in the hallway he lingered. Listening to the sounds of the house, he thought of going back out through the kitchen in the hope of seeing her again, stopped only by the possibility of encountering Mrs Remington or Mrs Sullivan and being unable to offer any plausible reason for his presence. And he was angry with himself for behaving like an infatuated schoolboy, angry too that he had somehow let himself feel the need for someone when in the years after the war he had convinced himself that this would never happen again, could never happen, thinking of emotional dependency only as a form of weakness, of dangerous vulnerability, when all that mattered was self-preservation and survival. Reaching the front door he turned round and took one last look into the house. He would finish the lake and when that moment came he would finish everything else.

18

The city is no stranger to fire. The cyclical riots and litany of burning outs; the houses in Farringdon Gardens ablaze; bombs falling during the Blitz that ignited firestorms; the incendiary devices and car bombs; the wavering flurry of the petrol bomb. This is a city that harbours the memory of fire in its scarred heart, that even celebrates through fire, but it is always fearful of what it brings. So when the first flames start in the Arcade the city's sleepers stir and lift their unseen faces towards it. In St George's Market the dead stored there after the Blitz because all the morgues were full, rise from their makeshift confinements and huddle together at the locked gates, regenerated by the threat of flame and what it brings. In the crypt beneath Clonard Monastery the sheltering women and children move closer together and look upwards at the sound, hoping to hide under an angel's wings. In the moments before the direct hit obliterates the air raid shelter on Hallidays Road, frightened people push up even closer and wait for the second that will send them into their final existence.

In the city's grandest stores – Robinson and Cleaver, and Anderson and McAuley – they gather on the staircase as if to have their photograph taken once more in sequenced rows, women in long Edwardian skirts and high collars on the lower steps, men in suits on the higher. In Arnott's, Thornton's and Sinclair's, in Brands and Normans, in tobacconist and haberdashery awakened shades press their faces to shopfronts long since gone and offer prayers for the living.

In the Tea Merchant's building, they turn their faces to the boarded windows that glow red round their edges then take the stairs to find a higher vantage point. Evelyn slowly turns the ring on her finger that Mr Russell has given her, wanting it to catch the new light filtering into their shadows. A gift for her loyalty and hard work was how he described it, but they both know that's not what it's really for. As the flames catch and spread in the Arcade she hears once more the clatter of her heels on the tiled floor. He thinks the ring is a down payment, but there would have to be many more, and even then the final purchase might never be completed. Billy moves a little too close to her, pretending he's only intent on viewing the fire. She feels his breath on her neck but it's not the way she feels her husband's breath when he comes off his shift and slips his body into her heat, stains her with the city's drunks and petty criminals. She could, if she wanted to, just lean back a little but she'll make him wait, wait as long as Russell who even now seeks to take charge of this impromptu gathering by declaring the source of the fire, though they all already know.

Billy looks at the back of Evelyn's neck, its paleness above her collar, the little down of hair that he wants to blow hither and thither. He smells her scent and wonders why even now when all else has gone this desire should remain and wonders too if desire is the one thing that never fades. So more than anything, more almost than any Saturday afternoon goal, he'd like to squirm his hand under her blouse and feel the soft ripple of her flesh. The sweet spot of the ball, catch it right and everything is released, the sweet spot his hand might know so that he too might be released, released forever, even as the flames rise and rise. And Eilish stands a little way off and clicks her Rosary beads – it is a burden to see things coming and not be able to tell anyone, and who amongst them would truly want to know what the young man's visit portends? Even in their vanished world, change is never good. And so much change is coming.

Agnes, who has never married and collects money for charity, wants to ask the flames why someone has never loved her and why no one ever gives anything to her. Wants to tell them that the reason she does her charity collections is because she still hopes that something, something so very precious, will be given to her in return. And somewhere in the city, an old man rises from his afterlife and thinks of a black curdled sea bursting into flames and tar babies being pulled aboard with fish hooks. In the mirror of Anton's barber shop a small boy with a wonky haircut and sweet-scented hair steps back from the glass and walks further back, so he's tiptoeing again across the shingle towards the sea that stretches to some unknown place that will hide him again from the world, keep him safe.

They didn't see the smoke from the car – from their distance it was just part of the flaring night. But as they were driving down again from their vantage point Alex took a call from Anton telling him about the fire in the Arcade. He swore aloud and asked Ellie to drive him there. By the time they arrived a cordon had been set up but even from a distance they could see the fire's intensity and feel its heat palming their faces as the smell of the funnelling smoke inveigled itself into their hair and the folds of their clothes. Alex wanted to go closer trying to assert his ownership but wasn't allowed, and what was the point? There was the sound of buckling and cracking, of things collapsing in on themselves and glass splintering and breaking.

A crowd had gathered, some of them coming out of nearby pubs still clutching pint glasses. On the other side of the street he saw Anton and Rosie, and taking Ellie's hand he pushed through the throng until he had reached them.

'It's gone,' Anton said. 'The shops, the equipment. Everything.'

'Shit!' Alex said softly, the syllable a slow stream of breath as he dropped the comfort of Ellie's hand.

'Can't they stop it?' Rosie asked, and he could tell she had been crying.

'It's too far gone,' Anton said. 'Look at it, it's too far gone. Gone to hell. All of it.'

They stood in stunned silence for a few moments, watching as flames broke free again from the roof in an angry defiance of the hoses that were turned on them, followed by what sounded like an explosion inside, making the fire crew draw back a little as if at any moment an engulfing firestorm might burst out of the warping and glowing shutters.

'How did it start?' Alex asked.

'We don't know,' Rosie said. 'We just don't know.'

She started to cry and Ellie put her hand on her shoulder.

'Fuck, Anton, I'm sorry,' Alex said, but Anton only looked at him in a way that made him feel uncomfortable before he turned his face back to the fire. Other occupants of the Arcade appeared and when they came towards them mostly they didn't say anything, but simply shook their heads in a quiet show of disbelief. Some tried to find comfort in hugging while others held themselves apart, trying to understand what was happening in front of them.

'What am I going to do?' Anton asked.

No one answered.

'I've a mortgage to pay, and bills. A child to provide for. What am I going to do?'

Other voices joined in, describing the desperation of their circumstances, of valuable items and equipment that had been lost. Some started talking about insurance and whether they had any or whether they were covered by the building's. Alex found Ellie's hand again and gently steered her away until they gradually managed to push through the crowd.

'There's no point staying here,' he told her. 'People are upset and some are going to get angry. We should go, wait until the morning to see what state it's in and what can be done for everyone.'

He knew it looked once more as if he was walking away from something, when the truth was he walking towards it. But he couldn't say any of this to her. Not until he knew for certain. So when they reached their house he went in but didn't take off his coat, telling her that he needed to go and let his father know about what had happened. When she asked why couldn't he just phone, he said there were things he had to discuss as a result of the fire. Things they had to talk about. He knew from her expression how unconvincing his voice sounded, but she didn't ask any more questions. She told him she was tired and that she would go to bed, that he should try not to be long. Then holding her coat to her face said she could smell smoke off it.

When he arrived at his parents' home his mother was already in bed while his father sat watching television with a drink in his hand.

'Did you forget something?' he asked.

'There's been a fire in the Arcade.'

'I heard it on the news a few minutes ago. Sounds bad,' his father said, but his attention was still on the programme he was watching.

'It's destroyed. I was there. I saw it.'

'As bad as that? Do they know how it started?'

'I was wondering if you knew.'

There was no going back, but he thought of the huddle of people standing watching their livelihoods go up in smoke. People he liked.

'Why would I know?' his father asked, pausing the television and turning to look at him directly for the first time.

'We both know you wanted those tenants out.'

'So you think because I'd prefer to have a vacant site as a resource to sell if development kicks in, that I torched the place. Alex, do me a favour.'

'Well, did you?'

'Alex, you've been watching too many box sets. Too much *Breaking Bad*, too much bloody *Sopranos*. It's scrambled your brains. This isn't fucking Dodge City. Get real. I can't believe you asked me that. In fact I'm going to try and forget you did, tell myself that you're under pressure with the wedding.'

His father was always stronger than him. He didn't know whether he was telling him the truth or not. And he always held the trump card that his son was biting the hand that fed him. But he wasn't ready yet to let it go and feel once more a failure in both his own and his father's eyes.

'So you'd nothing to do with it?'

'No, Alex, I'd nothing to do with it. Scout's honour. Is that good enough for you?' his father said, then threw the television remote along the settee.

Alex knew his father didn't do shows of hurt feelings. If he had any he kept them well hidden, so the gesture felt self-consciously theatrical. But he didn't know what to say, didn't know how to call his father a liar. Didn't know whether his father was a liar. He felt like he was flailing into ever-deeper water.

'Sit down, Alex. Tell me what's in your head. Get it off your chest.'

He knew if he sat down and re-entered the relationship that existed with his father, nothing would change. But he didn't know where any other path would lead him.

'You always saw those people as a nuisance, always wanted them out. So a fire did that for you. Whether you'd anything to do with it or not.'

'Of course it's better for me and the business and just in case you've managed to forget it, what's good for the business has always been good for you too. Very good, I'd say. But the idea that somehow I decided to burn these people out is crazy, just crazy. And believe it or believe it not I don't like seeing history erased. The Arcade was something that could have been made special again, brought back to a better life with the right investment.'

'What'll happen now?'

'The insurers and the Fire Service will investigate how it started. I'll probably be an old man before anyone actually pays out. And then the structure will have to be made safe. A bloody nightmare if you ask me.'

'But what about the people?'

'You mean the tenants? Listen, Alex, they were paying less than the going rate on rent. And if you really want my opinion I think you took your eyes off the ball as far as the Arcade is concerned. Sometimes I think it was more of some hippy commune than a commercial enterprise. And the city is full of rental space – they'll find new premises.'

'They'll need money for new starts.'

'That's what banks are for, Alex. We're not running a charity.'

'I never thought we were. But I liked the people there.'

'Well, that's a surefire recipe for disaster. You can like people all day long but it's not the basis for running a business. Like them in your personal life. Like them all you want, but don't let that cloud your judgement or you'll be done over. Done over big time!'

Alex sat down and stared at the silent television. It was obviously a documentary about a police investigation. A tooled-up phalanx of officers smashing in a front door. Evidence in bags, a forensic team in white suits. A blank-looking young man in a hoody slouched on a police station counter while presumably being read his charge. The bad guy getting caught. The terrible inevitability of being found out and publicly charged. The DNA of a life laid out as irrefutable proof. But he told himself he wasn't a bad person, that sometimes he tried to do good things, that all these should be taken into account before judgement was passed. He'd do his best to help Anton and all the others find new homes – he'd plenty of contacts in the city. He'd do his best and he'd try harder for Ellie than he'd ever tried at anything before.

His father was still talking but he wasn't listening any more. It was the same speech he'd heard since childhood, full of direct or implied criticism for his failure to fully emulate everything his father had achieved. Part of him wanted to walk away, to step out from under that shadow and the relentless flow of words. Step into his own silence, but he knew he wasn't yet brave enough to risk losing everything that made his life comfortable. Perhaps he never would be. And he couldn't expose Ellie to less than she was accustomed to, or start their marriage off with a surge of uncertainty.

'What's wrong, Alex? You don't seem yourself. What's going on?'

His father's question pulled him back to the present. He wanted to tell him about the photographs Ellie had looked at, to ask him about everything they truly represented, all the pretence. But never in his life had he talked to his father about what was in his head, frightened that it would just be considered another example of weakness, some pathetic distraction from what was really important. He couldn't start now.

The arrested man was led to his cell, where he was viewed from a high-up camera that showed him looking around himself and then lying down on a thin blue mattress, his head propped in the pillow of his hands. Alex told his father he was OK and that he needed to be going after he used the bathroom. His father simply nodded and reached for the television remote. As he climbed the stairs he could hear the police interview taking place and a repeated, monotone

'No comment'. The same stairs he had climbed as a boy so many times. He paused on the landing. There was light visible under his mother's bedroom door. He remembered the drawn blinds and the half-light, the bottles of pills on the bedside table, how soon she would be on the mend and right as rain. Yes, right as rain. He felt a sudden impulse to knock on her door and speak to her, and when she asked him if he was all right, he might be able to sit on the edge of the bed and tell her that he wasn't, that he hadn't been for some time.

He walked past his father's room towards her door, but stopped because he remembered the man in the club house. His mother different in his presence to the person he knew. Perhaps everyone had their secrets, secrets that belonged in the shadows. Perhaps you should let them nestle there. Yet even thinking about them brought them back into existence, each time dragged them closer to the light, and he had an inescapable feeling that as his wedding day grew closer the distance grew ever shorter. Taking a step closer to the door he raised his hand to knock but held it motionless. His coat smelt of smoke. He listened but even though the light said she was still awake there was only silence behind it. And what would she say to him except everything would be OK, that despite the half-light and the drawn blinds, despite the seclusion, despite the bottles of pills, everything would be all right? It was what you told your child. It was what you told yourself.

19

When Allenby told Gregson that Remington had ordered him to get rid of Crawford, his foreman bridled at the news, before sheepishly revealing that they were brothers-in-law.

'He's a good worker. Sometimes he lets his mouth run away with him, but the rest of the men look up to him,' Gregson said. 'If you fire him we could have trouble.'

'I think we'll find that the men's first loyalty is to their weekly pay. Why did you never tell me you were related to him?'

'It never came up. Is there no other way?'

'It's what Remington wants. I can't just ignore him.'

'Well, I can't be the one telling him.'

'Send him to the cottage – I'll do it. I don't have a choice, James.'

Gregson trudged away, his reluctance evident in each of his steps. Allenby studied the body of men labouring below him in the bed of the lake. The work had come on at a pace helped by the good weather. He looked for Crawford but at a distance the men were indistinguishable, all of them wearing similar clothes, their very movements replicating each other. Despite the length of time the excavation had taken he had got to know very few of them, had never made the effort nor thought it worthwhile. He didn't know their first names or anything about their families. It wasn't like in the trenches where, in time, everything would be revealed because a man's secrets had few hiding places. For a time at least, he had even been required to read the men's letters home, so before long he was intimate with the names of wives and children, the details of family births and deaths, with recurring jokes and bits of gossip. And if men baulked at expressing deep passions or words of love that would pass before another's eyes, sometimes it slipped out from between the lines. Hawley always wanted to know about the work of the farm, about the livestock, even about a particular field – how it had ploughed or what sort of crop it had yielded. Allenby's own letters home were few and the ones that came to him dry and sparse. His parents were Quakers and regretted that he had enlisted. The hours of silence in the meeting house where thoughts were meant to turn to God had never served their prescribed purpose and even in the plainest of settings his imagination had always wandered. But perhaps there would always be some pocket of silence at the core of his being. In the trench more life had flowed around and through him than he had ever experienced but he couldn't go back to that way of living, didn't want his own life entwined with those of other men. The cost was always too great.

He couldn't ever go to the cottage without hoping somehow that Cora would be waiting for him, but if anything he had seen her less and less. Mrs Sullivan's husband had recovered from his illness and her increased presence in the house reduced the opportunities for meeting. Some weeks he didn't stay in the cottage, didn't put the oil lamp in the window. And

Wickets and Rodgers were growing impatient – there were commissions in Belfast they wanted him to lead on. Alastair Wickets had been out twice to inspect progress and suggested a few corner-cutting measures, but as Allenby had pointed out, everything came down to the size of the lake Remington had insisted on. Wickets had made a joke of it, advising him to move the marker poles some dark night. But they valued their commercial relationship with Remington's expanding business empire, and he knew they wouldn't risk damaging that.

★

Crawford was broad-shouldered and when he stood in the doorway of the cottage he blocked the ingress of light. Allenby stood in front of the hearth and wordlessly signalled him in. Crawford took off his cap. His face had spots of mud on one side.

'I'm letting you go,' Allenby said.

'Why?'

'I've been told to by Mr Remington. Apparently you got into some sort of scrap with his son in McCartan's. As a result he doesn't want you working here.'

'You're sure it's not to do with the men asking for more money?'

'No, it's because of whatever happened between you and Eddie Remington.'

Crawford looked about him as if checking there was no one else present. Allenby wondered if he was going to beg for his job and hoped he wasn't.

'Did Mr Remington tell you what happened?'

'No, he didn't.'

'Eddie was in McCartan's with one of the girls who works in the house – tall, dark-haired. By all accounts he had been throwing back the drink for a right few hours and then whatever the girl says to him, he starts laying into her. Knocking her about. I told him to stop but he didn't listen and then he starts swinging at me. I didn't have much choice but to defend myself.'

'And you hit him?'

'I hit him. He was swinging and windmilling, knocking over glasses, swearing at everyone – he called me all the names of the day. So I put him on his back and then the girl was shouting at me as if I had started it and telling me I had killed him. Don't know why I bothered. And you're telling me now that's going to cost me my job?'

'I don't have a choice. I'm sorry,' Allenby said. 'The decision is not down to me. I've had no problem with you. The best I can do for you is pay you to the end of the week and hope you find something else.'

Crawford shuffled his feet. It looked like he was going to say something but instead drew the back of his hand across his mouth and put his cap on his head, but when he got to the door he paused and turned.

'They say you were in the war. So I imagine you're good at following someone else's orders. Maybe, though, there's something else you should think about.'

'And what's that?'

'I know about the baby. Know that you found it and buried it. Might be a few questions asked if I were to make that known.'

Allenby tried to keep his face impassive. Crawford moved to one side of the doorway, allowing a stream of light to enter.

'You'll know then that it was remains that have been buried for probably hundreds of years. I'd say we'll find more before this job is done. I simply reburied the bones – did it with due respect and so on. And you need to be careful you don't take on more than you can handle, more than is in your own interests, especially for a man looking for employment.'

Crawford hesitated as if he was going to say something but then he was gone. Part of Allenby wanted to call him to return and give him his job back, buy his silence. Later he would think of his failure as the moment when the planned schedule began to fall behind, as if life held itself in a kind of balance and a wrong decision or a poor judgement could upset that same balance. An hour later Gregson arrived to tell him that the men had downed tools and wanted Crawford reinstated. Allenby resisted the desire to rebuke Gregson for his indiscretion, unsure of how the argument might unravel. Work stopped for three days before they sullenly returned, but Allenby knew they came back with less willingness and a greater readiness to give the impression of going through the motions without ever fully offering their previous level of commitment. An unprecedented late fall of snow stopped work again and as it filled the bed of the lake it looked to Allenby that nature was trying to reclaim what he had taken from it. He didn't stay at the cottage but retreated to Belfast and each morning went into the offices of Wickets and Rodgers where he was greeted by his colleagues as if he had made a temporary return from exile in some far-off land.

He realised that he missed the office, the focus on work that, unlike the lake, could be accomplished separately from so many issues beyond his control. He didn't want the responsibility of being in charge of so many men, didn't want in Cora's words to be at Remington's 'beck and call'. But he thought too of his absence from the Manor House as his chance to wean himself off her, to try to regain some control over his feelings and clear some more prudent path to his future. A future that was safely solitary. But there were other times when he lay in his bed at night on the edge of the city wanting her beside him, wanting to have her there in the comfort of a proper bed. Once, as the early morning light began to break, he heard Hawley's voice singing outside his window, singing about packing up your old kit bag, about the Mountains of Mourne sweeping down to the sea, and then it was her voice telling him that everything was all right, her arms holding him, her breath on his face shushing him, stifling the cry in his throat.

In the week before Easter she came to him early one morning with a letter. He was standing at the side of the lake watching the men arrive and wishing he was back again in the Belfast office. She performed the half-curtsy that she reserved for encountering him in public. He assumed the letter was from Remington but when he opened it he saw that it was from her. All the Remingtons were going to Scotland over Easter and she had been given the Saturday and Sunday off. She was asking if they could go somewhere on a day out, a trip to the seaside perhaps, 'if he liked'. He studied the neat script that he found hard to associate with her and felt ashamed because the request sent him spinning into possible excuses. To go together on such a trip would immediately suggest that their relationship had found an existence beyond the private world of the cottage and that frightened him. But to go forwards seemed to represent as much danger as to try belatedly to withdraw. And he told himself that he owed her, owed her a day out even though he also began to think that this might be the time to try and find a neat ending to something that felt increasingly reckless.

During the midday break, one of the men produced a football and soon some of the marker poles were set up for goalposts and a kickabout started. Allenby didn't approve, fearful of another broken leg, but said nothing. There was more enthusiasm than skill with lots of flailing limbs, the ball punted high in the air at every opportunity and goals cele- brated in an exaggerated manner. His attention on the game was interrupted when he saw Cora coming from the walled garden with an armful of daffodils Walter Clarke had obvi- ously cut for the house. He called out and when he reached her they retreated amidst the trees bordering the gravel path. Under a canopy of dense branches and brindled light that fil- tered and flickered across her face he told her she was to take the mid-morning train to Belfast on Easter Saturday and they would meet in the Queen's Quay station. They could take a train to a seaside resort. He saw the excitement in her face. For a terrible second he thought she was going to hug him or offer him one of the flowers but she restrained herself and simply nodded to show she understood. Then she was gone before he had time to decide whether he was being a fool or had done the right thing.

When he saw her hurrying through the platform gates, paus- ing only to let her ticket be inspected, he realised he had only ever seen her naked or in her maid's uniform. Dressed in her own clothes she looked different, almost as if she had suddenly become someone else, and he wasn't sure if he fully knew the person now approaching him. She wore a light-coloured skirt that reached her ankles and showed the narrowness of her waist, a cream blouse with fussy sleeves that puffed at the shoulder, cherry Oxford shoes and a hat that looked a bit like a straw boater. She had clearly made an effort but there was something about her clothes that struck him as a little shabby. It was the first time also he had seen her markedly self-conscious and as she approached and put a quick hand to her hat he suddenly didn't know how to greet her. The station was crowded with arrivals and groups waiting to board their trains. And before she made the decision for him he extended his hand to shake hers. She looked at it for a second, then not looking him in the eyes took it briefly in her own.

They had half an hour to wait before a train would take them out of Belfast and eventually to the seaside, so he found them a space on a little bench. They didn't know what to say to each other and despite everything that happened in the cottage they were awkward and tongue-tied and already he was thinking that he had made an enormous mistake, that nothing existed or could ever exist between them apart from what flesh determined. There was an extended moment of silence and then he felt her hand discreetly take his and hold it under a fold of her skirt. His first impulse was to withdraw it but she tightened her grip and he yielded. She leaned lightly against him so they were sitting shoulder to shoulder, stiffly upright as if waiting to have a formal photograph taken, while in front of them families and groups of friends intoxicated by unfamiliar freedom and temporary release from the grind of mill and factory conversed animatedly with each other. He told himself that no one would notice them in the excited throng but he longed to be back in the cottage, the fire the only source of light, their voices whispers against each other's skin. He saw that the leather on her shoes was cracked and the heels worn down.

'So, Mr Allenby, what's your plan for this fine day?' she asked.

'I don't really know. Enjoy the train journey. Have a walk along the front. Find somewhere we can get something to eat maybe. Have a drink. Look at the sea. Does that meet with your approval?'

'Anything that gets me out of that house meets with my approval.'

As the time for their train's departure approached they joined the queue that already stretched back from the gates in a regimented line. It was obvious the train was going to be crowded and when the gates were opened the order of the queue was replaced by a rushed scramble towards the carriages. Some of those who had boarded hung out the windows trying to suggest that their carriage was already full. Allenby steered her further along the platform, his hand on her elbow, cursing himself for not buying first class tickets even though he knew he hadn't done so because there was less risk of encountering someone who knew him. She held on to her hat as she hurried and she was laughing. They found a compartment occupied only by one other couple and sat opposite each other at the far window, but before long three young men piled in and their breathless uncorked exuberance frothed over everyone whether welcomed or not. It was too late to find somewhere else so Allenby simply sat back and stared out of the window.

The three young men – they looked to Allenby as if they were in their early twenties – joked with each other and were excited like children on the first day of their holidays. It reminded him of how young recruits had acted after completing their hopelessly inadequate training and embarking for France. A trip out. Home by Christmas as heroes. It made him despise these three, their fatuous self-absorption rendering them oblivious to what others their own age had endured, and yet he knew that such feelings were stupid, that they had every right to their day's pleasure.

The train moved off and Cora swung her foot against his and smiled, but as they passed the densely packed rows of terraced houses he could hardly bring himself to look at her. The whole idea of a trip out had been a mistake from which there was no easy way out. But perhaps it was the right place, somewhere far away from the Manor House where he would be able to tell her that what existed between them was over and that they should both go back to the lives they had before, for better or worse. He started to compose words in his head, but none of them sounded right and above all he wanted to avoid a scene or angry recriminations.

The three young men took out tobacco and rolled cigarettes, one of them offering a tin and papers to his fellow travellers. The other couple declined but Cora accepted and rolled herself a cigarette with a proficiency that was clearly the product of experience although he had never seen her smoke. They worked in Gallagher's cigarette factory on York Street – 'there has to be some perks,' one of them said. They asked Cora where she worked and for a moment he panicked that she would tell them the truth, but then she retorted that it was none of their business, with just enough humour in her tone that the men laughed. He saw how easy she was in their company and wondered if she would have preferred it if the day ahead were destined to be spent with them rather than him. But almost immediately the thought made him feel jealous. Perhaps in him she too had come to the wrong place, the one with the blue-coloured light. Perhaps as a result he had brought her only potential misery. He tried to tell himself that pleasure was inevitably succeeded by pain. When he looked at her she made her eyes wide and blew smoke at him, and he wanted to put his mouth against hers and have her essence flow through him. Make him alive once more, to the core of his being.

The young men played card games using a cap as a makeshift table, and the journey slipped into a steady unravelling of countryside and drumlins accompanied by the waxy fistle from the flick of the cards. After a while Cora rested her head against the glass and began to doze, her mouth an open pout, her hat held in both hands like a plate on her lap. The light coming through the compartment window enhanced the paleness of her skin and streamed deeply through her hair, flaring its redness so intensely that he thought if he were to touch it he might burn his hand. He wanted her to open her eyes so he could see again how green they were. The young couple opposite him who wore wedding rings were slumped against each other, also in a doze despite the world dashing by outside, cattle bolting, startled by the noise and smoke of the passing train. Eventually there was a glimpse of the sea between buildings, and then the curve of a bay in full view. Eventually the young men grew quiet. He realised then that they would normally have completed half a day's work by now, and that all of their bodies carried the weary imprint of their labour even on their day off.

Tiredness was something he understood. The men he knew could find sleep in almost any position, curl themselves into any nook or cranny, almost immediately becoming oblivious, for however short a period, to what was going on around them. The compartment was heavy with smoke and he wanted to open the window but couldn't without disturbing Cora, so he sat back and waited. Then as they got closer to their destination the Mournes reared into view and the young men grew animated again and one of them opened the window and stuck his head out. Suddenly everyone was awake as the noise of the train rushed in. Cora leaned forwards to try to get a view of the mountains, and to keep her balance she placed her hand on his knee. Allenby, meanwhile, thought only of the Hawleys who farmed somewhere under those same mountains and he felt like a revenant, returning with some sacred memory of their beloved son, some hopelessly inadequate offering to the gods of place. And he couldn't bring the final moments to them but only their child's voice in the morning or late at night under the unblemished stars. Then what suddenly intruded into those memories of Hawley was a night when, watched only by a hesitant moon, he buried the remains of a baby. Whose child was it? He had been the one who disturbed its sleep and somehow that connected him to it however unwillingly, part of its story now, without ever knowing how that might end.

He looked at Cora and felt ashamed for the thoughts he had harboured, when the truth was that if she knew what his hands had done she would leave him in an instant, because what happened in the cottage had made her an unknowing part of all the terrible things he had seen and the terrible things that had found their origins in him. So what did it matter about the cracked leather of her shoes, the tiredness of her clothes? What did it matter about her accent or anything else when she had given him so much and in return had taken so little? A day out was to be the only reward she asked for. He could not spoil it for her or be mean of spirit. Let the train speed them towards the sea, let the train speed them to the mountains and the day unfold itself, whatever ending it brought. He smiled at her and without sharing any words with the rest of the carriage asked her if she was happy.

'Yes,' she said. 'Happy enough to sing.'

And then with a voice full of feeling she sang the final verse of 'The Mountains o' Mourne', her voice lilting and holding all their attention.

There's beautiful girls here, oh, never you mind,
With beautiful shapes nature never designed,
And lovely complexions all roses and cream,
But let me remark with regard to the same
That if of those roses you ventured to sip,
The colours might all come away on your lip,
So I'll wait for the wild rose that's waiting for me
In the place where the dark Mournes sweep down
to the sea.

Everyone clapped, and she blushed a little. Then in deliberately slapstick style, she two-handedly plonked her hat on her head with an exaggerated force that made the others laugh. It felt as if in that moment he had tumbled headlong into some world he had never even known existed, and he tried to tell himself that it was somewhere he might be able to dwell, separated from what had gone before, and as he looked at Cora he felt a pride in her, momentarily yielded to sentimental thoughts that were reflected in the blue sweep of a cloudless sky in a world that perhaps existed beyond the one he knew. But he was not someone much given to indulging in sentimentality and once more his eyes wandered over the worn tiredness of her clothes and everything that was at odds with what he thought of as her inner self.

People poured off the train and out of the station. This time it was Cora who was hurrying him on, impatient when he paused to look back at the red-brick building with its clock tower and a spire that always reminded him of a church. Everyone seemed in a hurry, whether to shake off the lethargy of the journey or to cram as much into their day as possible. They crossed the road and entered the main street that was full-stopped by the mountains above the town. Shops and street stalls alike were doing the best trade of their year. Cora took everything in, wanting to look at it all as if frightened of missing something, and when she pointed things out in shop windows he tried to share her enthusiasm even though much of it had already begun to feel tawdry and frantic.

Sometimes the pavements were so crowded that they came to a momentary halt. Young women let loose from mills and factories walked in lines with linked arms, while separate groups of young men tried to engage them in conversation or doffed their caps in an elaborate show of greeting. From the open doors of a bar that had a knot of customers packed into its entrance came the sound of music. Two horse-drawn open carriages passed them, full of elegant women holding parasols aloft with the demeanour of those temporarily elevated to royalty.

They passed the first row of shops and came to the sea and its stone-littered beach. Families were camped out on the sand or sheltering against the wall of the promenade on tartan blankets with baskets of provisions. The sea was far out. Cora hesitated at first and then without saying anything hurried onto the sand.

'Do you want to know a secret?' she asked him when he caught up with her.

'Tell me.'

'I've never been to the seaside before. I suppose you think that makes me stupid or something.'

He told her it didn't and then she said it was a bit of a disappointment, not really up to very much, not what she had imagined.

'It looks lifeless,' she said. 'Flat as a pancake.'

'It's a creature of moods. You're seeing it in good weather. It's not always like this.'

But then she was striding towards the water, telling him that she had come all this way and she wasn't going home without putting her feet in it. He tried to dissuade her by telling her that it would be freezing, that they should go somewhere to get something to eat, but she was determined and there was nothing to do but follow her across the stone-laden foreshore. They passed a young boy in swimming shorts who was tiptoeing over the pebbles as if they were made of glass, while his parents sat silently apart watching his progress. Then without ceremony Cora hitched her skirt up, balanced on his shoulder to take off her stockings and stuffed them inside her shoes.

'What are you waiting for?' she asked.

'I'll mind your shoes.'

'No, you have to do it too.' And then when she saw his reluctance, 'Please, George.'

It was one of the few occasions on which she had used his first name – he had no choice but to take his shoes and socks off and join her at the water's edge.

'Are there crabs?' she asked before she let the water touch her toes.

'I think you'll be safe.'

Gathering up her skirt in both hands she cautiously stepped into the water before grimacing at its coldness.

'It's freezing cold,' she said, turning to see if he was following her. 'And it just goes on forever. Like a giant lake without any sides.'

He watched the water trill around his toes and the sand pressing between them. She reached out and took his hand. He would build his house by the sea. A house with large windows so that the sky and the sea could flow in and every day would be filled with light that somehow in time would also flow into him and make him wholly himself again. She was squealing and gripping his hand tightly and suddenly he swept her off her feet, held her tightly in his arms and stepped further into the water. She was screaming and laughing and he pretended to stumble before carrying her back to the sand. She slapped him playfully on the arm when he set her down.

They made their way back to the main street and joined the crowds. He asked her if she was hungry, and when she said she was he told her that they would go and have something in the hotel behind the station. They walked back the way they had come, but when she saw the stateliness and scale of the building she asked him if he was sure. He wanted to do it for her, to take her somewhere grand even though part of him knew that it would be for his pleasure as much as hers. She smoothed her skirt and straightened her hat as they approached the door that was opened for them and as they entered he felt her move closer to him. But almost immediately they were told that the restaurant was full and unless he imagined it he thought the head waiter had looked a little too closely at Cora. They were welcome to take a seat in the drawing room and wait until a table became free and even though he felt her hand tug at the hem of his coat he accepted the offer. So they sat on a velvet sofa in a crowded room decorated with large vases of flowers and oil paintings on the wood-panelled walls. Everyone had looked at them when they entered and Cora removed her hat and held it almost like a kind of shield.

'Have you ever been here before?' she asked, her voice a thin whisper.

'A couple of times at functions. Do you know who else has stayed here?'

'No, but it must have been someone with plenty of money.'

'Charlie Chaplin.'

'You're pulling my leg.'

'No, he really did. And not so long ago.'

An elderly gentleman rustled his newspaper. A maid wearing a uniform identical to the one Cora wore in the Manor House served tea and shortbread to a dog-collared minister and his wife. Pipe smoke skirmished with the mote-filled light from the large windows.

'I don't like it here,' she said. 'Let's go somewhere else.'

'There'll be a table soon.'

'I don't want a table. I want to go.'

'We'll never find anywhere else with the crowds out there. And you're hungry.'

She didn't answer but instead stood up and walked away, leaving him with no other option but to follow her.

'I'm sorry,' he said when he caught up with her. 'We'll find somewhere else.'

'Did you want to show me up?' she asked. He started to mumble a denial, but before he could finish, she went on: 'The only way I belong in there is with an apron on or serving guests. What were you thinking?'

They walked on in silence. Halfway along the front there was a boarding house with a table outside, where two women sold them corned beef sandwiches, two Paris buns and two bottles of lemonade. They sat on one of the wooden benches facing the sea and all her anger drained away as quickly as it had come.

'A feast fit for a king,' she said, holding on to her hat with one hand as a sudden breeze blew off the sea.

'A feast fit for a king,' he repeated.

'All we need now is an ice cream.'

Two men on stilts walked by, a third following behind passing out handbills for a funfair. She asked if they could go.

'Why not? You can go anywhere you want today.'

'The top of Donard?'

'It takes a couple of hours and you haven't got the shoes for it. It's steep at the top, steep and cold.'

'We'll just do the funfair then.'

But for Allenby it was a bottomless pit of noise with shrill screams rending the air from people on the rides, demented music from a street organ and throbbing machinery. The air itself smelt rancid and mechanical, infused with oil and petrol. It felt like an unfolding hysteria slipping outside his control. He hesitated at the grass-trodden entrance as a dizziness started inside his head. He tried to blink it away, to focus on her tumble of red hair as she walked ahead, even the worn heels of her shoes. They had been billeted in the park, done their training there, and suddenly the faces of the crowd were pushed aside by other faces, men he had stood beside and shared that time with, but they were also the faces of men who hadn't come back. Men who would never stand again between the mountain and the sea. Men whose letters he had once read, whose thoughts he had become a part of, whose loves and fears he had come to understand. And it wasn't just Hawley because there were so many others. Men he saw now as clearly as he saw the sky above. All of them coming towards him with their letters held in their hands, the words streaming across their faces. Once, he had climbed Donard when its summit was snow-capped, but the whiteness now was a snowfall of lime dusting the dead.

She was staring at him and he tried to smile at her, but she knew that something was wrong. Taking his hand, she led him away from the entrance.

'I'm sorry,' he said.

'It's all right. Did you see someone you didn't want to?'

He shook his head. How could he tell her that he had seen the dead?

'We trained here. Before the war. Memories I suppose. That's all. Just memories.'

'We'll go somewhere else,' she said as she pressed the warmth of her hand into his.

But he didn't want to walk back into the town with its crowds, and he had already had the thought that he might at any moment without knowing it walk past Hawley's family, his mother and father who had held the letter he had written to them and believed what it said, took whatever comfort was possible from its lies. So he led her up the path that bordered the river, through a forest of pine, birch and oak trees, and when they got to the bridge they stood leaning on the stone parapet and watching the white-crested water course through the rocky channels.

'We'll not go any further,' he said, glad to be alone with her undisturbed except for the occasional groups of hikers ascending to the summit or wearily making their way back down. She told him her shoes were hurting her and she wanted to rest but when without saying anything she led him off the path and through a maze of trees, he understood immediately and was excited by the knowledge of what she had in mind. They went deeper to where there were only small pockets of sky visible and the noise from the funfair was ever fainter, smothered by the thick canopy of trees and overhanging branches. In a small clearing they sat on a bed of moss and pine needles, the air spiced with the scent of the trees. She kissed him, then took off her hat and pulled the pins from her hair. He asked her if she was sure and she said she had always been sure with him, and in that moment he told her about the house he was going to build, about the windows where the sea and the sky would flood in. He had never ever told another living soul and didn't know whether she understood what he was describing even though it appeared that she was listening intently. It was on his lips to tell her that he wanted her to live in the house he would build but in the seconds of his silent hesitation she kissed him again and the moment was gone. She slipped off her undergarments and, unbuttoning him, straddled him, easing him in slowly with the movement of her hips. A small vista of sky was visible above her through the branches that stirred in the rising wind. She moved rhythmically on him, from time to time leaning forwards to kiss him, and then taking his hands from her thighs, she held them level with her face and kissed them both. He slipped one out from her grip and lightly traced his fingers along the side of her face, around the lobe of her ear and then into her hair that fell loosely across her shoulders.

'This is what you must remember,' she said. 'Always.'

He nodded and his whole being was reduced to the meeting of their bodies and when she asked him again to say her name, he did it in rhythm with his own movements, again and again. When he came she smiled down at him, putting her face close to his.

'Am I your wild rose?'

'You're my wild rose.'

She made a joke about thorns and then taking a handful of pine needles let them fall a few at a time on his chest and across his brow, ran her finger across his bottom lip. A strengthening wind ebbed through the trees, fretting the branches and the window of sky and suddenly the whole world seemed so intensely alive to him that he was frightened by its reality. She held his head against her chest and he felt the beat of her heart, the speed of her breathing.

'Better than paddling?' she asked.

'Yes, better.'

'And warmer.'

'Much warmer.'

She lifted herself slowly off him and lay down in his arms.

'You realise we've never done this in a proper bed.'

For a foolish second he thought of going back to the hotel or one of the boarding houses and paying for a room but he knew it was a fantasy. Not just because everywhere would be booked but because they had no rings or luggage and he would not expose her to the judgement that would inevitably ensue. Despite the rising wind, it was warm and sheltered enough for both of them to fall into a doze, above them the small glimpse of sky veined by the shadowed striation of branches.

'Bloody babes in the wood,' she said when they both stirred then looked around her as if to confirm to herself where she had woken. 'Could you not build your house in a forest, a forest so deep that no one would ever know it was there?'

'I want it facing the sea.'

'But the sea is cold and grey.'

'It's not grey, it's blue and green and lots of other colours. And you can't have a forest without a wolf.'

'I've met enough wolves to do me, thank you very much. And I'd have thought you'd have had enough water after spending all this time digging a lake.'

'Except there's not a drop of water in it yet. Not a single bloody drop. Sometimes I think it'll never be a lake.'

She stood up and fixed her clothes, brushing down her skirt with fierce skites of her hand, then mustered her hair into a semblance of order. As he stood up, a cascade of fine pine needles fell away from him.

'I like it here,' she said, gesturing with her hand, 'the trees, the river, even the bugger of a mountain. Maybe I should have been a country girl.' And then she grabbed his arm and told him, 'I'm never going back to the mill. So help me God, I'm never going back.'

He didn't know what to say, but seeing the sudden serious-ness of her face nodded to show he understood and there was part of him also that didn't want to go back to any previous existence, wanted only to stay in the moment. He knew they had to return to the town, which was filled with people like them who had escaped for the day but who before long would also be funnelled back to the life that was theirs. If he could think of the means of escape from the things that were in his head then perhaps he might live differently, even accept the possibility that happiness could exist, that despite everything he had conditioned himself to believe, his life might be shared with someone else. Instead he told her that they should go if she was to catch the last train back to the village and the Manor House.

On the main street they saw young men who had taken too much drink and who were held up by their friends, or who slumped in the spaces between buildings. He didn't want to share a compartment with any of them and when they eventu-ally reached the station he bought first class tickets and shared the journey back to Belfast with the minister and his wife they had seen in the hotel, a woman with two children who all fell asleep with her arm draped round them – there was something about her that made him think she was a war widow – and an older man who read a book about David Livingstone and acknowledged no one else's presence. He saw Cora studying the children and wondered again why she could never have any. It was one of the many personal matters that were lodged deep in both their pasts which they knew instinctively they could not talk about, as if to do so would risk opening fault lines between them.

As they reached the city it was cradled by dusk, and the slumbering backs of the terraced rows seemed oblivious to the noise and smoke of the train in any perceptible way, except once when pigeons flurried out of their coop and fanned across the grey tiers of slate roofs. When they got to the station there wasn't much time before Cora's train, and he was almost glad because neither of them knew what to say, so they stood nearly as awkwardly as they had that same morning. Her train was called but they didn't kiss, and instead briefly brushed hands before letting them slowly ease apart, and then she was walking away. At the gate she turned briefly, raised her hand and smiled back at him. It was one of the images by which he would always remember her. He waited until she was finally out of sight before he left the station.

In the morning there were pine needles on his pillow and in the folds of his clothes.

20

It was a full two weeks before Alex was allowed to view the damage in the Arcade, and even then permission was granted reluctantly and only in the company of someone from the Fire Service. He was given a yellow safety helmet to wear and when the shutter was prised up he swore involuntarily at what he saw – everything collapsed in on itself in a blackened chaos as if the building had gorged on its own innards then violently expelled them, the tiled floor buried under a layer of acrid debris, shopfronts vanished, and in the few places where the glass had not shattered, it was darkened into blindness. The steel beams of the roof still clung on in an open fretwork through which the sky was visible. Everything original and decorative had been consumed, the remains twisted and distorted into obscene shapes, the upper floors a series of gaping black holes.

Alex paused outside the remains of Anton's barber shop. Inside, two skeletal metal chairs still sat starkly in position in front of where the mirrors had once been, their remains now stripped of leather. Everything else was a flare of charred waste. There was nothing that could be salvaged. Nothing that could be saved. He thought of his father's love of a blank slate and turned to the man accompanying him.

'Do we know how it started?'

'Not yet – there's still a lot of clearance to do. Once we establish where it might have begun, then we'll be closer to answering that question.'

'Do you think it could have been started deliberately?'

'Too early to say. But as likely as not we'll find it was faulty wiring. What I do know is that it was a hell of a fire. Sad to see something so full of history destroyed like this.'

'Do you think it could be restored?'

'That's a question for the architects and the planners. But you see what I see – it wouldn't be easy.'

Alex walked on as his companion took a phone call, pausing just long enough to warn him to be careful. He went slowly, picking his steps until he reached a section that was strewn too thickly with fallen debris and he turned back the way he had come. The acrid smell seemed to intensify with each minute he stayed and he felt a sickness loosening in his stomach. He wanted to be gone, be free from the destruction that clamoured all around for his attention.

Afterwards he tried to phone Anton but he didn't pick up. Nor did Rosie. And he was glad because he didn't know what he would have said to them. The insurers wouldn't be allowed inside until the building was rendered fully safe, but he imagined the renters would only be covered for their own contents if they themselves had taken out policies. He told himself the place was run-down and that there were probably faulty electrics in some of the shops, probably a whole catalogue of possible defects that might have been responsible for the fire. But when he left the building he carried the smell of smoke with him on his clothes and on his skin, so after a while he went home, showered and changed. The house was strangely silent as if intent on preserving its privacy so that he felt like an intruder in his own home. Every noise he made, every step he took seemed to leave an imprint, an unwelcome disturbance, and he realised that in time others would come to live inside its walls and its spaces would be layered with the presence of different lives. Perhaps they would find things – a little faded smear of the original colour of paint on a wall, the slight indentation where a picture hook had been, or the smooth patina of wood where their hands had brushed it every day – things that might make them wonder for a few seconds about the lives that had preceded their arrival. He tried to look forward but found himself trapped between the unwelcome memories of the past and anxiety about the future. And there were secrets that he didn't believe could be hidden. He thought back to the Tea Merchant's, where he had been able to see exactly where pictures had been taken from the walls and floor coverings removed. There was always some trace, some DNA that could be forensically recovered and finally identified.

*

He stumbled through his stag night, forcing himself to pretend he was enjoying it. After early evening food and drinks they went to an escape room. They were on the *Titanic* after it had hit the iceberg and they had an hour to complete all the tasks – radioing for help, sealing watertight doors, organising lifejackets, getting to the lifeboats. Find the clues, find the codes. Find the code to save yourself. Matty, who had in effect appointed himself best man before being asked, thought the choice of game was funny and Alex had to go along with the jokes. Since announcing his engagement to Ellie, he'd found that he was finally able to understand how much he disliked Matty. Disliked the way he sometimes tried to act as a surrogate older brother, someone who was always telling him what he would like, what he should do to have a good time. Disliked the way he wore a fake Rolex and drove cars that were too flash despite the fact that they were all growing older. And it had been Matty who had first encountered the girl in the tent so it was easy to let his dislike fester because it gave him someone to blame.

Afterwards in a city centre hotel that was once a linen warehouse they had more drinks in the company of a Dutch women's hockey team who were on tour. A squad of young women, mostly with blonde hair and muscular bodies burnished by the sun. He was glad they were there, because his friends soon tired of cajoling him into having a good time and focused on the young women, who were also intent on enjoying themselves. At one point, Matty came and sat beside him. He rested a hand on his shoulder and nodded towards the women, whispering, 'Low-hanging fruit, Alex. Low-hanging fruit.'

'That's what she was, wasn't she?' he said.

'Who, Alex?'

'The girl at the festival. The one we never talk about.'

'So why are you talking about her now?'

'Do you think about her?'

'No, I don't think about her and neither should you. Why the hell are you talking about her now? We were trying to look out for her, that's what I remember.'

'I don't think that's what we were doing.'

'Call it what you want but don't beat yourself up about something that's not worth remembering. You should be enjoying yourself, not moping round talking shit. And Alex, we were all high as kites and if I remember right she was the highest of us all.'

And then he was gone. Gone in pursuit of low-hanging fruit.

A few minutes later Alex found himself in conversation with Aleta. She told him that she didn't believe in marriage when she heard it was his stag night, that she worked in advertising and that Dutch people were the tallest in Europe. She talked and he listened, nodding his head in order to pretend that she had his attention. A scab on her right knee was the only visible imperfection on her skin, an imperfection that she would touch lightly from time to time as if she couldn't quite believe that it existed. And Amsterdam was cursed by stag dos and the city was planning to do something to discourage them because they didn't want the city polluted by drunks in stupid costumes who behaved badly. As he glanced around the bar she appeared oblivious to the fact that her team mates seemed increasingly gearing up to finding their own bad behaviour, lurid cocktails and colourful shots proliferating on tables. According to her, Belfast was an interesting city – they'd been to the *Titanic* museum the previous morning – but she'd like to see more of the coastline, see the Giant's Causeway, then was disappointed when he told her it was only a pile of boring stones not worth the effort of going there.

He thought her pretty in a fierce sort of way, wasn't sure he would have liked to face her as an opponent when she was armed with a hockey stick. Then she told him she would like to hear traditional music and asked if he wanted to go on somewhere. He wanted to tell her that he didn't, that even though there was an iceberg lurking in the darkness he didn't even want to get into a lifeboat, that he didn't know the code to anything and that the clock's hands were moving forwards and then back again. She looked at him with her sharp blue eyes and then swallowed what was left of her drink in a way that said it was decision time. So he lied and said he couldn't leave his stag night, and when she said that it looked as if his friends had already left him, there was nothing he could do but shrug his shoulders, feign disappointment and wish her well for the rest of the tour. When she left him to seek out new company, he took the opportunity to slip away, stopping outside briefly to look at the former linen warehouse. For a strange second he thought he heard the sound of women singing, their voices blending and rising against the encroaching night and then he saw the faces looking down at him, fixed forever in stone. He struggled to remember their identities but didn't get further than Shakespeare and Michelangelo. The faces of famous men – no women – destined to stare down for eternity at the city's inhabitants.

His phone pinged. It was Ellie asking him if he was having a good time, and when he told her not really and that he was going home, she asked him if he wanted to meet her. Her hen do had petered out early and hadn't been much of a success either. Her sister had arrived drunk and eventually they'd had to summon her partner to take her home. They weren't far away from each other and if they walked towards each other they would meet halfway. In less than five minutes he saw her coming towards him still wearing a bride-to-be sash and tiara. He was as glad to see her as he ever had been, and had to force himself not to rush towards her with outstretched arms like some romantic cliché. But they hugged long and tight then sat on one of the seats in front of the City Hall. He knew she wasn't drunk, but nor was she entirely sober.

'What's it all about?' he asked her.

'I don't know. It's like a list of things you have to tick off, one after the other, until eventually you're married. I think I've let myself get stressed out about everything just like you have.'

'Sometimes I think we should cut it all out, just go somewhere and get married.'

'Like Las Vegas? The way the builder's son did?'

'No, somewhere nice. Italy! Or somewhere even further away with a beach. Somewhere just for ourselves.'

'What about our parents?'

'I don't think mine would mind much. They'd probably be secretly grateful.'

'I couldn't do it to my father. I owe him this day.'

'I know. We're nearly there. And it'll be good.'

'So you're going to give it your best shot?'

'Cross my heart and hope to die. My very best shot,' he said as he straightened her plastic tiara.

An older man and woman stopped and congratulated them on what they thought was their wedding day, and momentarily brushed them with their sweet smell of alcohol. They didn't tell them they hadn't yet got married. The man went to walk away but turned to share his well-rehearsed joke.

'When we were newlyweds, our marriage was like a deck of cards. All we needed were two hearts and a diamond. Now all she wants is a club and a spade.'

'Don't you pay any attention to him,' his wife said, pulling at his arm. 'Enjoy your day.'

They waited until the couple were gone before they really started laughing.

'Do you want to go home?' he asked her, hoping she would say yes.

'Seems a bit of a waste to go home on a night when we're supposed to be out on the town.'

'Where do you want to go?'

She thought for a while and fixed her slipping tiara back in place.

'The zoo. I want to go to the zoo.'

'It doesn't open at night.'

'That's all right, because I want to free all the animals. Let them all out of their cages.'

'Tigers and lions as well?'

'All of them. Every last one.'

'And why do you want to do this?' he asked, smiling at her and speaking in a faux-serious voice.

'Because it's not where they belong. It's not where they should be, and because it's what my mother once said she wanted to do.'

There was a moment's silence. Alex had rarely heard Ellie speak of her mother and he didn't know what he should say, so instead he held her hand. She wanted to talk to him about her mother but she didn't know what it was she wanted to say, except that her absence at her wedding assumed an ever-greater sense of loss. They sat in silence for a while until slowly they were absorbed by the city and somewhere close by the women's voices that once stirred the linen warehouses seeped out through the walls of the building and garlanded their silence. Then other sounds were swept along in the slip-stream of time. The clack and rattle of trams in Royal Avenue with their advertisements for Hudson's soap and Alexander King's Best House Coal, the tinkling complaint of bicycles over cobbles, the cries of hawkers, the soaring and falling falsettos of boys selling the evening paper and then the unbridled ugliness of angry crowds flowing towards the building behind them. But they heard only their own uncertainties, their unwillingness to speak the wrong words.

21

Allenby found some consolation for the misery of constructing the lake in overseeing the building of the boat house. It wasn't dependent on the vagaries of the weather, nor did it require the labour of an army of men. Skilled workers had moved in – Wickets and Rodgers had even found him some Italian craftsmen to lend their skills to the wood and glass. They had originally come to Belfast to work on new churches and had decorated the Crown Liquor Saloon, and if the boat house wasn't like any building he would have constructed for himself, at least it was a change from the monotony and frustrations of burrowing in the earth. And everything was suddenly blessed with a swathe of better weather. The lake itself was almost ready and the men had an easier time constructing a pathway round its contours and helping Walter Clarke with planting. In scenes that contrasted vividly with what had gone before, there were days when they laboured in their shirts with their sleeves rolled up and caps set aside. And if they didn't like the Italians, they mostly kept it to themselves. He had even discreetly found a job for Crawford with a local foundry, buying his silence about the discovery of the baby. He knew Gregson was grateful for his intervention.

The attempted legal action by Stewart had eventually come to nothing, a piece of news communicated to him personally by Remington with ill-disguised pleasure. But as the work had progressed towards completion he was called back to Belfast, and a junior member of the firm dispatched to temporarily stand in for him. One of the firm's most experienced architects had been struck down by tuberculosis and Allenby was needed to oversee an important project he had been working on for a city centre bank. It irritated him to think that he had been called away so close to the moment when the lake would finally exist, but he also knew it was a sign of his growing importance in the practice. And in the intervening months it was also true that he had seen less of Cora, but his workload allowed him to attribute this to circumstances, rather than his own actions. Mrs Sullivan had taken on more staff to prepare the Manor House for the open day. Everything appeared to be in a state of high alert as the day assumed an ever-greater importance for the Remingtons. He told himself that perhaps the time with Cora had passed, that both of them had derived something that brought them a fleeting comfort. However, he also knew that some fundamental part of him still wanted her company, but without any public scrutiny or embarrassment, because he had never lost the sense of danger that their relationship created. Sometimes in his wilder moments he actually thought he might build his house and then ostensibly employ her as a housekeeper, although he knew her sense of pride would hardly allow her to accept that pretence.

One of his colleagues in the office had tried to act as a matchmaker, and invited him to a concert in the Ulster Hall with his wife and her younger sister. She had been amiable, pleasant and just for a few weeks he had been tempted. Tempted to accept the strictures of the world and fall into conformity; but he knew he would be deceiving her because he didn't feel whatever it was he imagined he was supposed to feel and that in time that absence would lacerate them both. He had a litany of deceptions in his past, and no wish to add another one to the list. So one night over gins he made his escape by confiding in his colleague that he believed the war had damaged the prospects of any shared future life, and then clouded his responses to subsequent questions with vagueness about the things he had seen. The lie was made easier by the fact that he could believe, in part at least, that it had its origins in truth.

When he was eventually able to return to the Manor House to inspect the finished boat house, Mrs Remington joined him and gave her enthusiastic approval. When Eddie, who also accompanied them, trailed his hand along the freshly painted walls in a gesture of bored indifference and asked her what she intended to use it for, he was told he must wait and see. Allenby realised that she didn't really know the answer to this question, and the building, like the lake itself, was merely part of some imagined route to greater social standing, an effort sustained by boundless wealth to demonstrate to the world that they were entitled to their rightful place. That cognisance should be taken. But he told himself it was a matter of no consequence and soon he would be permanently gone.

He would have been happier if no members of the family had been present when the day eventually came to divert water into the lake, because he suspected they anticipated some tumultuous Niagara Falls torrent to suddenly roar into the excavated basin. In reality, it resembled little more than the slow filling of a rusted bath. But all the Remingtons were there with the manor staff lined up behind them, as if waiting to greet a visiting dignitary. He scanned their faces, but there was no sign of Cora or Ida and he didn't feel able to enquire about her without drawing unwelcome attention. In the moments before he gave the signal to temporarily divert the river, he had a sudden vision of the water trundling into the waiting basin only to disappear down some invisible sump hole. His nerves did not abate when Remington senior approached him to ask, 'So when does the tap get turned on, George?'

'Any minute now. But it's not going to be a speedy process. We have to let it fill gradually over a drawn-out period of time so as to reduce the risk of too much pressure and damage on the monk and overflow.'

'Nothing has been speedy about this whole escapade,' Remington said. 'But at least Lydia likes the boat house and when the woman you live with is happy, you can get on with everything else in peace.' Gregson came running along one of the paths and gave him the thumbs up. 'You're on your own aren't you, George? Too busy making lakes and throwing up buildings for you to latch on to someone. You know what they say, don't you?'

Allenby shook his head.

'Marriage has many pains, but celibacy has few pleasures.'

Allenby felt the weight of Remington's hand on his shoulder. He didn't know what to say in response to the offered wisdom but before he could think of a reply there was a loud cheer from the waiting labourers, and as water started to flow into the lake some of them threw their caps in the air. Allenby walked closer to the banked edge and watched as the water seemed to meander and move half-heartedly, almost reluctantly, into the basin. But gradually it increased in speed and volume and quivered forwards across the bare earth like the slithering motion of snakes, seeking out the restraints of their new home.

'It's very mucky,' Remington said. 'Not quite somewhere you'd want to paddle your feet.'

'It'll clear in time. Clear enough to have fish swimming in it.'

But as Allenby stared at the water and tried to decide when to shout to Gregson to stop the initial flow, he saw only a shell-gouged crater filled with a splurge of winter rain. For one terrible moment it felt as if his feet were struggling to find a hold on the rim of the crater, and he was beginning to slide slowly downwards towards the trapped frieze of sky that swirled in the bottom and trembled like mercury with every new explosion that ripped the earth's core. And at first he thought it was Hawley's voice he heard slowly rising up from the lake. The gurgle and lisp of the water filling his throat and mingling with the dying rasp of his breath, his innards spreading across the sodden earth. But then he knew it wasn't Hawley. It was the cries of a child and he knew it was the child he had lifted out of the earth and buried again. He wanted to calm it somehow, still it before others heard it too, and it was coming from below the water. It shouldn't be there, he told himself, because he had lifted it in his arms and buried it elsewhere under the darkness of night.

'Are you all right, old man?' Eddie asked, and after Allenby registered the words he simply nodded but part of him wanted to grab him, push him into the water and hold him under. It was Gregson's shouts that brought him back, as he waved his arms for attention and wanted to know whether he should stop the flow. Allenby shook his head as if he had just suffered a blow or was trying to shake off a deep sleep, and then told Gregson to wait for just a few more minutes. He looked around again to see if there was any sign of Cora, but there was none. He wanted to think she might be waiting for him in the cottage and that if she came to him once more and lay with him before the flames then what he felt inside could be eased away and he might find oblivion in the refuge of her body.

'You look like you could do with a drink,' Eddie said.

'It's just wanting everything to work as it's supposed to,' Allenby said without looking at him. 'That there's actually going to be a lake with water in it after all this effort.'

After a few minutes the flow of water stopped and Allenby stared down at the frothed brown surface. Remington senior and his wife had already turned back to the house with Mrs Sullivan and the housemaids scurrying after them. Eddie lit a cigarette but didn't offer him one.

'So we'll have a lake for this bloody open day after all. A lake with sparkling clear water and fish swimming everywhere. If we have gondolas and mermaids perched on them it's not going to make a spit of difference.'

'No, I don't suppose it will,' Allenby said, loosening his tie.

The labourers were moving away from the water's edge at Gregson's instruction, returning to their work on the path. Two men were hammering planks of wood on the jetty.

'Was the war as bad as they say?'

The question was unexpected and when Allenby turned to look at him, Eddie turned his face away and held the cigarette out from his body as if there was a danger it might catch his clothes.

'Yes, it was bad. And do you know what really mattered, Eddie? You had to hold your end up. Do whatever was needed. And do you know why?'

Eddie shook his head and looked intently at him, a little spiral of smoke filtering into the space between them.

'Because if you didn't there was a price to be paid, either by you or some other poor bastard. Now if you'll excuse me there are things I need to check on.'

Allenby walked away from Eddie, towards Gregson. On the path he encountered Walter Clarke.

'A long way off your drawings, Walter.'

'In this game, you need patience. Nothing happens overnight. It'll come right in its own time. And as for the planting we've done, that'll take years to establish. I wouldn't go telling the Remingtons that, though, because patience is one thing they don't have. It will be like the drawings in time, and the water will clear pretty quick. Was young Remington offering his advice?'

'He asked me what the war was like.'

'If you have to ask you weren't there and can never know. What did you tell him?'

'Nothing really. Nothing that he could ever understand.' Allenby hesitated before he asked, 'Walter, do you ever look at young men like Remington and think they should have been the ones who didn't come back? That the wrong ones died?'

'Every day, and there are times when I see someone striding about like a peacock, or listen to them talking big in a bar, I want to push their faces deep into the mud. And there's an anger rushing through me that I have to smother.'

Allenby nodded but was conscious that in talking about the war he was in danger of crossing one of his red lines. Suddenly there was a volley of shouts and laughter – two of the men had stripped down to their vests and underpants and were cavorting in the water, splashing each other as if they were at the seaside. Their limbs were ghostly white against the brown of the water. Others were thinking of joining them until Gregson berated them and called to the two men to get out. Allenby wanted to tell him to let them be – there had been so much misery in their labour – but he wouldn't publicly undermine his foreman's authority. He thought of the day when Cora had paddled in the sea and made him join her, thought of her under the trees and felt the need of her flare anew.

Afterwards he went up to the cottage, but he didn't have the key and the door was locked so he was reduced to staring through the window. He saw only emptiness looking back at him, and the mottled glimmer of his own reflection.

22

Alex stood perfectly still in the shower, feet apart and both hands pushed against the tiles, letting the water sluice over him. If he waited long enough he told himself that the fug would wash away. He had spent the night in his parents' house and this day of all days he needed a clear head. He watched the water running through the dark hairs on his arms and remembered the rain on the last night of the festival. They were all coked up – Matty was like a walking dispensary, dishing out whatever their collective funds had been able to purchase. He told himself they were young, that he wasn't with Ellie then, that just maybe it was all an hallucination. That it was the drugs coursing through their bodies. Rain coming down and nowhere to shelter.

It had started just after the end of the music and fireworks, with the smell of sulphur hanging over the site as the crowds started drifting away. The squelch of their feet in the mud, the desire that the night shouldn't ever come to an end. She was wasted on drink or drugs, probably both, and she latched on to them as if they were her oldest and best friends, throwing her arms around them and saying that they were the nicest, coolest boys she had ever met. Matty had to hold her up when she tried to dance to the music that was no longer playing, her arms flopping like a marionette whose strings had been cut.

'Who are you with?' Matty had asked.

'Amber. I'm with Amber,' she said but where Amber was she didn't know. One second Amber was her best friend, the next a bitch she had never liked. Nor did she know where her tent was as the aftershock of the music vibrated in their heads and mixed with the adrenalin and everything they too had taken. Something was already stirring – he felt it even now in the shower until it was replaced by a surge of shame. With her dark hair beaded with the rain and plashing across her face, her cut-off denim shorts and T-shirt, she looked as if she had washed up out of the sea. Was it flotsam or jetsam that you were allowed to claim?

'We'll take her back with us,' Matty had said, and for a second it felt like they were taking care of some stray puppy that had temporarily attached itself to them. And she was intent on being playful, elaborately transferring her embrace and attention to Will, draping her arm across his shoulders so that when they walked it looked as if they were in a three-legged race, in danger of stumbling at every step. When did their kindness end? Was it ever kindness? Deep down, did they always know? They never talked about it, never alluded to it, because to do so would only make its existence real so he only knew how he felt now, standing under the water and hoping it would all wash away. He was last to have her. Have her while the other two stood outside the tent and waited smoking in the darkness, their exaggerated shadows flaring briefly when someone with a torch walked past. And it wasn't a crime – no one forced her as she bound her arm tightly round his neck, and if she called him by the wrong name and talked of things he couldn't follow, she didn't tell him to stop. Not once did she say stop or push him away, because that would have made it something else, something for which he couldn't ever make himself responsible or bring into the life he was about to begin with Ellie.

It was a hired suit, hired shirt, hired waistcoat and hired tie laid out on the bed. The outfit that he and his groomsmen would wear and which would make them all look the same, and as he finally moved his head out of the water's flow, he thought that in that tent that's what they were. All the same. So where was she now and what was her memory of that night? Perhaps she had been able to find the forgetfulness that eluded him. His feet left damp prints on the bathroom tiles, and it felt that even today it was following him. And he knew then that whether you wanted it or not you were joined with someone else forever, like some fusion of particles, lodged in memory that had no delete button, no trash in which to vanish the file. He would never see her again, barely remembered what her face looked like, but she would come to the wedding, take her place with all the others, and he was powerless to prevent it.

He tried to tell himself it was just a matter of letting time pass, until eventually the memory of the girl would grow fainter with every passing year. Why, then, was he thinking of it on this of all days? And why did it press so sharp-edged and glittering like a piece of mica, when everything else still felt fogged from the night before? He was a good person, a good person who, like all good people, had once done a bad thing. He got dressed and the unfamiliar clothes gave him the sensation of wearing a disguise, of temporarily assuming someone else's identity. He went, not to the mirror, but to the window and when he opened the curtains he stood perfectly still and let the sudden stream of light pass through him.

It was the same light that varnished Ellie's room – the room that had been hers as a child – and crystallised her wedding dress so it looked both cold and beautiful to the eye. Her make-up and hair had been done earlier in the morning, so she was alone with the photographer, a man called Tom. No one wanted an album of endlessly stiff shots of relatives any more, the type of photographs she encountered when they did an old person's house clearance. Those jobs always made her feel as if she was an intruder, prying through the private accumulation of a life. What they wanted was a more natural record of the day – something unusual, and yes the word she was searching for was 'creative', something that even aspired to art. She had liked his website, and the fact that his son Luke would do a video of the day swayed it for her. Tom was taking a photograph of her shoes – he said they looked as if they were made of icing sugar. He had already taken one of her wedding dress just after it had been eased out of its protective sheath and hung on the wardrobe door. She was wearing it now as she went to the bedroom window, its rustle coiling inside her head as if her bare feet were crimping snow.

Outside in the garden her bridesmaids were sharing a cigarette, holding and passing it at arm's length so the smoke didn't infect their dresses. She could hear her father down below – he had Prince's 'The Most Beautiful Girl in the World' on repeat. It was undoubtedly the most out of character thing her father had ever done – she had thought the only Prince he was aware of was royalty. She was a little embarrassed, but gradually her consciousness of the music faded, replaced by a longing for her mother. She told herself she would be waiting at the Boat House, waiting without her turquoise turban and with all her dark hair grown back, and she would let her child brush it once more, lifting the strands, moving along their length and then letting them fall gently back into place. What was the sound the brush made? Was it the same electrical charge that shocked so many things into life? Her mother had thick black eyelashes – Ellie had liked to run the tip of her finger lightly along them, a touch that always made her mother blink. That's what she wanted more than anything – that under her daughter's quickening touch her mother would blink, once more open her eyes and see her youngest child dressed for her wedding.

'You've got a great day for it,' Tom said before he suggested taking a photograph of her reflection in the mirror of the dressing table. He angled her towards it, touching her shoulder so gently that she wasn't sure whether she had imagined it. 'Mirror, mirror on the wall, who's the fairest of them all?' he said before the camera clicked.

She stared at her reflection, knew that she couldn't let sadness overshadow the day that lay ahead, because it risked overwhelming her, but it was made more difficult because there was something else that she wanted her mother to hear. She would tell Alex after the ceremony when they found a private moment and she was sure that whatever words she used would also be heard by the person who had brought her into the world, and whose years of absence had narrowed and constricted so much of it. She would walk out with Alex along the wooden jetty and tell him. That would be the place.

'How long have you been working with your son?' she asked.

'A couple of years. We keep an eye on each other. Good to keep your kids close, but it's just until he's able to find his own thing, whenever he works out what that is.'

'Have you other children?'

'I have a daughter.'

For a second she thought he looked distracted, as if he was going to say something else, but the moment passed.

'What are you like with wildlife, Tom?'

'Wildlife? I sometimes take photos of Saturday-night revellers for the Paradiso's Facebook page, but that's as close as I get. Why do you ask?'

'There are two swans on the lake.'

'And you'd like a shot of them?'

'Just an idea.'

'I've seen photos where their necks form a heart. Bride and groom with a swan heart. Maybe a bit tacky. But that would be the money shot. I could Photoshop it for you.'

'I want everything to be real.'

'No problem. Just turn towards me. Look towards the window. That's it. Perfect. I once did a wedding themed on *Game of Thrones* – all cloaks and swords – and they had a falcon or some bird of prey at the ceremony. Delivered the rings to the best man's arm. But judging by the way the couple were bickering at the end of the night I'd say winter was coming and coming pretty soon.'

'Have you ever done photographs of a bride who changed her mind?'

'You're not thinking of doing that, are you?'

'No, no, I'm not. But I am nervous. It's like it's someone else wearing this dress, not me.'

'Everyone gets nervous at some point. This is a good time to have it – get it out of the way,' he said as he continued clicking the camera. 'I did do photographs once of a girl who had a last-minute change of heart. When the car came she made the driver take her to the airport and she got on a plane to Ibiza.'

She shook her head, part in disbelief and part in wonder.

'Was there another man involved?'

'I don't think so. She just had a change of heart. A pity she didn't have it a bit earlier, that's all.'

Ellie stared at her reflection again, worried in case the make-up artist had been too enthusiastic, but reassured herself that all was as she wanted it.

'You've been lucky with the weather for it,' Tom said as he looked at the last couple of photographs he had taken. Then her father was calling that the car had arrived. Perhaps now he would switch off the music but then she realised he wanted to play it as she came down the stairs in his well-meaning piece of theatre. She didn't begrudge him if it helped with the absence they both shared. She looked at her phone, expecting a text from Alex, then wondered if pre-ceremony communication infringed one of the many wedding codes and rituals that seemed to regulate every aspect of the day.

'Let me go first,' Tom said, 'so I can get you coming down the stairs.'

She was alone and paused to glance around the room for a final time, knowing that after this day she would be somehow different, even though outwardly nothing much would have changed. The chirping voices of the bridesmaids rose ready to greet her as a descant cutting through the music. The most beautiful girl in the world. Only a father could believe that. As the scent of her flowers flurried about her, she stared at the room in which she had grown up and, catching her reflection suddenly flaring white in the mirror, was startled, as if she was looking at someone else, her own ghost made only from tiny particles of light and moving through a different world, unsure where was home and what she must do to get there.

★

At the Boat House they are glad that their early morning wait is nearly over. It isn't the coming and going that discomforts them – they are used to that. It's the brightness of the light silvering the water that mirrors the sky and troubles it with its constantly changing reflection. It's the fractured noise as well – the wheels of trolleys on the gravel; the laughter and joking of the staff who amuse themselves by sometimes carrying the trays on their heads, secured by one hand only; the small tractor, its trailer loaded with stacked chairs leaning at precarious angles.

The weather had been kind but there is always rain in the head of the young woman with the tattoos. She holds herself at a distance from the others and has no name. She doesn't want to be there – it threatens to bring things back when perhaps it is better that they fade out of definition. Once, as a child, she'd seen a puppet show performed behind a sheet where the shadowy silhouettes grew large and hands fluttered like the wings of giant moths. The sides of the tent suddenly illuminated the way some lighthouse beam swept across the blackness of the sea – that's what she remembers. That is all she is able to allow herself. She takes her place amongst the other late arrivals, threading their path along the edge of the water, just as Alex knew she would.

Who are they all, these forming fragments of memory? An old friend long estranged; a boy in school who had once said something cruel to him; the first girl he ever kissed at a school disco, her lips a shock of softness pressing him into a startled new awareness of himself; a grandfather with shallow breathing holding out to the very end in his hospital bed; a woman's face sheened by rain and a splash of neon glimpsed from a night bus. Someone who had once done him a kindness. The boy with the skateboard. Anton and his son. Evelyn and Billy, Russell and Eilish who clicks her beads as she says the Rosary. All those who worked in the Tea Merchant's and who without his full knowledge have become part of his life. A young boy with a bad haircut, because the barber is watching a horse race. On and on, like the pulse of a distant star that sears a fleeting image of itself into one's consciousness before spinning into the dark distances of memory.

They come for Ellie too. The minister who had placed his hand on her head at her mother's funeral. An old man locked in confusion, starting at every sound, his eyes a skittering search for what makes sense. He too is also frightened by the water. The young man in the underground car park who swore at her. The woman who brought the ring that Alex will place on her finger, the ring that looks like no one else's wedding ring and that had once belonged to Evelyn. Ellie had never sent it to auction, but rather had bought it at the estimate price and then never charged the owner seller's commission to salve her conscience. An older woman with sad eyes who once served her in a shop and whose hand just for a second touched hers as she handed over the purchase. The people in a black and white photograph – guests at a wedding – she found in a writing bureau that the auction house was selling. The mother and daughter from the restaurant. Those whose hands have carved the furniture she sold, or decorated the pottery with careful steady strokes, those who set the precious stones in the jewellery that lives on after those who made it have passed. And walking through them always, her own mother with her black hair uncovered and full, waiting to take her rightful place in the Boat House.

The ghosts assert no importance of rank, make no attempt to press for position. And afterwards they will filter away silently, leaving nothing behind but a delicate disturbance of air, a slight tremble on the surface of the lake – no one wants to be thought of as a ghoul or voyeur and the presence of happiness is always a closing door. Only a woman cradling a child will linger, watching from a distance that is made of nothing but longing for a different ending to the story.

She travelled in the wedding car with her father. He was quiet, surprisingly nervous, repeatedly checking that his wedding speech was in his inside pocket, asking her if his spray was sitting straight. She wondered what he was going to say but knew she couldn't ask him. Sometimes cars sounded their horns when they stopped at traffic lights, and they got a thumbs up and a flash of lights from the crew of a fire engine. When they arrived at the Manor House slightly early, their driver had to do a lap of the grounds to avoid them meeting their guests on the way to the Boat House.

'You're used to standing in front of people,' she told him. 'Everything will be all right.'

'I'm supposed to be the one telling you that. But I only stand in front of people when I'm selling something and I'm not selling anything today. And I'm certainly not giving away anything either.'

'That stuff about giving your daughter away is long gone – just like promising to honour and obey.'

'Glad to hear it.'

'You like Alex, don't you?' she asked, but she knew that even asking the question betrayed her uncertainty.

'I like anyone who makes you happy, Ellie. And it looks to me that Alex makes you happy.'

He was going to say something more, but hesitated. They were pulling up in the car park closest to the Boat House.

'Ellie, I wish your mother was here for this day. Here to see how beautiful you look and how wonderfully you've turned out.'

He angled his face away from her and she thought there was a danger he was going to cry. She tugged at his sleeve so that he had to turn and look at her.

'I do too, Dad. I do too, but I think she's here with us. And there's a comfort in that.' He nodded and composed himself again. The driver said that if they wanted a few more minutes he would do another circuit, but she told him no and instead spoke to her father, understanding that at that moment she needed to be the stronger of the two, even if it required a pretence on her part.

'We'll do this together,' she told him. 'Walk in together and smile at everyone. And I don't doubt that the day will be, in your favourite words, a very fine example of a wedding. A very fine example indeed.'

'Let's do it, Ellie,' he said, lightly patting her hand. 'Best foot forward. Let's do it.'

Then after passing a thank you envelope to the driver, they got out of the car. As the Boat House doors opened for them, they stepped into a room blossoming with light and flowers. The large windows behind the registrar who stood waiting for them afforded unbroken visions of the lake that seemed to flow almost into the building, so it felt as if they were walking towards water and a sweep of sky, as white flowers blazed against her. Paul Weller's 'Thinking of You' started to play.

Alex half-turned with the smile that always made him look like a boy. Her father held her arm firmly and she felt guarded and safe in the space that still separated her from her future husband. Now time was racing and they were making promises to each other and exchanging rings, the rings that had been inscribed with their private messages for each other and which they had incorporated into their vows. On his were Heaney's words: 'Within our golden ring', and on hers was engraved: 'To the very edge of time and beyond', and she was pleased by his choice, even though it sometimes made her think of *Star Wars*. And despite what she had said to her father she tried not to think of her mother or glance at the empty chair beside him because she knew it might overpower her.

After the ceremony, the day was filled with snatches of conversation with their guests, all of whom said the same things to her and to whom she gave the same replies, seemingly endless photographs and drinks sipped from glasses as she moved about but never finished because someone needed her presence and she forgot where she had set her drink. When they were called for the meal she was nervous for her father, worried that he might speak for too long, bore his audience, or worst of all be overcome with a surge of unaccustomed public emotion that he wouldn't be able to control. The seat beside her at the top table where her mother should have sat was occupied by her sister who, as usual, was drinking too much. Before the speeches started Sandra took her hand and told her that she had always been there for her and always would be. 'No matter how things worked out.'

Then her father was rising with his speech in his hand and his reading glasses poised to slide off his nose at any moment.

'It is a foolish speaker who outlives his welcome and comes between his audience and their food, so I don't doubt you'll be relieved to hear that I intend these comments to be extremely brief. So I'd like to welcome you all to the wedding of Alex and Ellie – I think the only time we ever called Ellie "Eleanor" was on her birth certificate, so Ellie's the name I choose to use now.

'Right at the start, I want to say that we are saddened by the absence of one precious guest, Astrid, my late wife and Ellie's mother. But I know with absolute certainty that she would be proud of the daughter she brought into the world, who we have seen blossom into this beautiful young woman. I am also very proud of Ellie and the person she is – intelligent, thoughtful, hard-working and indeed someone who is occasionally confident and resolute enough to steer me in the right direction. Although I also occasionally feel her elbow in my back pushing me towards retirement, and who knows she may well be right. When that day comes, I know the business will be in good hands.

'I am pleased she has found happiness with Alex and I promise you, Alex, that I shall do my very best to be a very fine example of a father-in-law. Thanks too to Eric and Angela, who have welcomed Ellie into their home and their family in a kind and generous way. As you know, my business in the auction house is based on the gathering and selling of things that are old – Eric often tells me that most of it should just go in the nearest skip – but setting that aside, I'd like you to think for a moment about how some things survive and endure through time, sometimes hundreds and hundreds of years. And what is it that allows something to survive when all around it there is decay and decline? Well, I suppose it's because it has been valued and treasured, protected as best as possible from extreme conditions, never taken for granted and a special place set aside for it. Alex and Ellie, I believe that's a guide to how a marriage might also endure and flourish, through sickness and health, through good times and bad.

'And before we have a traditional toast to the bride and groom and I bring the gavel down, I just want to say that we, like the rest of the world, have come through some dark and difficult days, days where families lost loved ones and families were separated and isolated. Now as we move towards the light of what will hopefully be a better future, we can rejoice in the marriage of Alex and Ellie, and all the other marriages and all the other births that bring us together again. So I ask you now to stand and raise your glasses to Alex and Ellie.'

As her father sat down amidst the applause Ellie took his hand and told him he had done well, and now all that she wanted him to do was enjoy the rest of the day. He simply nodded and squeezed hers in response.

★

Later, as the evening light slowly settled and then lengthened into dusk, she took Alex's hand, walked out along the wooden jetty and stared out at the water. He had discarded his jacket and tie, and when she shivered a little with the cold he draped his arm across her shoulders. When she looked back to the Boat House she could see couples dancing and hear the incessant pound of the music. A few guests sat outside on chairs, a little gauze of blue smoke wreathing their heads as if a mist was seeping off the water. She took his hand.

'I don't see the swans,' she said.

'Perhaps the noise scared them off.'

'It went well, didn't it?'

'It was great! And it's not over yet. There's still dancing to do.'

'And there's something else as well,' she said, turning to face him.

Taking his hand she placed it where new life was beginning and when he asked her if it was true she simply nodded before they embraced, then pulled him closer because she knew he was already nervous of holding her too tightly. The water on the lake seemed to shift and tremble for a second as she stared at it over his shoulder. There was cheering from the Boat House. But there was something else. Perhaps it was an echo of the music, or did it come from the Manor House? She couldn't be sure, as just for a moment, while still in his arms, she thought she heard the faint crying of a child, and then it was gone.

'We can't tell anyone yet. It's too soon,' she said, unable to hide her shivering. He led her back towards the Boat House, towards the start of their married life.

23

Wickets and Rodgers had both accepted their invitations to the Manor House open day, and Allenby hoped they would be pleased by his work. Mr Wickets had hired a photographer to take pictures for the firm's records and he was required to pose with both partners at various locations. Allenby told them that the softening of the lake's edges with trees and shrubbery couldn't be achieved overnight but he was confident Walter Clarke had landscaped it skilfully and that, in time, the drawings the gardener had done would become a reality. If there weren't yet fish in the lake then the water was clearing and settling so that the idea of it no longer seemed such a remote possibility. When Allenby's eyes occasionally turned to the recently con-structed drumlin, he told himself that the planting there had permanently sealed what he knew was buried below it. The weather had been kind, with a late summer's day still laced with a vestige of heat and light that skimmed over the lake and played upon its surface. The red glazed tiles of the boat house glinted brightly as the sunlight polished them.

'So, George, you'll be glad to see the back of this lake,' Mr Wickets had said to him but he had only smiled in reply. 'Good to get you back into the office – there's lots of work coming in so it'll be all hands on deck for the next year at least. Now where do we get a drink?'

Allenby had pointed them up to the house where a large marquee sat pitched on the front lawn, its bleached white canvas beginning to tremble and stretch a little in the rising breeze. Outside it were trestle tables covered in linen table-cloths and decorated with vases of flowers. Various house-maids scurried about serving the guests while to the right of the marquee a seated brass band played, the light reflecting off their instruments. Allenby had already realised that the area was roped off, so was clearly reserved for those guests deemed worthy of entry. And while the whole village had been invited, they were confined to other areas of the grounds where a tent serving beer and lemonade had been erected. Swing boats and donkey rides for children and stalls offering various forms of entertainment had been set up. On the way to the Manor House he had seen a poster advertising a children's fancy dress competition, and as Allenby walked towards the marquee his passage was obstructed by children in a variety of home-made costumes. A Pierrot clown, Britannia with a dustbin lid for a shield, a pirate with eye patch and wooden cutlass, two Charlie Chaplins – one complete with a small dog – and a young suf-fragette with a sash demanding votes for women.

Taking a seat at one of the outside tables he harboured the hope that Cora would appear and serve him. The realisation that after this he would permanently leave the Manor House unsettled him. He hadn't seen her in a long time, felt the guilt of not having contacted her and wondered how he would feel if she came to him now. Perhaps she might be able to slip away to be with him even for a short while, but then he asked himself why he couldn't just ask her to come with him. Come with him and be damned. But there was no sign of her, and he didn't recognise the young woman who approached to serve him. When she brought him a glass of beer he asked her if Cora was about, but she told him she didn't know anyone of that name.

'Come to see the circus?' Eddie asked, collapsing wearily on the seat opposite Allenby and pulling a silver hip flask from his jacket pocket. He went to pour some into Allenby's glass, but he put his hand over it. 'You don't want to rely on this pish they're serving to do anything for you,' Eddie said. It was obvious from his slurred speech that he was well on his way to being very drunk.

'Too early in the day for me,' Allenby said. 'And my bosses are here.'

'I wouldn't worry about them. They're both tucked up in the boat house – reserved for VIPs, naturally – and probably busy getting sloshed. You'll be pleased to know that the old man told them you'd done a good job even if it was done at a snail's pace. So maybe you'll get to do another one.'

'I'm never doing another one.'

'But you're the expert now, George. The expert on everything, I'd say.'

Eddie's voice was edged with resentment but Allenby didn't respond and instead thought about how best to extricate himself. Sandwiches were being served, and as one of the housemaids passed with a platter Eddie made a sudden grab at her arm and the neatly arranged contents somersaulted onto the grass.

'You clumsy bitch,' Eddie hissed, then staggered to his feet.

Allenby stood up, his fist clenched. He wondered if the moment had finally come and he heard again his sergeant telling him what it was he had to do, but there was someone else's hand on his shoulder.

'For the love of God, George, get him to his room before he makes an even bigger spectacle of himself than he has already.'

Remington looked at his son with disgust, then walked round the table to where he was standing and, putting his face close to his, said in a voice that Allenby had to strain to hear, 'On this of all days. If you embarrass us again on this your mother's special day there'll be a price to pay. And pay you will, if you have to sweep the factory floor to earn your crust for the rest of your days. George, see him to his room, and Eddie, if you know what's good for you, you'll stay there, or so help me I'll swing for you.'

Allenby took him by the arm and when Eddie tried to shrug him off he tightened his grip and eased him away from the table, saying as he did so, 'You heard your father, so let's go and not attract any more attention. There's a good chap.' When Eddie stumbled, Allenby held him up then kept him moving away from the tables and up towards the house. Halfway across the lawn, Eddie doubled over and emptied his stomach.

'You'll feel better for that and sleeping it off.'

'I can hold my end up. Hold it up as good as anyone,' Eddie said.

'Of course you can. Now, just a bit further.'

Allenby felt as if he was in a three-legged race, the ones he remembered from school sports days. Part of him knew that if a water-filled crater had opened up in front of them he would have pushed Eddie into it. He had to stop himself thinking of all the men he didn't bring home, when an accident of timing meant that someone like Eddie was born in a time of peace, guaranteed to survive. Survive and waste his life. In the distance the brass band was playing a tune he did not recognise. Eddie tried to pull himself free from his grip but Allenby propelled him on, refusing to let him stop again.

They entered the house through the back door. The kitchen was deserted but the signs of chaotic industry were everywhere. He responded to Eddie's request for something to eat by telling him that he'd have something brought to his room, then steered him into the hallway. The house felt hollowed out, abandoned like some silent ship drifting far out at sea. Every part of him wanted Cora to appear from one of the rooms, but although she pressed against his consciousness with every one of his burdened steps, all that he encountered was an emptiness. And there was no time in the house, as if all the clocks had suddenly stopped, so he didn't know when she had first come to him or how long it had been since he had seen her. And if there was no present time then he had no awareness of future time, and when he tried to imagine what lay ahead for him there was only a blankness, a snowy whiteout with no horizon, or one of those mornings when the mists seemed to emerge out of the bowels of the earth and render the world void and without form once more.

Step by step they laboured up the stairs. He remembered the night he had climbed these stairs behind Mrs Sullivan, Cora coming into the room to light the fire, her hair the strongest colour in the grey wash of the room. When they reached the top he let go of Eddie's arm for a moment. He thought how easy it would be to push him into a tumbling, neck-breaking fall. He thought too of the little skeleton he had buried in the earth, of the life it had never known, wondered what hopes and dreams had been buried with it. It disgusted him to be so physically close to Eddie – the smell of alcohol on his breath and the splashes of vomit on his jacket. It disgusted him too to think of the man taking the women who came to work in the house, but he knew he had no right to moral superiority, saw again the blue light and stairs less grand than these he had climbed but which represented the same journey nevertheless, however breathless and desperate it was when the face you were looking at was yours in death. And he had taken Cora, someone he wasn't entitled to take whatever her willingness, had taken her while knowing he would never allow her access to his life beyond the expression and absorption of his need.

They reached Eddie's room and when he thought of resisting and slurred something about not being a child, Allenby propelled him through the door and pushed him onto the bed, removed his shoes and covered him as best he could with the eiderdown. He had already seen a key, and after he shut the door behind them he locked it. When Eddie blattered against it like a little boy and promised to be good, Allenby told him to sleep it off, that he'd feel better if he slept it off. He started back down the stairs but then paused and turned around, arriving eventually at the room in which he had spent his first night in the Manor House. There were two suitcases now, and clothes and possessions strewn round, but rather than the damp coldness he associated with it, the room was warm even though no fire had been lit. A pair of white shoes had been kicked off at the side of the dishevelled bed, and what looked like a bride's veil was draped over a chair. He thought of the hessian sacks on which he had first known Cora, and he realised that the word he had used in his head was 'known', rather than something sexual. He told himself that had to mean something. Going to the window, he looked down at the world outside and the people below moving in seemingly random patterns, heard the band playing 'Pack Up Your Troubles in Your Old Kit Bag'. In France the men had invented their own profane version and they sang it with raucous abandon at every opportunity. He wondered why the profane so often existed in such close proximity to things that felt sacred and if there was any real difference between them.

People were promenading round the lake, children in fancy dress were lining up to be judged by Lydia Remington while the brass band suddenly fell silent as if the needle had been taken off a record. Down at the boat house he thought he saw something to which he couldn't give a name, as figures whose faces he could barely discern clustered in small groups or stood alone, their presence a kind of tremulation of the air. Were they the men who had laboured on the lake, or the men he had taken to France? What about all those he had left behind who now had no faces or human existence? He blinked his eyes and then they were gone, as if dispelled by some breeze off the lake. His hand touched the glass but his fingers left no print, as if he too was nothing more than a fleeting breath of air.

Suddenly he had the feeling of disturbing someone in the room, of intruding in something that was private. He turned and looked at the ruffled bed, remembered how he had smoothed the print of Cora from the pillow; for a second he heard whispered voices in his head and then went back into the corridor. As he walked towards one of the stained-glass windows at its end, coloured light speared in and quickened the carpet's flowers into a kind of bloom. He paused and turned back the way he had come. He had a vague idea where Cora's room was, and after trying several doors he eventually found where some of the maids were living. There were three beds pushed tightly against the walls, leaving very little floor space. A cord bisecting the room acted as a clothes line from which hung various undergarments. Battered suitcases were pushed under the beds and from their open lids poked glimpses of clothes. A pair of shoes and a gauzy concertina of stockings rested on a bedside chair. Someone had stuck a magazine picture on a wall of some film star he didn't recognise, and on one of the beds was a Bible.

Allenby walked slowly round the room, touching nothing but taking everything in. He remembered how once in France he had come across an old deserted farmhouse. The remains of an evening meal still sat on the kitchen table, a knocked-over chair and pulled-out drawers cascading their contents onto the floor were evidence of the owners' sudden departure. A small bird in a cage, the door swung open but the creature showing no desire to escape. Photographs left behind and all the paraphernalia of a life that had departed. Did they ever return? Had Cora once lived in this room? As much as he tried he found no sense of her, nothing he could latch on to, and that emptiness seemed to magnify and then extend through his being.

He went back out, down the stairs, then quickly through the kitchen where two young women were so frantically busy that they barely registered his presence. The brass band was playing again. On the path back to the festivities he met Walter Clarke lolling against the wall of the cottage garden. He had forsaken his gardening clothes for a tweed jacket and was in the process of lighting his pipe, angling himself against the red brickwork to shelter it from the rising breeze. There was no one else to ask. He knew it meant revealing what he had always hoped to keep hidden, but remembered Cora saying that Walter Clarke knew everything that happened. That he was one of them. There was no other way, and if Clarke judged him then he would accept his verdict because there was no escaping its truth.

'Seems to be going well,' Allenby said.

'If you like that sort of thing.'

'You don't?'

'I've had enough of bands and speeches. Haven't you?'

Allenby nodded. He tried desperately to think of how he could ask about Cora without it being obvious.

'Lots of changes around here. New faces.'

'They brought in more girls to prepare for today.'

'I didn't see Ida and Cora.'

'Both gone. One day they're here and one day they're not. That's the way of the Manor House.'

'Suppose they went back to the mill.'

'Couldn't say.'

Clarke took the pipe from his mouth. Allenby scuffed his shoe through the gravel then offered some compliment about how well the planting was going.

'Long way to go but we'll get there in the end.'

'Wonder why they let them go when they were bringing in more help. Seems a bit strange.'

'There's a lot of strange things go on in the Manor House, George. But I imagine you know that already.'

It was useless to try further. He told Clarke he had to return for some photograph that was going to be taken, but then as he started to walk away he heard him say, 'They don't always leave in the same way they arrived.'

Allenby turned to face him, but Clarke was already disappearing through the gate that led into the walled garden.

24

She had been sent from the Manor House quietly and without interrogation. Mrs Sullivan had sensed it long before it was physically obvious and it wasn't obvious until very late. Perhaps Sullivan had previous experience to guide her, or just some sixth sense. In the end, she wasn't sent back to the mill but to a farm just outside the village that was owned by Sullivan's sister and brother-in-law. Ida had already departed, taken to the station early one morning to catch the first train back to Belfast. They had been kept apart so there wasn't time or opportunity to talk to each other. When she had asked Sullivan about Ida's departure she had been told brusquely that Ida's mother was unwell and needed looking after. But she knew it wasn't true. No letters or messages had ever come for her. If anything she believed it was because Ida had embarrassed Eddie in public or simply that he had grown tired of her. Perhaps she had been foolish enough to reveal that she held expectations of a shared future.

As she sat in a back room of the farmhouse that was furnished with nothing more than a single bed, a chair and a washstand, she wondered if the same fate had befallen her and then felt ashamed that she had thought Ida foolish for harbouring such hopes. She hadn't seen Allenby in months, knew he had gone back to Belfast and, when she understood her condition, had no easy way of contacting him. And if she had, what did she expect? That he would come running and place a wedding ring on her finger? She remembered the trip to the seaside, recalled the moments in the railway station when he had been awkward, embarrassed by their being together, always holding something of himself back. And if she liked him more than anyone before, perhaps when it came to it he was no different from all the others.

Nor had she been sent to the farm to rest, because it was soon obvious that she was there to work for her board and lodgings. But only ever inside the house. So all the house and kitchen work was her new responsibility. Sullivan's sister Meredith watched her constantly and when she said she needed air, or asked to go outside, she accompanied her, but not as a companion. She had already seen how Jonas, Meredith's husband, looked at her and without him saying anything she knew he thought of her as loose, potentially available to him if the opportunity arose.

'Keep your head down, do as you're told and work hard for your keep,' Meredith had instructed her, as Jonas stood just behind his wife, leering.

When once she raised the issue of going back to Belfast, they sent for Sullivan who told her that she must stay where she was, that she'd be looked after. That the child would be taken care of. How they knew families who would take a baby and bring it up as their own.

'There's those who would have packed your bags for you and thrown you into the street,' she said, 'but in the circumstances the family are willing to make some provision.'

And then she understood that Sullivan assumed Eddie was the father. But what difference did it make who the father was; he still wasn't going to be there to see his child. How could he have left the Manor House without even telling her that he was going or when he would be back? She tried to hate him but kept encountering things that prevented the full flourish of her hatred. He had always treated her gently and with what she liked to construe as respect. Sometimes she had even felt as if she was the dominant partner, as if she was leading him out of himself to somewhere he wanted to be. But it was all gone now with this child growing inside her, a child she thought she could never have and which would imprison the rest of her life even more than it already was inside the boundaries of the farmhouse.

The weeks turned slowly into months. She had no communication with the outside world except through the pages of the local newspaper that appeared occasionally on the farm. When her chores were done she would rest on her single bed and sometimes as heavy rains squalled against the house and berated the slate roof, she thought of the fire in the cottage and tried to warm herself with the memory. But already that consolation was ebbing away. She had never felt as lonely as she did here, and when she looked out of the farmhouse windows, the surrounding fields seemed to stretch to an endless emptiness. She thought of running away, tried it once, but the two dogs Jonas kept tethered in the yard betrayed her and when he brought her back to the house he held her arm tightly and pressed himself against her, leaving her repulsed by the broken stream of his breath and the smell of the farm that seemed to permeate every item of his clothing.

And even if she could have escaped, where could she have gone? She had no money, knew no one in the locality other than those who belonged to the Manor House. She thought of harming herself but there was some stronger impulse inside her that refused to give up. The closer the time came, however, the more she turned her thoughts to finding him and she knew that her only hope was to return to the Manor House, comforting herself with the idea that just maybe if she could do this then there would be a lamp burning in the window of the cottage, the cottage that had felt more like home than anywhere she had ever known. And perhaps he hadn't left her after all, but was ill, or battling something from the war that had returned to snare him. There were times when she was with him that she saw sudden shadows flitting across his face, things he could never talk about but which she registered in unexpected moments of silence. She tried to create as many reasons as possible, told herself that when he had said her name again and again it had really meant something. And when Sullivan visited her sister on Sunday afternoons she tried to make herself as unobtrusive as possible so that she could hear and perhaps glean something that would help her, listened intently when they talked about the success of the open day. How Eddie had got drunk and disgraced himself.

*

He watched for her as often as he could escape from work. He had created a list of the mills and one by one he turned up at each of them at closing time, when the hooter signalled a sudden surge of employees, mostly women, pouring out towards freedom. He tried to find a vantage point from where he could scrutinise the people streaming towards him. But there were too many faces in what became a torrent of workers embracing their long-awaited escape. Some of them linked arms, some sang and shouted at others. It was a river in flood, and he had to frantically push himself back against a wall to avoid being swept away. Sometimes at a distance he thought he saw her but when she drew closer he knew it wasn't her. And if he approached a woman on her own and offered her Cora's name, they shrugged him off with their faces pinched tightly into suspicion. They could tell from his clothes and voice that he wasn't one of them, that he represented authority, so instantly they were wary of him and unwilling to help even if they could. But he kept on trying. Mill after mill. Standing in the rain and the cold, standing when the fading of the year's light made everything look spectral, until the cold penetrated him and he felt the sadness of diminishing hope. And with that came the bitterness of realising too late that what he had found with her was what he had always wanted, and that all the other concerns with which he had tried to force himself into her rejection no longer mattered to him, that they had withered into nothing like the autumn leaves shrivelling on the city's trees. He remembered the light he had put in the cottage window and wanted some signal that would burn brightly and call her back to him again. But now there was only this heaving mass, a blur hurrying to wherever they called home, and the only sound he heard was the clack of their shoes on the rain-slicked road.

She waited until the farmhouse was silent. But it was never truly still because there were mice or perhaps worse scuttering about in the eaves, the snoring of Jonas and the springy squirm of their bed as they tried to burrow themselves into a deeper sleep, the stretch of some pipe or beam while from outside the lowing of cattle and other creatures of the night slipped through the walls of the house despite their thickness. Sometimes she heard them make their bed complain even more loudly with Jonas's snort and snuffle like some penned animal feeding at a trough and her angry breathless rasps before they collapsed into a discordant duet of ragged breath.

The dogs were tethered at the front of the house in two roughly hewn wooden kennels and, mindful of what had happened before, she made her way to the kitchen at the back. The few possessions and clothes she had were pushed inside a pillow case she had hidden under her mattress. She carried her shoes for fear of making noise in the corridor. She had to pause for a few moments while her eyes adjusted to the darkness of the hall, but she knew there was a three-quarter moon and hoped it would help her find the way. The child felt heavier, pressing against her, stretching her in ways that were strange and frightening.

Outside she felt suddenly swallowed by the night, infinitesimally small in the face of the boundless darkness. Every star seemed far-off and cold to the eye. She had to clamber over a stone wall and cut across fields until she was able to safely reach the road into the village. She stayed close to the hedgerows, glancing back over her shoulder whenever she heard a noise, never sure whether it was real or imaginary. In one of the fields a horse, startled by her approach, jolted away into the darkness. She thought of the time she had seen the sea with him. The endless darkness reminded her of the ocean now.

Sometimes she stopped to rest but she didn't linger long because she started to shiver and knew she had to keep going, had to reach the cottage, had to believe that there would be a lamp burning in the window. She remembered the time he had told her about the house he wanted to build – the light-filled house with its large windows looking out to sea – but she didn't care about that. She would have been content to live in the tiny cottage with him. She'd clean and make it pretty. Make it so pretty he'd forget about wanting to live anywhere else. So she struggled on, trying to ignore the complaints of her body and silence all the doubts rushing through her mind. Hold on to the light, she told herself. Hold on to the light and never take your eyes off it. Let it guide you through the darkness.

He was distracted at work, finding it hard to concentrate on anything in the way he needed to. One of his colleagues asked him if he was well, and he had tried to make a joke at his own expense. But the reality was he didn't want to be in the office and on several occasions had invented a reason to visit the Manor House, claiming he needed to check that everything was working properly. Walter Clarke had left his post and gone back to England, and his replacement knew nothing about the staff who worked in the house. If Clarke had gone, however, his legacy remained and the planting he had overseen was establishing and beginning to hide the man-made origins of the lake. Allenby stood at the water's edge but any sense of pride he felt at what he saw was eroded by other thoughts about what he had lost. Once, he went to the cottage and found it unlocked. It seemed so much smaller than he remembered and for a moment he struggled to understand how such a space had opened up such a vast emptiness inside him. A vastness that now felt collapsed in on itself like some derelict house with empty rooms that had no hope of finding the life they once held.

He tried to think of his own house – the house he would build some day. At home he started to build a model of it from card and wood, but each of its rooms also felt empty and without purpose. One night he took the model and flung it into the fire, and then spiralled into such lowness of spirit that just for a second he thought he had been happier in the trenches. There at least, all he had to do was stay alive and try his best to keep as many of his men safe from harm as he could. One Saturday he took the train and retraced their Easter steps, where in the face of inclement weather the resort was stripped of the crowds who had thronged it months earlier. And on the street he saw Hawley's face everywhere, so there was no respite but to find a bar and sit over a drink before he took the almost empty train back. When he reached Belfast he stood for a few seconds and remembered how he had watched her walking away, tried to conjure some spell, some incantation that would bring her out of the nothingness and let her walk towards him once more.

The cottage door was locked. There was no light in the window. She held her face against the glass but saw nothing inside. And something was happening to her. It was too early but something was happening. She put her hand against the bricks and angled her body forwards trying to find a steadier flow of breath. She had to find shelter, and for a moment thought of knocking on the Manor House door but knew she couldn't step back once more into that world. There were no lights on in the house and yet it seemed to loom over her, holding her in its unbroken gaze. She had to get away and so she followed the path down to the lake, trying to stifle her cries from the pain pressing against her. In places the slight shift of the water's dark surface bore a trembling flurry of light, as if a star had just melted into it.

The doors of the boat house were unlocked. The clean-up from the night before had not yet started, so the tables were still littered with glasses, discarded favours and debris left over from the wedding feast. White-faced flowers leaned out of their silvered vases as if weary of holding up their heads. A pair of red shoes, thrown off and never reclaimed, nestled under one of the chairs. The night was passing and it was nearly time for another day to slowly emerge as the shadows and moonlight skirmished then melded into the milky oneness of dawn. She huddled in one of the corners and pushed her back against the wood, and with every moment it was harder and harder to muffle the cries that came from deep inside her and with them the voices telling her that this was the price she must pay for allowing herself to be noticed, for believing that love could ever change what was forever fixed. For thinking that she might live in a house by the sea with someone who loved her. She had always been good at hiding things – under her mattress in the house was a silver thimble, a silk handkerchief, a coin she had found in one of Eddie's coat pockets. But she knew that nothing could hide this shame, that it would seep through all her future days.

It happened just as dawn crept inside the boat house. She took it in her arms and looked at it only long enough to know that it was a girl, and then wrapped it in the pillow case. She begged the child not to cry, hushing her gently over and over, then carried her out to the lake and gently hid her in the water.

25

The day was almost over, the last dance ending. Her father had already said goodnight to her with a kiss on the cheek before going up to his room. She had thanked him for the day and he told her she was welcome and then left before his emotions got the better of him again. She hadn't seen Alex's parents for a while although remembered how, earlier in the evening, Eric had done some noticeably energetic dad dancing, waving his arms and skipping, hopping on his feet like a child playing an odd form of hopscotch. She knew there was some new tension between Alex and his father, but didn't know exactly where it was coming from. She was too weary now to ask about it, unwilling to let it intrude on her happiness. The white train of her dress had a little seam of brown where it had trailed across the ground on their way to get their photographs taken.

Already Alex had started behaving towards her as if she had acquired a new fragility. Then when she got up to join in the final dance he held on to both her hands as if she might topple over at any minute; all they did was a kind of sedate sideways shuffle. Many of the other women had discarded their shoes, but she kept hers on even though they rubbed her heels.

She was glad the photographer had left with his son because only the die-hards remained now, and some of them were the worse for wear. There was nothing in the lees of the day that would have made a good photograph. Hopefully he had already got everything he needed. She suddenly thought she would have liked another photograph of her wedding dress after the day was over, so she would have one of it hanging in all its perfection on her bedroom door, then wearing it at the wedding ceremony and a final one with its creases and brown seam. She didn't really know why, but perhaps it was something to do with the strange way time had passed today, some moments going so slowly while others rushed headlong forwards. It had felt at times as if the hands of the clock were confused.

Alex pulled her closer and she wasn't sure whether it was because he needed to wrap his arms round her to safeguard against whatever was in his worried imagination, or because he just felt the need to be near her. 'Within our ring, within our golden ring,' she whispered to him and he replied with, 'To the very edge of time and beyond.' Some stupid part of her mind started into an awareness that the inscriptions suggested different directions, but she dismissed it and held him tightly. Now the music had finally come to an end and the brightness of the turned-up lights encouraged everyone to set out towards their rooms in the Manor House, their cars or scheduled taxis. Ellie pulled Alex's sleeve to make him linger at the back of the crowd, wanting to talk to him about the child they were going to bring into the world. Suddenly, however, there was his best man and groomsmen clamouring round him asking him to help with someone's car that needed a push. He showed reluctance until she encouraged him to go, and then she was glad because now it was her mother she heard calling to her, whispering her back to the lake, and as she walked towards the water there she was, standing in front of the trembling reeds with all her black hair grown back and stacked on her head in a precarious balance, her outstretched hand holding out a silver brush.

'Brush my hair, Ellie,' she says, and she's smiling through every passing year and vestige of time, and her skin is moon-washed and without blemish. Her hands flutter like the wings of small birds about to take flight. 'Brush my hair, Ellie.'

So Ellie takes the brush and moves it through the thickened quiver of hair. As always, she pauses to run the tip of her finger along the thin white line of her mother's scar. And there is music playing but she isn't sure of the song at first, then she knows it is Joni Mitchell's 'Little Green', a prayer for a lost child. It always makes her sad but her mother smiles at her and shakes her head, saying that she mustn't cry. And her mother tells her she looks beautiful, that her dress is perfect, and when in reply Ellie touches her lashes lightly with the tips of her fingers, they both close their eyes for a second. When she opens them Ellie sees herself cradling a baby and it's a girl, as she always knew it would be, and her mother places her hand lightly on the baby's head in a blessing and then she is gone. Gone back through the years that slowly close over her once more until there is only the breeze skimming the surface of the lake, worrying round her dress.

There was no car that needed pushing, and Alex looked back to where he had left Ellie but his friends' hands propelled him on until they reached the trees. And they were giving him a joint to smoke – special quality someone said, as if it was a final wedding present – but he held up his hand to indicate that it wasn't for him, knowing he couldn't smoke even a cigarette because he was going to be a father and couldn't bring any toxins near his child. And there was something else – he no longer wanted to be part of anything that reminded him of what had happened, or the people he had been with. He wanted it all gone because that was something else he couldn't bring near his child or allow to tarnish what lay ahead for him. He made a joke of his refusal and ignored theirs in return, then went to find Ellie.

Ellie wasn't on the path and when he went into the Boat House she wasn't there either. There was a pair of discarded red shoes and Ellie's veil draped over the back of a chair. Empty glasses and bottles littered the tables. Their extravagance of a cake, now half-consumed, sat sagging in the corner. The DJ was packing up his equipment and staff were clearing glasses. He didn't want to embarrass himself by asking if anyone had seen Ellie, inadvertently advertising the fact that he had already lost his bride, so he went outside and called her name, then walked towards the lake.

They come once more to meet him. And he's walking again across the pebbles of the beach trying to place his steps as lightly as possible to avoid the sharp-edged shingle. Behind him his mother is reading her book, his father struggling to pump air into an inflatable. The clicking noise he half-hears is Eilish doing her Rosary beads. She has seen already what his arrival portended and what will befall the place in which they live but can say nothing to Evelyn, Russell, Billy or any of the others because she is the only one able to see what will come. The young woman with the tattoos stares at him but isn't sure, is never sure about the faces or anything else and she is glad of that. But the time has gone and with its passing all those who have gathered now fade away, and so as he saw Ellie standing at the water's edge there was only the slightest of shivers, a shiver that might have been caused by the wind rising off the water.

'Are you thinking of going for a swim?' he asked.

'Too cold and dark.'

'And who knows what lurks in its depths.'

'I haven't seen the swans, have you?'

He shook his head and draped his arm over her shoulders, leading her away from the water. They stayed linked as they walked back towards the Manor House. In the lobby they met guests who weren't staying overnight and who said goodbye to them shaking Alex's hand or patting him on the back and he wasn't sure whether it was because they were wishing him luck, or because they thought he had done something worthy. There were times when he had thought of inviting Anton, Rosie and all the others from the Arcade to the evening festivities, but he knew the lingering tensions caused by the fire made that impossible. He wondered how Anton's son was, and then realised that he would likely never know what future the child faced.

He wanted only to go with Ellie to their room. Placing his hand on Ellie's back, he felt the soft silk of her dress and then tried to guide her gently away from the lingering wedding guests. One of them was complaining that their taxi hadn't turned up, others held slices of wedding cake in little decorative boxes. Some of the women carried their hats in brightly coloured handbags. One of his cousins was asleep in a chair, both legs draped over its arm.

They took the stairs, Ellie forced to gather up her dress in both hands so that she didn't trip on it. That they were married suddenly felt unreal, as if they were characters in a story about their own lives. And he was weary, more weary than he could ever remember. When they reached their room he couldn't find the key at first, and for one terrible moment thought he would have to go back down to the front desk. But eventually he pulled it from an inside pocket and they stumbled inside, into a room that felt like an unexpected haven. Together they flopped backwards onto the bed and lay staring up at the ceiling. The silence stretched over them and had to be broken. He wanted to say important things to her but didn't know what they were and it was too late already for anything else.

'I've given up smoking,' he said.

'Again?'

'I mean it this time. I've really given up.'

'What's going on between you and your dad?' she asked, turning to look at him.

'Just stuff. Just stupid stuff.'

'Well, that explains it.'

'Let's just talk about us,' he said.

'Can we get in the bed? I'm done in.'

He had to help her out of her dress, and watched her while she hung it up. For a second as she stood beside it and smoothed it with the palm of her hand, it looked like there were two of her in the room.

'Ellie, maybe it's not the right time to talk about it, but I'm thinking of leaving my father and going into business on my own. Or even starting something that we could do together eventually. Something new. Just us. No parents looking over our shoulders.'

'How long have you been dreaming of this?'

'Since the fire. Maybe longer.'

'And what type of business have you been thinking about?'

'I'm not sure,' he said, suddenly feeling foolish, and as a distraction let his hand touch the dress she had just taken off, his fingers lingering in its softness.

'Well, that's bound to be a success. And it'll need to be a success to provide for this little one,' she said, cupping her hand over her stomach. Then she came towards him and he lightly laid his head where their child was growing. She stroked his hair as if he too was a child.

'It's going to be a girl,' she told him, studying his face to gauge his reaction.

'How do you know?'

'I just do.'

'A girl is good,' he said. He knew he would be glad whatever it was, but told her again that a girl was good.

In the bed, they lay in each other's arms and neither of them felt the need for anything more. The day had been long and they were spent. They had the rest of their lives ahead of them. The room was not fully dark, and from outside, car park lights filtered against the closed curtains so she could still see the white sheath of her dress with its little seed pearls on its bodice and sleeves. During the day, one of the seed pearls had worked itself loose and she hadn't been able to find it.

Before long Alex slipped into a deep sleep, but despite her tiredness Ellie's was broken and disturbed by strange dreams.

Sometime before dawn she woke. The room was too warm, too bright, her dress a silver glint even in the shadows. She got out of bed and walked to the window, pulled back the curtains a little but couldn't open them. Only a sliver of the lake was visible through a break in the trees. Her hand drifted once more to what was beginning to grow. She could hear it again. When she glanced back at her husband under the white sheet, it looked as if he was sleeping beneath a deep drift of snow. She heard him whimper. What dreams sifted through his sleep? Why did he not hear what she heard? She wanted to wake him and ask why a child should be crying, ask him if it was their child. Her outstretched hand touched the coldness of the glass before the world suddenly fell silent, then, taking it away again, she watched her handprint slowly fade, wondered if the swans were together somewhere in the darkness.

26

Time shuffles itself lightly like a pack of cards. Who can tell what sequence it will deal? Who can tell what will fall across future days? As Allenby gets in his car outside Allenby and Rodgers, where he is now the senior partner, he tries not to think of the passage of time or the days that will come, because it feels as if there are too many of both. Too many days to fill, too many rooms in his house by the sea that hear no voice but his own with the ever-shifting light a parabola of silence. His searching had ended many years before, when he forced himself to admit there was no point in adding another futility to a world that was overflowing with them.

And with each year her memory doesn't grow any less real, but her face is fading. Sometimes it feels as if a slow tide is coming in and erasing what had once been drawn so sharply in the sand. He knows that with time there will be an even greater vagueness, and that too feels like a betrayal just as advancing age diminishes the reality of who he once was.

He wants to tells himself that the journey he is about to take is business but knows it is a lie, and such a blatant lie that he is embarrassed by it. Whatever the reason that will see him journey once more to the Manor House, it has little to do with business or money and part of him wishes the invitation had gone to some other firm. It is the first time he has ever driven there, and as he sets out he recalls all the journeys he made by train and the strangeness of how a life can be changed by some chance occurrence. Heavy rain. A fall across the line. A single night spent in a house. The fire she lit in his room. The sparking of it into life, the flare of her hair, all tumbling into everything that happened. And as always there is another light falling across the memory, one that he's never been able to erase. Blue lights and red lights. The separation of one from the other, the attendant pulse of guilt that he's never been able to fully subjugate. Where did she go? What happened to her? Why couldn't he find her? Was that to be his punishment?

The city watches him go, the way it watches all journeys through its being. Faces in empty buildings and shadowy unused rooms turn towards his movement through the streets. All of them know his story, whispering it across the endless empty nights when they meet on dust-laden back stairs. He is a murmuration, a threaded link between spaces and moments. Evelyn stands at a window and turns a ring on her finger, a ring for which she has not paid the hoped-for price and perhaps never will. She tells herself it can't be taken back once given. That someday she won't have to hide it from her husband. In a solitary room an old man tries not to think about the black-throttled sea and the tar babies sliming across the iced-up deck. These and so many others silently watching, their lives layered so thickly in the city's strata that they reach up to the very surface of the present.

Allenby passes the Arcade, with its beautifully polished tiles and glass roof, its green marble and black granite and in which Alex will see his childhood self walking towards him out of the mirror. He drives on, past the mill, where each long day flax dust inveigles its way into lungs, and outside which he stood night after night in the raw coldness as winds swept in from the Lough and poisoned the air. Past the railway station from where they had set off to spend a day together. Their only day. And if he had known what was to come he would have found a way to give himself fully to each of the hours and also sought some way to preserve its moments, pristine and protected from the relentless course of time.

Nothing in the village appears to have changed other than a few different names on the shops and pub. After the city it feels quiet and undisturbed, wedded only to the turning of the seasons. In the fields the crops are harvested and the stubble is a hard spiked yellow bristle, like sandpaper. But the light is soft on his eyes and the narrow roads with their drowsy hedgerows, drained now of the excitement of colour, feel at first as if they're funnelling him towards a deeper slumber, until gradually that illusion fades as he draws ever closer to the house. He looks at himself in the mirror and sees a man with grey hair and a tightening face, colour leeching from his eyes. And then what he experiences is the first retch of fear so that his hands tighten on the steering wheel and there is a dryness in his mouth and that carries him even further back, so far back that he has to stop the car and stand for a while at the side of the road. A horse drifts aimlessly about a field before breaking into a gallop, its heels kicking up spurts of dust. He puts his hand on the roof of the car and takes strength from its solidity, the coldness of the metal. As he stands looking into the fields he thinks of going back to the city, of having someone else come and do what needs to be done. But that too would be a betrayal, and he knows already there have been too many of them.

The wrought iron gates are rusting and chained. He struggles with the key because his hands are shaking but when they're slowly pushed open, their reluctance marked by a scrape and then a high-pitched whine, he starts the drive to the house, careful to avoid the potholes. Grass and weeds pepper the gravel and on either side of it the overgrown shrubbery and trees have encroached so close that branches brush against his driver's window as he passes. Then he steers round the curve and sees the house again after all these years. There is something sunken about it, as if it is slowly smouldering into the earth on which it stands. Slates are missing and buddleia and weeds sprout from the sagging guttering so it looks as if the roof wears a planted fringe. All the windows are boarded up but still it feels as if it holds him in its gaze and he wonders if it recognises him now that he too has been changed by time. The Remingtons are long gone, both dead, and when everything passed to Eddie it took little time for him to fulfil his father's pessimistic assessment. Business ineptitude, mounting gambling debts and reckless parties to which people arrived empty-handed but left with bags and pockets full – all hastened the house's demise. Forced to sell to pay his creditors, left with a pile of bank loans outstanding, he had, according to popular belief, decamped to Australia. It was rumoured that he ran a working man's bar now under an assumed name, marooned in some desolate, sheep-farming outback.

The new business owners of the Manor House intend to turn it into an hotel. They have asked Allenby and Rodgers to submit a design, but he has already decided that it is a job for some other firm. There will be questions asked about why he should turn down such a lucrative opportunity and he will have to invent answers, but he knows he cannot return to supervise work here, cannot walk back through all the years that have passed. So when he reaches the front door, he takes the key out of the lock and lets it slip back into his pocket because he has already gone inside, along the hallway with its floral carpets and wood panelling, into the kitchen where there was the sweet smell of apple tarts and steam rising from a giant pot on the range; up brass-rodded stairs and past the stained-glass window that colours the light; along corridors and bedrooms where secrets are hidden; into the room where he first slept with her that night, another man's clothes laid out at the end of the bed for him to wear.

But it is the lake that draws him, and so he slowly steps away from the front door, moving backwards at first as if leaving the presence of someone he dislikes. He follows the gravel path, the very same path that Alex and Ellie will tread towards the Boat House to make their promises of love many years later. His steps are cushioned by the swathe of leaves that has fallen, and it is through the spread of bare branches that he gets his first glimpse of the water. It is steeped in a greyness, almost motionless except for a slight swell that sifts through the reeds. A heron stands further along the edge of the lake, as still as if it has been turned to stone. He walks out along the wooden jetty, stepping over a gap where a plank is missing. Water frets below his feet. It's as close as he can come to the lake that flows round him like time. As close as he'll ever be to the daughter he will never know he had. He thinks of the men who laboured to bring the lake into existence, of all the other men, their lives splayed like leaves across broken fields.

All those men. All of them turned to shades. A sudden wind is cold against his face. He listens for voices, of some remnant of those gone before, but now there is only an unfolding silence. The year is turning at the insistence of time. He knows nothing can be done to stop it. So more leaves will fall, more light seep away, and all he can do is say her name. Say it gently over and over like he said it once before and hope that even now as the words vanish into the eternal stillness of the water, that somehow, somewhere, she will be able to hear, and despite the coming darkness know that he tried to find her.

She hears his voice saying her name, hears it through the years even when she's not expecting it – walking down a street late at night, when the wind trembles the glass in the window of her lodgings, or in the moments before her weary body falls into sleep. Sometimes she hears it so clearly that even the frantic din of the mill can't subdue it. In the backstreet room that she rents is the drawing of the lake she took from the cottage after he had gone. Its colour has faded over the years just as her hair has slipped into grey, but from time to time she takes it down from the mottled glass of the mirror and holds it close to her eyes, eyes that no longer see as clearly as before. Sometimes too there is another voice, and when its cries filter through her dreams she returns to the water in search of her child. But she is gone and can't be reached, no matter how much she tries. Then she dreams of walking out into the water and being with her forever, but when she wakes in the half-light of the early morning, she feels a sadness that time hasn't eased any of the pain. She wonders if he ever built his house beside the sea, remembers how excited he was when he talked about it, wonders too if her memory is still part of him, or whether someone else has long since taken her place in his heart.

His voice feels suddenly weighted, vanishing below the surface of the water. He knows when he leaves he will never return, so let others be the ones to breathe new life into the house, let others repair the demesne and tend anew to the lake that so many men's hands struggled to create. He tries his best to make the memory vanish, but remembers once more the night he walked across the basin in the darkness and lifted the bones of a child, how he buried it in the earth without prayer or ritual. On the slopes of its burial mound now grow alders, downy and silver birch, rowans with red berries waiting for birds to scatter their seeds. In the attenuated light, the white bark of the silver birch is like the seam of his scar. The scar that no one has ever seen except her. Suddenly the grey heron frantically flaps itself into flight and skims across the surface of the water until it gradually lifts itself higher and vanishes towards the distant bank. As he turns away again, time stills and settles once more so that his departure is marked by nothing other than the stirring of the wind and the slow passing of the day's light.

The Invitation

The tale is told and now I prepare a table in the heart's imagination. It's not a wondrous feast or banquet, but it is all that I can muster in these my autumn days. So now it's done, let the invitations be sent. Let all these be asked with humility and grace, asked to come and sit at the table, travelling through worlds and time to take their rightful place.

All those who are lonely and without love. Those to whom life has been unkind and those who know the sadness of loss. Let them come. The two gravediggers who waited at a distance to fill my mother's grave and stood leaning on their long-handled shovels while the snow whitened their hair. My father as a smiling young man, when he was happy and dapper in his suit. My mother, who will not take a seat but move with kindness amongst those women whose need is greatest. Let them both come. The children who think they have failed and are told they are failures. Let them come, with those who go hungry in order to feed their children. Let my own children and their children come also and find a place. My two brothers.

The women and men who rise at dawn to clean offices and hospitals. Let them come. Those who stand at bedsides and care for the dying. Everyone who came when the world was closed and brought and delivered, who were a human voice at our door. Let them come. The nurses who put the needles in my arm and did long shifts. All those who died alone without family or friends to comfort their leaving.

The woman with no name whom I have seen every Christmas Day for countless decades when I drive into the city to collect my brother, and who is walking regardless of the weather to visit the cemetery. Let her come and take her place. Let the risen one she loves also be there at her side. And there will be a place for those whose lives were taken in our cities, towns and villages and a sacred seat for all the children whose future days were stolen from them. Let them come, and with them all those who mourn the unrelenting desolation of lost lives. Those without a home who sleep in doorways and hostels and those who seek to provide for them. Let them come, and those who travel vast distances to escape what afflicts them. There will be a place for you. Those to whom I was unkind and are able to forgive and accept this offering. All those who have strewn kindness across my path. Please come. And for all those who came out of the holy mystery that is the imagination, and found their life on the page there will be a seat ready at the table. Swift the detective trudging through the Belfast snow; Connor Walshe the taken boy who wanted to go home; Catherine married to a dreamer and seer of visions; Maurice running to hold on to life in the face of loneliness; Tom driving snow-blinded by grief and trying to reach his son; Michael and Donovan standing at the edge of a desert under the unblinking stars that look down on all our end. All those too who generously read the words and whose faces I never see. These and so many others. Let them all come.

The young woman I see running as if she's always trying to reach somewhere in the distance. The old woman who sits alone in her garden and waves as I pass. Let them come. The solitary walker on the early morning beach who says hello, and in so doing acknowledges that I am alive and not a passing shade. The barber who cut my child's hair and anointed me with his sweet-smelling oil. The elderly optician who told me I needed glasses and gave me a silver coin because I cried. That same young boy riding home on the bus with his mother wearing his new peach-coloured glasses, washed in the light of the world. Let these too be called. The young boys who played football after school under an autumn sky in the space in the park between the cycle track and trees, on that day when the world arched over me intensely real. Let them come. The young woman nursing a child in the cold on a Dublin bridge. The women and girls we made get on boats and planes, carrying their sadness to strangers. All those women who created art in words and on canvas and were lost in history, confined to the shadows. Let them come into the light and have their rightful place. So many others. So many others. Let them all come.

And you too must take your place, take it at the head of the table, dressed in white, rubies in your hair. Most beautiful, most full of grace and intensely brave, who silently shows us how to find strength in the face of what seeks to damage the body and how to stand true against the malice of all those who trade in hate. Let your love and kindness welcome each in turn and may your love, that is not bound or lessened by time, continue to bless me through all our days. In this world and beyond.

© Mark Jones

David Park is the author of ten novels, a novella and two collections of short stories. *The Healing* won the Authors' Club First Novel Award. *The Truth Commissioner* was awarded the Christopher Ewart-Biggs Memorial Prize and his novel *Travelling in a Strange Land* won the Kerry Group Irish Novel of the Year. *The Light of Amsterdam* was shortlisted for the International Dublin Literary Award. He received the American Ireland Fund Literary Award and has been shortlisted for the Irish Novel of the Year four times.

His work has featured on BBC Radio 4, both as short stories and twice as the Book at Bedtime and is published widely in translation. He has received a Major Artist Award from the Arts Council of Northern Ireland and an Honorary Fellowship in the Seamus Heaney Centre at Queen's University, Belfast.